Keeper Of Stones

All rights reserved; no part of this publication may be reproduced, stored in a retrieval system, or transmitted in any form or by any means, electronic, mechanical, photocopying, recording or otherwise, without the prior written permission of the publisher.

Published by Tribes Press 2025

This paperback edition first published in September 2025

Copyright © 2025 Ger Moane
Cover Design by Ana Slattery

You must not circulate this book in any other binding or cover and you must impose the same condition on any acquirer. The moral right of the author has been asserted.

Tribes Press policy is to use papers that are sustainably sourced from manufacturers with EU Ecolabel and FSC® certification.

ISBN 978-1-912441-68-6

www.tribespress.com

To Sonya,
Le Grá

Author's Note

Inspiration for this novel originates in the rich heritage of ancient Ireland, in particular the magical Tuatha de Danann, and the mystical Newgrange. Boann, a goddess of the Tuatha, gave her name to the river Boyne, and the three mounds at the bend of the Boyne - Newgrange, Knowth and Dowth - are called Brú na Boinne, where Brú refers to a magical place of hospitality.

Stories of the Tuatha de Danann (the People of Danu) are rich in descriptions of glorious other worlds such as Tír na mBan (land of women), Tír na nÓg (land of youth) and Tír na mBeo (land of the living), worlds of abundance, sensuality and fabulous natural beauty. It is said that the Tuatha withdrew from mortal life into the Otherworld of the mounds, thereafter, referred to as the Sídhe, to live forever alongside humans as fairies or supernatural beings.

These stories go back to childhood, with school tours to Newgrange and stories from Celtic mythology such as the Children of Lir. I only later discovered that the mounds of Brú na Boinne go back to the Neolithic or Stone Age, five thousand years ago, long before the Celts arrived and before the mythology of the Tuatha de Danaan was written down in Ireland between the sixth and the thirteenth century.

Newgrange stands as a magnificent monument to that Stone Age culture and has excited people's imaginations for centuries. It stands on a hill overlooking the Boyne, with a covering of white quartz and beautiful carved stones which surround its base and fill its interior. At sunrise on Winter Solstice, usually the twenty-first of December, sunlight slowly shines up the long passageway and illuminates the inner chamber, a beautiful event that speaks to the sophistication and wonderment of the people who built it.

All over Ireland there are cairns, standing stones, stone circles, wells and carvings on stone, often on hilltops, that evoke a sense of awe and connection to the land and to the people who placed them there. Could it be that Newgrange and other structures were built during a time of abundance and peace, like the worlds of the Tuatha de Danaan?

My fascination with Newgrange was ignited in 1989 when Marija Gimbutas, a renowned archaeologist of prehistoric Europe, visited Ireland. She not only challenged the view of Newgrange as a tomb, but also presented a vision of a peaceful, egalitarian, earth-centred culture in which a mother goddess, representing the earth and nature, was central.

She referred to this culture as 'Old Europe'. She presented extensive archaeological evidence from all over Europe, showcasing a rich culture where houses were filled with shrines featuring goddess figurines and pottery decorated with goddess symbols. She saw Newgrange as the earth's womb, and the art carved on its stones as symbols of the goddess.

This put Irish neolithic culture in the context of Europe – our links with Malta (called Melita in the novel), in particular, intrigued me. Although goddess-centred, she did not argue for a matriarchy, which is a hierarchy of women/mothers, but for an egalitarian women-centred or matri-focused culture. A great deal of archaeological and, more recently, genetic evidence supports her views about the communal nature of prehistoric society, in contrast to the view that a hierarchy possibly coerced people to build monuments that were reserved for elites. We can now see Newgrange and other monuments as places where people gathered for healing, ritual and community, rather than solely as tombs.

The visit by Marija Gimbutas gave momentum to a journey that had begun earlier, while studying for a PhD in Berkeley, California, which at the time was a hotbed of radical thinking, from the radical feminist philosophy of Mary Daly to what was then called the new age healing approach of Barbara Brennan. I was inspired during the 1990s by workshops and writings on feminist and goddess spirituality in Ireland by Mary Condren, Anne Louise Gilligan and Katherine Zappone.

Several worldviews and spiritual movements, such as goddess spirituality, paganism, wiccan, druidry, Buddhism/Taoism and shamanism have continued to flourish in Ireland. They share a love of nature and of nature-based spiritualities and have evolved and developed over the years to share practices that include the wheel of the year, honouring the land, visits to ancient sites, meditation, rituals and ceremonies. Over the years, I have participated in numerous workshops in these areas, trained as a shamanic practitioner, and visited ancient sites all over Ireland, Brittany and Malta, all of which helped to imagine the world of ancient Ireland.

Visions of an egalitarian society are, unfortunately, in contrast to the lived experience of many in Ireland (and elsewhere) in the 20th and 21st centuries. Patriarchy, capitalism and colonialism are what I call systems of domination in my book *Gender and Colonialism, a Psychological Analysis of Oppression and Liberation,* which is almost a mirror image of this novel.

That non-fiction book goes into detail about how hierarchy and domination operate, and are linked to despair, anger, helplessness and mental health problems. It describes pathways to liberation and develops a new approach in psychology, namely liberation psychology, which has become an international movement. Exploring these topics over decades with colleagues and students in UCD in psychology and women's studies, and as an activist in feminist and LGBTQ+ groups and communities, provided insights as well as personal experiences of solidarity, pride, joy, courage, hope and humour.

Fortunately, many of us have experiences of joy and solidarity, the opposite of fear and competition, in our everyday lives. But what about a whole culture and society that would place love, cooperation, harmony with nature, healing, and art at its centre? Musing about an egalitarian culture brought me back to the dreams of the Tuatha de Danaan, the world of Old Europe, and the human potential for cooperation, creativity and joy.

This is evident in the intentional communities that I experienced over the years through political activism and involvement in women's and lesbian lands and communities, and also in the collective elation at Newgrange, palpable every year as people gather for sunrise on the morning of Winter Solstice.

A longstanding interest in energy approaches to healing, including classes over the years in Tai Chi and Taoism, shiatsu, and bioenergy, fostered a view of the human body and the earth as an energy system. This seemed to offer a unifying worldview with roots in ancient times.

All of this fed into writing a novel about the world that built Newgrange, which I believe had a cosmology that cultivated collective harmony and joy, and a different way of being.

Note: My author website provides more exploration of these topics and can be found at germoane.com

There was a time when you were not a slave, remember that.
You walked alone, full of laughter, you bathed bare-bellied.
You say you have lost all recollection of it, remember...
You say there are no words to describe this time,
You say it does not exist.
But remember.
Make an effort to remember.
Or, failing that, invent

Monique Wittig Les Guéillères 1969

Briona's Journey

Wheel of the Year

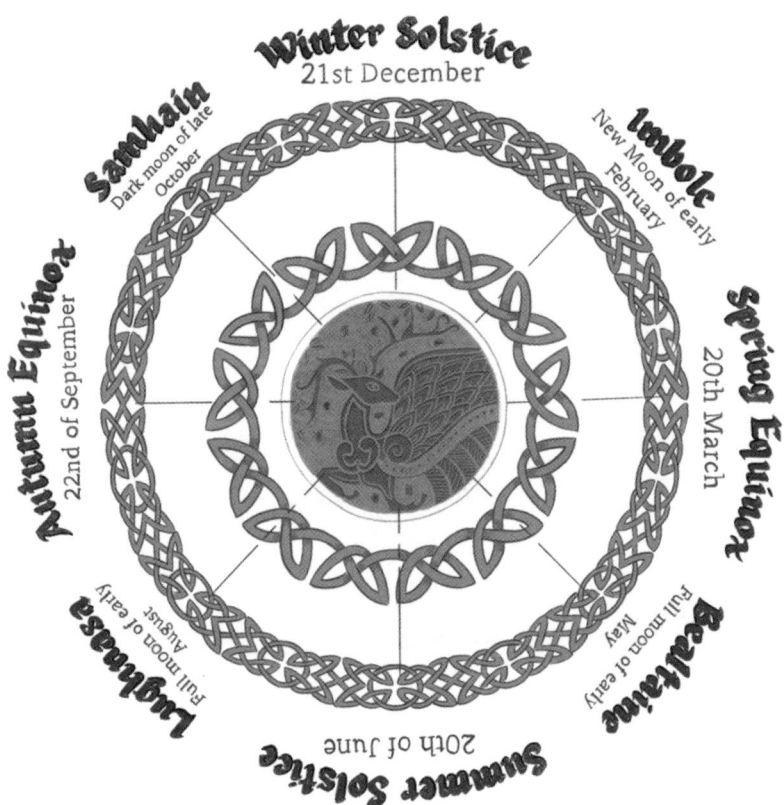

-1-

Dreaming at Imbolc

The sound of drums beating low and soft wafts through the forest. It's the call of the Dreamhouse. My eyes open. Hazel poles woven with reed and bark curve above my head. Layers of fur and Dori's warmth beside me keep me snug. Embers in the fire smoulder, sending wisps of smoke snaking through a small hole in the roof. Dori squeezes my hand, and we smile at each other. Today is the new moon of early Spring and the start of Turas, my passage to becoming an adult. It will take me on a journey to place my birthstone on Newgrange, the great mound at Brú.

I jump up and pull on a tunic and two layers of wool. I put twigs on the fire, wrap deer fur around my body and step outside, pouch and boots in my hands. The soft throb of the dreamstone in my pouch tells me that there are dreams to share this morning. The earth pulses beneath my feet with the beat of early Spring and the crisp morning air chills my face. Leaves and twigs rustle on the ground and buds peep from branches. Two doves sit side by side on the branch of an oak tree, heads bent towards each other, ready to start the work of spring, flying back and forth, building their nest. Shivers run through my body. Brú is a long way from home.

"Briona!" Shula calls me over as she steps out of a nearby hut, pulling fur across her shoulders. I put my boots on and hurry over for a big hug. I touch her necklace of polished bone and the soft leather band around her red hair. We fall in step and walk shoulder to shoulder in tune with the drumbeat.

"It starts today!" Shula exclaims, her eyes glistening. This is her year for Turas too - we were born the same year, and this year the Bright Star returns to the place in the sky where it was at the time of our birth.

"The dreamers are calling us," I say as we quicken our pace.

"They may have news about our journey," Shula adds.

We often talk of our journey to Brú - we love to hear about the glistening mound that lights up with golden sunbeams at Winter Sun

Standstill, the shortest day of the year. Our great wish is to be inside the chamber with our birthstones when sunlight glides up the passageway, filling everywhere with light.

The Dreamhouse appears, a tall circle of tree posts set side by side with a woven roof. It is tucked into the forest at the edge of our settlement and is the place we go to share our dreams. A small group waits to go inside. We stand together and face the rising sun. We raise our arms as we look towards the Fast Star which glows low in the sky. My breath stops as its light shines into my eyes. I wonder what it tells me about Turas - of places we may visit, who we may meet, how the stars move and what they say about our destiny. The door opens and Mona, Keeper of Charts, appears, an indigo band around her long grey hair.

"Welcome," she says, smiling as she waves us inside.

It is quiet, though some people talk in low voices. A small fire burns in the centre of the room. The reds, yellows and blues of rugs on the walls around us glimmer in the flickering light. The Dreamers lie on their backs, covered with furs. A gong rings out. We lie down and pull rugs over our bodies. Gentle drumbeats give the signal to settle and start the slow breath that connects us to the dreamers. Eyes close, bodies relax, and heads drift as we match our breath to the beat. The drums pause and a gong sounds three times. I see the vision that the Dreamers share.

A small boat arrives on the seashore. Six figures in dark cloaks jump out and pull the boat on to the beach. They move quickly up the shoreline, gather hand-sized stones and place them in a circle around the boat. One of the figures removes a cauldron from the boat and sets the boat on fire. They stand in a circle and watch flames rise as black smoke billows into the sky.

Longing fills my chest - I want to be there on that shore and find out who they are and why they come here. Will we meet them on our journey to Brú? Gongs sound again. The dream fades and we slowly open our eyes and ears to the colours and sounds in the room. Mona moves to sit on a big chair near the door. Her bright blue robe sparkles as lights dance on tiny crystals sewn into its front.

"Our Dreamers see that Voyagers may come to our island later this year." Mona raises her hand as she speaks, and the room falls silent.

"They come from across the ocean as the prophecies foretell. This year Stargazers say there will be a Grand Cross of stars that brings big changes."

My heart quickens at these words, a mixture of excitement and fear stirring within me.

"We must all stay clear and balanced," Mona continues in a grave voice.

The room goes silent. She often reminds us to keep our bodies clear and balanced, so that the life force, Beo, can flow through us. We attune every day to the stars so that we know when Beo is strong and look for stones that hold the strength of Beo.

Mona rises from the chair.

"There is more to tell at the Imbolc celebration tonight."

We need stillness for Imbolc, when every year we celebrate the rise of energy at the start of Spring, but I'm unsure how we can stay calm with this news.

We leave the Dreamhouse and stand in a group, eyes bright and full of wonder. Currents ripple between us - excitement, joy, questions. We wonder where the Voyagers are from, who they are and if they can block our energy. The picture of the six, with their boat on fire, black cloaks, and rising smoke, stays in my head.

"Where are they from?" Someone asks.

"Mona said they come from across the ocean," I remind the group.

"Black cloaks and smoke rising - not a good sign," murmurs someone.

Some people lower their eyebrows and their shoulders sink. Others move away.

"When will we meet them?" I ask Shula.

"Wait for the celebration," Shula replies, her hands spreading wide as she gestures toward the path leading to the Cistin. "Mona will tell us more later when we go to the stone circle for the lighting of the new fire."

Shula's eyes glaze over, and she stares at the river.

"I see a journey," she says, her voice distant. "Downriver... boats... people..."

Shula has the gift of second sight and often has visions of what is to come.

"Where? What river?" I turn my head quickly, eager to hear more. She raises her arms.

"Rivers wind, twist and turn," she murmurs, her voice soft. She pauses. The rising sun glistens through her hair. Then she turns and grasps my arm. "Someone is missing at Brú."

Hairs rise on the back of my neck. Her eyes widen.

"Energy like lightning. Sun goes dark." Shula shakes her head, then puts her hands to her head, breathing heavily.

"Are *we* there in the chamber?" I press, my voice barely above a whisper, my fear growing.

"I didn't see inside."

"What can stop us from being there?" I ask, my heart racing.

"Blocks in our energy, these Voyagers, an accident, someone who…"

"We *must* be in the chamber," I interrupt. "It's our passage to become an adult.*"*

We turn to walk towards the Cistin but Shula hesitates.

"What if the Voyagers take our place in the chamber? Brú is *so* far away. Are we ready? Are we strong enough?" she asks.

"*We are,*" I say in a firm voice. "We have our first blood flow. We're old enough!"

"But who knows what challenges we may face?" Shula mutters.

"Every year people travel to Brú for Turas. We can do that too." I assure her. Her breath slows and her steps steady. "Let's go, I'm hungry."

I pull Shula's arm. I want to stop these questions, but as we walk back through the forest unease ripples between us.

When we arrive at the Cistin people are excited, they already know of the dream and the Voyagers. We help ourselves to big slices of bread and handfuls of dried apples and hazelnuts and mix them in bowls with juice. There is still enough food in our stores, but soon we may have fresh food from the big farmland downriver. I look for Murta, my father, he can calm us. He touches my shoulder, his blue eyes and curly black hair just like mine. We go to sit by the fire.

"Mona spoke of a Grand Cross. What is it?" Shula asks Murta, full of curiosity.

"It's when many stars line up," Murta replies, his voice calm and clear.

He is a stargazer - he often stays awake at night to go out on the river and watch the sky.

"Sun, Moon, Fast Star, Bright Star, Red Star..." Shula lists the stars and makes the sign for each.

"And Seven Stars and Swan Stars and Three Stars." Murta imitates her breathless words, his voice teasing.

Shula laughs, her eyes sparkling.

"But what's a Grand Cross?" she asks.

He holds up two fingers, crossed over each other.

"It's when the stars line up and make a cross with big energy."

"Oh? But a cross means stars are against each other," I say.

"Yes, it's harder for the stars to work together," Murta agrees, turning to me.

"Does this mean hard times for us on Turas?"

Murta twirls a piece of my hair between his fingers.

"Briona, you see hard times too often, trust the stars, they can guide you."

"I hope I learn to be a healer with stones or even a Keeper of Stones," I say, a wish of mine for a long time drifting through my head.

"Yes, you loved stones even when you were very young," he remembers, and his eyes soften. An image of us looking for stones by the river comes into my head.

Shula leans in and touches Murta's arm.

"Winter Standstill is so far away. I had a vision of twisting rivers and flashes of lightning," she says, her voice low.

"Ah, this year brings strong energy for you both. Turas brings many lessons; it tells you of your destiny."

"*Lessons?*" Shula says playfully as she tosses her hair.

"This dream of Voyagers... can they stop us?" I ask slowly.

"On Turas, you'll learn what you need." Murta smiles gently, not answering my question.

I glance at Shula, but she is looking into the distance as she slowly eats her food.

Dori comes to sit beside us. I grew up with Dori and Shula. Gara, their mother, is like a mother to me. Dori, Shula and I always have fun together in the forest, in the longhouses, on the river. We collect stones and twigs and bring berries and nuts and eggs to the Cistin, where Gara shows us how to make bread. Dori carves wood and I make signs on stones. Shula makes jewellery and we all look for plants to make dye. We have a special hut that we go to where we light a fire and sometimes stay the night. We talk about sparks we see between people, where energy between them draws them together and they go to the forest to share pleasure. Sometimes Dori and I have soft kisses.

We talk about the visit to the Dreamhouse and the dream of the Voyagers that we shared until Gara comes to the fire and Shula goes to sit beside her.

"Shula thinks Turas may be a hard journey," I turn to Dori, concerned.

"A lot can happen during Turas," Dori responds thoughtfully.

"She had a vision. She saw rivers with twists and turns, and someone missing."

"Briona, there are long rivers and different paths to Brú, you don't know what Shula sees, or what may happen," replies Dori.

"What if I don't get to Brú?"

"*Everyone* can go to Brú in the year of their Bright Star Return," Dori reminds me softly.

"This year isn't like other years," I say. "Who *knows* where Turas may take me." But then my eyes brighten, and my words speed up as I talk more about the Voyagers and the Grand Cross.

"You *want* to journey to Brú," Dori says, leaning in.

"Yes, like everyone with their Bright Star Return," I respond with a smile.

"You'll go, and you'll forget us," Dori says with a frown.

The words sting, sharper than I expect.

"I'll be back here after Turas," I say, feeling sure.

"Not *everyone* comes back." Dori's voice is gentler.

Tears prick my eyes as the name of my mother, Bríd, comes into my head. I close my eyes and take a deep breath. When I was very young, she went to the Summer festival and never came back. She slipped and hit her head on a rocky bank as she was getting into a boat to return to Carraig. Healers worked for days and nights, but Beo, her life force, left her body and she went to the Otherworld. Mona, her mother, wrapped me in my mother's fur and rocked me to sleep for many nights. As time passed my heart was not so sore, and I love to hear stories of my mother. It is hard to lose somebody - maybe that is why Dori fears I may go and not come back.

"I want to live *here*," I say, as my love for Mona and Murta, for Dori and Shula, for Gara and the clan in Carraig surges.

"You don't know what will happen on Turas. You may meet someone new."

"No, I'm sure to come back." I say, though in my mind doubt lingers. I want to see what the stars bring. I love Dori, but sometimes I wish for more sparks and to meet new people.

"I *know* you," Dori says, voice quieter now, eyes darkening. "When you travel, you'll change."

"Dori you're *family*," I affirm, but I can feel the tension between us.

"This year is different," Dori says, face reddening.

People beside us stand up and we turn to see movement at the river. We walk to where boats arrive on the riverbank and a group of people get out. Excitement rises as they pull their boats onto the shore. Their sheepskin coats show they come from the big farmland further downriver on the plain of Cill Dara. They are here for the Imbolc celebration with news and gifts of food. The air charges as people crowd around, eager to hear their news.

"*Come!* We should finish the preparations for the gathering!" Shula calls as she steps forward and raises her arms to the group. She has a special way of knowing when to speak so that everyone listens.

The group moves away from the river, and I lose sight of Dori. The visitors carry baskets of food for the festival, and they talk and laugh with the people around. We still have supplies of wheat, some dried fruit and nuts, and people are out fishing and trapping for more. The visitors bring dried meat and cheese from the farmland. My eyes are drawn to one of them, strong, with a lovely face, bright blue eyes, a ready smile and brown hair tied back with a red headband. A tingle rises in my body, my cheeks glow, and as I look and listen intently, I hear a name - Gormley. I move over to be closer, but someone pulls my arm.

"I see there is already someone new," Dori states, standing there with a flushed face.

"*What?*" I ask, surprised.

"You're looking at someone else," Dori asserts and nods towards Gormley.

"No, no," I protest. But there is a spark between Gormley and me.

"You want someone *new*," Dori repeats.

Maybe it is true. I sigh and shake my head. Dori turns and walks away. I don't follow - we can talk later. I stand and press my feet into the ground. Mona wants us to stay tuned to the low slow beat of Imbolc, but it is difficult with all this happening.

Further downriver people collect reeds to weave the wheel of the year. The rhythm of weaving can keep me calm. I go to help - take some reeds, cut them to arm's length, bend them over and wind them around until four arms rise out of a central web. Around me people sing songs of Imbolc, but I stay quiet. Spring is different this year, with little time for long easy stretches, talks with friends and walks in the forest looking for first buds and the beginnings of nests. Bright Star Return is a time to clear the energies that we are born with and to take our birthstone to Brú, to learn our destiny. It may also be a time to find love. Is that why my heart quickens at this visitor, Gormley?

The light fades by the river as the time for the Imbolc celebration nears. I gather my reed wheels. We walk up to the settlement where the hearth is cleared out and set with new wood from the forest. Benches are laid out around the central firepit. The Cistin is like a hive as groups prepare food for the feast. I go to a longhouse - its thick walls and strong thatched roof are built to keep us warm. A fire burns in the centre, candles are lit. Groups sit preparing clothes, passing around jewellery, stones, shells, feathers, barks and weaves in different colours. A pipe plays a slow tune, and someone beats gently on a drum.

"Briona, you bring wheels!" Shula calls, waving me over.

"Let's hope they bring good energy! *Even sparks!*" I say and everyone laughs.

"And fun and food!"

"These visitors bring sparks, especially the one with the red band," someone says, and I take a quick breath. They are talking about Gormley.

"The tall one is older; he looks like he already has a mate," another voice chimes in.

"Maybe the one with beautiful green eyes," someone else adds.

There is much laughter all around. Some years we are reluctant to leave the darkness of winter and go out for the Imbolc celebration when it is still cold and wet, but not this year. Already we can sense that this is a special year. I weave feathers into my wheel and wish for strength for Turas.

-2-

The Imbolc Gathering

"The moon rises soon," Murta calls into the longhouse.

We jump up and hurry outside. All around people are dressed in colours and sparkle with jewellery and bright stones. Some carry drums and pipes, while others have bones to click. Children run up and down, happy to show off feathers and stones from the forest. We head towards the river, eager for our first sight of the new moon that brings the stir of Imbolc energy. Excitement fills me as I gaze up at the moon's slim crescent rising slowly above nearby trees. The Bright Star shines beside it. Shula and I glance at each other, full of wonder about the year ahead.

Steady drumbeats guide us towards the forest as the evening light fades. Shula and I link arms and smile at the familiar faces of our clan as they mingle into the parade and wave at visitors who join in. When we reach the edge of the forest we make a long line of rows, with four or five in each row. The evening air is clear and crisp as we walk along under the crescent moon.

We enter the forest and start a low hum that pulses with the earth. Animals shift, little ones are ready to be born, roots stretch, and buds stir. A breeze drifts through. It gathers speed and brings a tremor to the air around us. Suddenly a large flock of ravens fly up from the trees in a rush of cawing and flapping of wings. They rise together, fill the sky, and then, swooping, swirling and gliding, they fly in all directions, scattering on the wind. They caw loudly as they fly overhead. Caw, Caw, Caw! Crackles run through the forest, through our bodies.

"Birds fill the sky, like dark clouds!" Shula exclaims and she drops my arm.

My breath quickens and I turn to catch Murta's eye.

"The stars bring strong energy this year," he says, taking Shula's arm and mine and linking us all together. Uneasy feelings are swept away as people surge forward, eager to hear what Mona may say about the year ahead. We arrive at the circle of big stones in the forest - they stand side by side as tall as me, gleaming in the flickering light of torches. A fresh pile of firewood in the centre of the circle awaits new flames.

At the entrance, Teelin and Ciara, dressed in deep blue Keeper robes, hold up a hoop of hazel branches that they have woven together. Ciara wears a hairband decorated with tiny crystals and Teelin, Shula's father, has a large owl feather in his headband. We step one by one through the hoop and hold out our hands for a small drop of honey to take into our mouths and swallow. It tastes wonderful, a hint of the feast to come.

Mona sits on a large stone chair covered in deer fur. Feathers of small birds of the forest peep from the indigo band around her grey hair. She wears the green Cloak of Spring with its wavy white lines, and three necklaces, one of polished bone, one of painted shells, and one of coloured stones. We settle on the ground in front of her.

Her voice rings out in the crisp evening air.

"We are here to light the fires of Imbolc.

To be at one with earth, sea and sky,

As the wheel of the year turns once more."

The familiar words soothe me. We come here at Imbolc to welcome the year ahead, greet newborns, and hail the start of Turas for those who have Bright Star Return. My heart starts to beat faster - Turas means leaving home and saying goodbye to Mona, Murta, Dori and all my kin. Am I ready? I shake my head to chase the doubts away and lean forward, ready to hear Mona speak about the dream of Voyagers from across the ocean.

"Stargazers see a Grand Cross of Sun, Moon and Stars.

Dreamers tell us that Voyagers soon arrive from far away.

They may join us at Teamhair for the Summer Festival."

Mona smiles and excitement billows through the group. Shula nudges me and smiles. At the Summer Festival we gather at Teamhair, on the Hill of Tara, from all over our island with visitors from far and wide. We stay there for many days with food and drink, drumming and dancing to prepare for Summer Sun Standstill, the longest day, when light reaches its peak. Mona continues.

"Keepers of Stones sense their energy as they come closer.

They bring crystals that pulse with stones at Brú na Bóinne.
They want to be there for the Grand Cross at Winter Sun Standstill."
People shuffle and turn to each other. This is new. Many visitors come to visit Brú for Winter Sun Standstill. These Voyagers are different; they have special energies that bring dreams and prophecies and reach the Keepers of Stones. Mona raises one hand to still our talk.
"This year there are two here in Carraig with their Bright Star Return.
They are Briona and Shula; they will join other Seekers and carry their birthstones to Brú na Bóinne for Winter Sun Standstill.
There they may meet the Voyagers."
Mona gestures to Shula and me to stand up. We glance at each other, eyes wide, stand and hold hands. Drums roll as Teelin and Ciara step forward and raise our hands to the sky. I gaze up to the stars that sparkle all around us and joy rushes through my body. We all come from the stars; our ancestors are up there with the stars. Now it is my time to journey to Brú and learn what the stars say about my destiny. People cheer and shout our names, wishing us good energy for Turas and our journey to Brú. I feel surrounded by love.
"Now you are Seekers," Mona announces to the gathering.
Teelin and Ciara turn us in a circle and people call back - Seekers, Seekers. Murta pats my back and beams at me as I sit down. The people around us smile and touch our shoulders, while others look over at us in wonder that we may meet the Voyagers.
Silence falls as Mona starts to speak again. Her voice rises and her face glows, lit by burning lights all around.
"The Grand Cross creates a shift in Beo, our life force.
This brings changes to our great culture.
Fear may enter our world."
We listen, spellbound by words full of fate. Ripples run through the group. Beo comes from the sky, it brings life, and it is always there, in our bodies, in stones, in the earth and water, in plants and animals. What is there to fear?

"We must stay tuned to earth and sky. Keep good Glan to channel Beo into stones for healing. We must keep the web of life together!"

We all want Glan - our bodies clear so that the life force, Beo, can flow through us for healing and prophecy. Now Mona says we need Glan for the changes ahead, that this year may disturb our lives. We are in this together; we all have parts to play in the changes to come.

Mona stands up and raises her arms out to all of us. Love shines through her face, lighting love within us. Teelin and Ciara join her, and together they chant the Imbolc wish.

"Let us charge this new year.
Send love to tribes all over our island
And to people in farther lands who gather for Imbolc.
Let us welcome the newly born in Carraig, five in all.
Let us wish for a good harvest, good health, and a good year.
Let us light our fire!"

Drums sound. We get to our feet and watch as Teelin steps forward with the Ceremonial Wand in his hand, lights it, and hands it to Mona. She holds the Wand to the sky and as she turns in the four directions the carved spirals on the Wand spin in the flickering flames and the Cloak of Spring billows out around her. She moves forward and lights the fire in the centre of the stone circle. As the flames rise, we open our throats and let our voices ring out in cheers and whoops. I watch in wonder as Ciara's body shakes and trembles with the force of energy that comes through the stone. That is what I wish for, to sense stones, to be a healer and a Keeper of Stones like her.

The crackling of fire gathers pace, and flames reach to the sky. The drums beat out a deep thud for the Imbolc dance, a slow dance for the start of Spring. Flat-footed, we stretch our feet out on the earth with each step, swaying ever so gently to the rhythms of drums. We weave through the standing stones, and when I touch one of them, heat runs straight through my body. Sparks of connection flicker - between us and the earth, between all of us on this island, between us and others in further lands, between us and the moon and stars. The Imbolc festival is the time of most harmony in the year - people are clear and settled after the quiet of Winter, unlike the chaotic high energy of the summer festivals. I love this time on the wheel of the year when we know that the Bealtaine festival comes next and brings us higher and closer to the ecstasy of the Summer Festival. Silently we thank the earth for the warmth of fire and a safe passage through winter.

After the dance ends, we cluster around the fire to make a wish with our woven reeds. Shula and I stand side by side, fingers entwined. We reach to the fire and burn our wish of entering the chamber of Newgrange on the morning of Winter Sun Standstill into our reeds.

"Who knows what may happen this year," Shula says, turning to me with a smile on her face.

"Who knows when we may meet the Voyagers," I add, raising my eyebrows in fun.

"Who knows how we may all fit into the chamber." Shula throws her hands into the air.

We both laugh and hug each other. For now, we feel the calm of Glan, our bodies relaxed and open, the energy of the stars flowing through us.

The elders usher us to walk back to the homestead for the lighting of the new fires. We walk in silent procession back from the forest as we shift from the stillness and quiet of winter to the awakening of early spring. Mona's talk of fear rings in my head, but the fear fades as the slow beat for Imbolc calms me and brings the tasks of early Spring into focus. It is time to repair buildings, walls and pathways, and get baskets, boats, nets, axes and knives ready for gathering, fishing and trapping.

My body fills with different rhythms as drums beat out the points on the wheel of the year. They build up through the fires of Bealtaine to the peak of Summer Sun Standstill, then break into the chaotic rhythms of Lúnasa. Suddenly I want to skip and leap around - Bright Star Return is here, Turas has started. Drums slow into the quiet beat of Samhain. At the beat for Winter Sun Standstill Shula and I turn to each other, eyes gleaming, faces beaming. This is our year to be there at Brú with our birthstones!

The drums return to the Imbolc beat just as we arrive back at the centre of the homestead. We stand in a circle as torchbearers step forward and light the new fire. Heat spreads out to us, into the earth, up to the sky. As the flames of the fire roar, a breeze catches the smoke and sends sparks flying.

Gongs from the Cistin announce that food is ready, so we move over to the tables laden with food and drink - bread, dried fruit, and nuts from our store. My mouth waters at the sight of platters of fish, and meat that the visitors brought. Huge pottery vats sit on a table, full of soup made from winter greens, alongside vats of mead. Shula and I pile food on slabs of bread, fill small pottery cups with mead and go to sit by the fire.

Murta comes to sit beside me and Shula, and Dori joins us. Murta turns to the group sitting around, eager to talk about Brú.

"The three mounds at Brú na Bóinne took many years to build," he begins. I catch Shula's eye. We often listen to his stories of Brú - he went there many times after Turas to learn about stargazing. "They face towards Sun Standstill and Sun Balance, and …"

"Tell us what it's like at Winter Sun Standstill." Shula interrupts him with a smile.

"Beams of sunrise enter only one mound, Newgrange, on the morning of Winter Sun Standstill. That's a very special time; it brings great joy. It's hard to describe, it's like the Imbolc and the Summer festival combined." Murta beams.

"Is the chamber big enough for us all?" I ask.

"Oh yes, the mound is *huge,* with a long passageway and a big chamber," Murta continues. "People travel from all over the island and from other lands to gather outside and watch as Keepers and Seekers enter the passageway. Seekers carry their birthstones inside. Sunbeams sparkle in every direction, and then they come out and lay their birthstones on the mound."

Bres, the tall visitor from Cill Dara, leans forward, his beautifully coloured hat glowing in the firelight.

"Not *always* joy," Bres says. "When I went to Brú, there were many changes."

"Things change after Turas and the journey to Brú," Murta answers. "We're adults, we've found our destiny, our purpose and we can have children."

"The life I wanted was gone when I returned from Brú," Bres continues.

"Yes, but Brú tells you your destiny, it helps…" Murta says.

Bres talks over him.

"I missed the chance to have a child and life with someone I loved…" he says with sadness. "When I got home, she was with someone else."

The group grows silent and tense. This is the first time we've heard from someone sad about their journey to Brú. Many people from Carraig travel to Brú in the year of their Bright Star Return, and when they come back, they glow as they talk about their journey.

"It's best that we do as the stars say," Murta says and looks into Bres' eyes.

"The journey to Brú isn't for everyone," replies Bres.

Murta spreads his hands and glances around the group. There is silence. We look to Bres, wanting him to say that his life is good.

"May the stars shine on you soon," says Shula and touches his arm.

He glances at Shula, shrugs and laughs.

"That child wasn't for me. Now I travel overseas, farm and fish, I hope to have a child soon," he responds and Shula smiles at him.

I look around the celebration and see Dori standing near Gormley, gazing at Neasa, another visitor from Cill Dara. They listen intently as she talks, her face glowing with excitement and her green eyes sparkling. Maybe Dori has a spark for her. I beam when I overhear Neasa telling the group that she and Gormley are going to Brú this year for Turas. Dori meets my eye and comes to sit beside me, putting an arm around me.

"Briona we all must be open to the flow of Beo," Dori says, softly, brimming with the joy of the Imbolc celebration and wanting to put aside the tension between us from earlier.

"Yes, especially now that I am a Seeker!" I say joyfully.

Dori glances back at the group of visitors.

"But Dori, you walked away from me before the celebration," I say in a flat voice.

"You turned away from me for visitors," Dori says, blinking in surprise.

"But everyone was excited to see the visitors," I say.

"You already have a spark with Gormley," Dori responds, voice rising. "He's going on Turas this year, *like you*."

"*And* Neasa. And *lots* of others," I say, eager to calm the conversation. "You'll go on Turas soon," I add.

"Yes, I know, but you are leaving me behind."

"You're always in my heart," I say, and reach out for a hug.

"This holds my love for you," Dori says, taking out a beautiful wood carving of a dove and placing it into the palm of my hand.

"There will always be love between us," I say, and squeeze Dori's hand. We hug and hold each other close with tears in our eyes.

Suddenly, the beat of the drums quickens, bringing us all to our feet.

"Come on, let's dance," Shula calls to us.

We all take hands as we laugh and join together in dance. There is much joy at winter ending and the sense of spring in the air. Our fears of the Voyagers and the changes to come drift away with the smoke of the fire.

-3-

Birthstones

I wake up in the longhouse and go to the Cistin with Shula and Dori. People sit talking about the wonderful celebration, with so much singing and dancing well into the night. Pairs drift in, soft with pleasure. Groups come in laughing. Just as the visitors from Cill Dara come to join us, Teelin comes over. He wears an indigo band around his grey hair with the feather of an owl - he is a Keeper of Ancestors.

"The Keepers want you to help at the Labyrinth," he says to me.

"Oh?"

"They need someone with a birth chart like you."

"Like *me*?"

"Your moon is in a good place, and they need someone with a still moon."

I hesitate. Surely, I'm too young for that, we only help at the Labyrinth after Turas. And I want to stay here at the fire and hear more about the Imbolc celebration. But Teelin gestures towards the forest. I stand up slowly and look in that direction.

It is then that the branches of a nearby oak tree call me. I stand with my back to its calm solid trunk and take a few breaths. Its roots pulse and branches whisper, they say to look for signs that lead to the Labyrinth. I take slow steps, my feet firmly on the ground, my eyes half open, and my ears alert. The forest sounds drift by, low hums, crackles, shifting breezes, and gentle rustling. And then the song of a blackbird, so beautiful my heart sings, lifting and lilting.

I turn my head at a sound from the left and catch a quick flash of movement. A deer stands, their big brown eyes staring at me. Our eyes meet. My back and feet tingle. The deer turns and slowly walks away. I step off the path and follow the deer. Trees loom over us, beautiful, longstanding, rooted deep in the forest floor. My breathing slows, as the light grows speckled and dim. The smell of damp earth fills my nostrils, and the forest sounds caress my ears as the deer's gentle steps bring me deeper into the forest.

Drumbeats call me to a clearing. I stop. Mona stands at a cauldron set over a smouldering fire wearing furs over a colourful gown. The cauldron is big, earthen, painted with white wavy lines and spirals. Mona stays in place, she smiles at me, and I step forward. Beams of light encircle us and charge the space around us. Suddenly Mona lifts a large jug from the cauldron and pours the contents over me. I jolt as the warm liquid soaks through to my skin. Smells of nettles and green leaves set my mouth watering. My body shivers, tensions flow out and I am open to the flow of Beo through my body. The familiar feeling of Glan tells me that I am ready to enter the Labyrinth.

Now I see it, nestled in trees behind Mona. Three curved domes built of wooden posts connect to make a spiral, revealing different entrances to the three rooms - one for keeping maps of stars and birth charts, one for healing and balancing, and one for dreaming. It is where I hope to be after Turas, where Keepers work with the stars and stones.

I follow Mona through a passageway of tall stones into a small round room. Fire lights up the bare walls and flickers on a pale blue robe laid out on a bench. Mona motions for me to change out of my wet clothes and put on the robe. She picks up a rattle made of bark with a hazel shaft and the hair of a deer and faces the four directions in turn - first east, then south, west and north. She shakes her rattle and speaks words I have never heard before. The outside world fades away.

We enter a large circular chamber in silence. Ciara, Keeper of Stones, lies on a rug on the ground in the centre. She is always in the Labyrinth; her long thin body can sense the energy of stones. Bright stones and crystals sit on the floor around her, and she is surrounded by a small group. Circles and spirals on the walls swirl in the candlelight, making my head spin. I close my eyes, my mouth goes dry - I'm unsure what to do, I want to leave. Mona is wrong to bring me here, I don't know how I can help. Drops sprinkle on me, my eyes open and Mona's steady gaze holds me and calms me.

Mona beckons me to sit at Ciara's feet and places a stone at the base of my back. It brings my focus to the earth beneath me. Rattling and drumming begin. Energies swirl around my head. I peek out from under my eyelids to see that some people sit on the ground while others stand holding stones, swaying slightly, with their eyes shut. I pick up a stone from the ground, it is slightly warm to my palm. Slowly heat rises in my body. I attune to the energy of the Bright Star, then the moon. They are opposite each other, like two strong rivers going in different directions, churning against each other.

The energies shift and change, and the currents attempt to find their channel, though they are still separate from each other. I sense them surge, meet and blend, then calm. Low hums rise in the chamber. Our throats open, pulsating with a hum. We become one harmonious sound, rising in volume. My head fills with the sound, my chest quivers, and my hips settle on the ground. Vibrations from others fill my body, as we blend into one with earth, sea and sky. The hum fades and silence falls. We are in stillness. Ciara lies without moving like she is in a deep sleep.

Mona starts a slow drumbeat. We stand, face the four directions and filter out of the chamber, leaving Ciara behind. I stand in a daze, shaking. Mona puts one hand on my shoulder and the other at the base of my back. A glow rises in my body.

"I know you didn't expect this. We needed a birth Moon with the right placement for Sos, for this balancing," she says.

"I always heard that we're not ready to help with Sos until after Turas."

"Yes, that's a good guide, but it depends. Sos is a balancing that brings the clashing energies of the stars to rest in harmony. We need to have good Glan for Sos. Good Glan means our bodies are clear of tension and open to the flow of Beo. But you already know this," Mona says. She smiles and slowly lifts her hands away. "For this balancing I needed someone with a strong moon placement in their chart. Only you and Ciara have a Birth Moon opposite to the Bright Star."

Mona knows the pattern of stars for all our births; she keeps charts in the Labyrinth. I take the robe off and put my clothes back on, they are warm from the small fire.

"Is that how Ciara has good Glan?" I ask.

"She stays at the Labyrinth, that is why she always has Glan, she clears tensions all the time. She is one of the best channels. You are like her," Mona replies. She takes my arm and guides me towards the door.

"This Sos is to clear the Labyrinth itself. We channel the energy that is left into the earth so that it is ready for new energies that flow at Imbolc."

"Can I have good Glan, like Ciara?" I ask.

"You've a good placement of the stars for Glan," Mona reassures me. "You know that Beo will flow through your body if you do the daily attunements and clear tensions."

I want her to stay and talk, say I can be like Ciara, but she hugs me and gestures towards the door.

"See if you find Shula and bring her here."

I wrap fur around me and leave with echoes of humming and warmth from Mona's hands still in my body.

I step outside and stand for a moment. A sharp breeze cools my face. My stomach rumbles, yearning for food, but there is very little in the forest, no berries or fruits at this time of year. I hear a rustle to the right of where I stand - a squirrel hops by, just awake from winter. I follow it with my eyes and there at the base of a nearby tree is a pile of earth that covers hazelnuts. I thank the squirrel with a smile. Stories say that hazelnuts can bring me wisdom for my journey to Brú. Sitting with my back to the tree, I chew the nuts slowly. Pictures of the Imbolc ceremony come into my head. I hope Turas will lead me on the same path as Ciara; she can sense energies from the stones and the lines of the earth.

When I finish the nuts I walk towards the Cistin, and as I do, I see Shula and wave her over.

"I was just at the Labyrinth," I say.

"You needed balancing?" Shula asks.

"No, I helped with Ciara's Sos."

"But you aren't *ready* for that. It's not your time," Shula's says as her eyebrows rise, and a flush brightens her cheeks.

"Mona says my moon is in a good place."

"Mona always says you are good."

"*Not always.*"

"She *always* picks you."

Shula tosses her hair over her shoulder and walks on.

"She wants us both at the Labyrinth now," I say.

"*Me as well?*" Shula stops in her tracks.

"Yes... let's go."

We walk in silence to the labyrinth. I know Mona has a special love for me. When I was very young, Mona came back to Carraig from Cill Dara to be a mother to me after my mother, her daughter, had an accident and went to the Otherworld. But Shula is wrong. Mona picked me for Sos because I have a steady moon, not because she favours me.

When we arrive at the labyrinth Mona leads us in our daily attunements. We face east with our feet firm on the ground and arms by our side. I picture a ball of hot energy in my belly. We turn to the south, then west and north. Our legs move; our hips sway and our arms rise. Heat flows up my back, over my head and down to my belly. I can sense the energy of the moon and the Bright Star, but stargazers attune to many stars - the Red Star, the Crystal Star, the Furthest Star, the Swan Stars and more.

Mona brings us into a big bright round chamber where there are many alcoves full of shelves with bones laid out. They are covered in markings - dots, lines, circles, and star shapes. Mona points to benches and we sit. She places a purple shawl across her shoulders and bows her head towards a bowl of water that sits on the ground with a plate of seeds beside it. She shakes a rattle for a long while then lifts the purple shawl over her head like a veil and throws some of the seeds into the bowl of water. Eerie calm enters the room. Mona gazes at the seeds and speaks in a whisper.

"At your time of birth, the pattern of stars matched the Grand Cross that comes this year. This gives you special energy to bring to the chamber of Newgrange at Brú na Bóinne for Winter Sun Standstill. You must have Glan to enter Newgrange. This is vital for our tribe to survive." Mona takes off the shawl and sits in silence with her eyes closed.

Hairs rise on the back of my neck at these strong words. Unease runs between Shula and me. We often talk of our Bright Star Return and going on Turas together. It is our chance to clear our birthstones and the patterns we are born with. We think of it as an adventure. But we also know that Bright Star Return brings challenges. Many energies come from the stars and mix together, making it hard to keep clear and have good Glan. Now Mona tells us that we have a special pattern in our birth chart, that we must be in Brú at Winter Sun Standstill to save our tribe. Questions swirl in my head. Mona opens her eyes and points to the shelves.

"Here we keep the birth charts. On the day of your birth, we marked the positions of the stars on these bones and charged your birthstone. Later, you will copy your chart onto a piece of deer bone and learn more about your energy patterns, and how best to keep clear for good Glan."

Mona gestures for us to follow her into another circular room with candles lighting. Tapestries hang around the walls. Whirling spirals, wavy lines and diamond shapes pile up on top of each other, circles within circles, lines radiating out from a central circle. So many images swirl around in my head, I sink into cushions on the floor. A spiral tunnel spins in front of my eyelids, a white light beaming at the end.

"Now, you receive your birthstone."

Mona places a stone in my hand. It has a familiar pulse, this is my birthstone, my connection to the Source of life. I lie there with the stone in my palm. Circles and spirals float in front of my eyes. The warm energy of the stone slowly seeps from my palm into my body until I feel like the night sky, full of twinkling stars. I tremble as white light pours from the stars into my body. Love for my clan brings a smile to my face - we all come from the stars. I want to stay here, full of joy and love.

Too soon the vision fades. I open my eyes and sit up. Two small wooden boxes carved with spirals lie on the woven cloth. Mona takes the white stone from my hand. Already, I miss it, I want it back. She places it in a box, puts Shula's stone into another, then squeezes out resin from the bark of a tree onto the side of the boxes to seal them.

"Now you have your birthstones. You're Seekers, ready to start your journey to Brú. Your birthstones bring your own distinct energy to Brú and help you with challenges along the way," states Mona.

"What challenges?" Shula asks, her eyes widening with curiosity and concern.

"This is for you to learn as you go."

"Do you keep our birthstones here until we leave?" I ask.

"You will leave for Cill Dara tomorrow," Mona says, her words landing like a weight.

"*Tomorrow!?*" I gasp, unable to hide the shock in my voice.

"Yes. I know it's sudden."

"We're not ready, *it's too soon.*" Shula speaks with a flush on her face.

I stiffen. Silence falls. People always leave for Turas in Summer, they go to Tara for the Summer festival, help at harvest and then travel to Brú for Winter Sun Standstill. Why go now? Even though it is the start of spring, it is still dark and cold.

"It's how the stars fall. How Spirit wants it." Mona's calm voice soothes the tension rising in my body. I close my eyes, and a picture of stars and white light fills my head.

"*But we're not ready!*" Shula says again, her voice rising with anger.

I open my eyes.

"This is your preparation," Mona replies steadily.

"*Tell us more!*" Shula asks, her face red. "You say too little."

I look at Shula with eyes wide. I don't like this news, or how Shula talks to Mona. I want the white light to stay in my body, but my heart is beating faster as Shula's anger rises.

"The Voyagers and the Grand Cross bring a lot of energy this year, we need you to be ready," Mona says. She reaches out and takes our hands. "You must trust that you'll learn more on Turas."

Shula pulls her hand away.

"I'm *not* ready," she says again, but in a calmer voice.

"Let's go to the fire," Mona says. She stands and we follow her outside.

Shula avoids me as she walks off towards the Cistin.

Mona pulls me aside.

"Did you sense the pulse of your birthstone?" she asks softly.

I hesitate; I have no words for the vision and the feelings in my body.

"I had a vision of a bright white light," I reply after a moment.

"That's the Bright One, the Source of life. You have a very strong connection," she says as she places her hands on my cheeks. "You have good Glan for your birthstone, for Bright Star Return."

I beam back; I can still feel the beautiful white light.

"Why don't we hold our birthstone every day? For that joy?" I ask.

"Such joy can only happen when the stars are in the right place, our bodies are clear, and our birthstones are charged by Bright Star Return," Mona replies. I want to ask her if I can be a Keeper of Stones. I open my mouth, but Mona speaks again. "Keep clear and look after your birthstone, your special white stone. Keep good Glan. There are many Moon cycles to Winter Sun Standstill."

She turns and walks out of sight around the Labyrinth. My breath stops. Why does she leave like that? A thread stretches between us and breaks. Mona always loves me. Can she help me with Turas, with Glan? Does she warn me when she says it is a long time to Winter Sun Standstill? The white light fades - I want to reach out and draw her back, hold my birthstone, feel her love.

I see Shula ahead in the forest and run to join her.

"*You* didn't help us to get answers from Mona." Shula says as she stops in front of me, her hands on her hips.

"*Why* did you talk to Mona *like that?*" I snap back.

"The stars show her it's time for us to leave. *Why did she not tell us anything before now?*" Shula questions.

"She only saw it *now*, at Imbolc," I respond.

"She says that the stars show her what is to come." Shula snaps at me.

"Maybe she was unsure until now!"

"We *need* to know sooner!"

"You didn't get a vision about us leaving soon," I challenge her.

"I don't see everything," she mutters, the tension between us rising.

"Mona says we must go *now*."

"Mona says, Mona says," Shula mimics, her voice full of anger as she looks away.

"No, the stars say. Spirit says," I assert and step towards the Cistin.

"You *always* do what Mona says. *No wonder she picks you*, you're her kin, she treats you differently," Shula says loudly. Anger flashes through me, a hot surge that flushes my face.

"*How* can you speak of Mona like *that?*" I ask, my voice steady.

We stand face to face, hands clenched. Shula looks down and shuffles her feet.

"This is not good for Glan," I finally say and reach out to touch her arm. We fall into silence. Shula knows that Glan comes from a calm body and our feet firm on the ground. The tension eases.

"*We* aren't ready. *I'm* not ready," Shula repeats, her voice quieter now, her head down and her hands hanging loose at her side.

"We have our birthstones. We can go tomorrow. Maybe it's a short trip, and we can come back soon," I say.

That calms us. But as we walk to the Cistin I wonder - why did Mona not tell us more?

At the hearth, people gather for the evening. I go with Shula and pile nuts and honey and slices of dried meat onto bread to take to the fire. Dori comes and sits beside us; we squeeze together as we talk about leaving. Soon people settle around the fire with food, enjoying its heat. Quiet conversations scatter about; children finish their meals and skip around before someone brings them to a longhouse where they sleep for the night. Does everyone know we leave tomorrow? Teelin starts to play pipes and is soon joined by the clicking of bones. It is lovely to sit surrounded by warmth and love. An ache rises in my chest - this has been home all my life. I look around at the circle of faces and across the settlement.

Near us is the Cistin where so much food comes and goes at different times of the year and beside it is the store for dry winter foods. There are always people at the Cistin - Gara and Murta are there now. Shula's eyes follow them and we suddenly have tears in our eyes.

"You're leaving," Dori states with sadness. "Who knows when you'll be back, who knows when we'll all be in the forest together again."

"We had so much fun in the forest," Shula says.

"We had good times and some not so good, like the day you cut your hand," Dori adds, eyes softening.

I laugh as a picture comes into my head of blood gushing from my hand after I accidentally cut it with an axe many moons ago. Shula kept me calm as Dori rushed to find a spider's web to put on the cut and seal it. Later Mona covered it with special bark to keep it clean.

Shula follows my gaze to the river, where several boats line up, log boats and basket boats for fishing and travelling down the river. She tugs my arm and points.

"Soon we start our journey to Brú," Shula says.

We squeeze hands and touch our heads together, watching the river flowing past the settlement.

I look away from the river towards the longhouses at the back of the settlement where we sit inside by small fires and sleep in the cold winter nights. Children play with dogs outside, enjoying the last of daylight. Beside them are wooden shelters where we make beads and pins, weave and dye cloths and rugs, make baskets and pottery, and carve wood. And my favourite place, the stone carving shed, where I love to spend time with Murta. Maybe we will come back soon, but who knows when.

The music stops and a drumroll sounds. Mona and Teelin appear out of the darkness and stand at an opening in the circle around the fire. They each carry a bundle.

"Shula, this is for you, may it wrap you in our love," Teelin says and as he steps forward, he looks at Shula and holds a bundle out to her.

Shula takes the bundle - it is a woven shawl with tassels at the ends; it is hard to see the colours or what is woven into it. She holds the shawl aloft, arms outstretched, and bows to the circle, face beaming. Everyone claps.

"Briona, this is for you, may it wrap you in our love," Mona says as she holds out her arms.

I stand up and walk slowly over, tears in my eyes. I take the shawl, turn to the circle and say, "Thank you". Sounds of clapping fill my ears as I return to the bench. The shawl is soft and warm in my hands, made of wool, a dark colour, maybe dark green.

Everyone gets up clapping and whooping and calling our names with words of love and wishes for our journey. We stand, hugging the shawls to our chests. We are wrapped in warm embraces and group hugs. Murta and Gara put their arms around us and squeeze us close. Dori gives us big hugs and smiles. We hold each other tight for a long time. Too soon Teelin and Mona encircle us and bring us away from the fire to the sleeping huts by the Labyrinth. They bring us into a hut and cover us with the shawls and then layers of furs and blankets. Mona sings songs as we fall into a deep sleep.

-4-

Travelling on the River

The faint light of sunrise says it is time to move. I sit up and touch Shula's shoulder. We wrap the woven shawls around our bodies under our furs and go outside with our packs. I press my hand on the precious box that holds my birthstone and step towards the river. Shula stops me with a gentle touch - it is time for our daily attunements. I take a breath and sense the ground beneath my feet. Good Glan today. I can sense the strong energy of the moon and the warmth of the Bright Star. When we're finished, we stand with arms around our shoulders. We open our eyes and take a slow, deep breath - we are ready.

At the Cistin, the visitors from Cill Dara - Gormley, Neasa and Bres - are already there. We stock up with bread, nuts and leftovers from the festival. Bres says we have enough food for all and points to the river. We stride down together, our packs thrown across our shoulders. I'm eager to see Murta waiting at the water's edge to come with us. Pebbles crunch beneath our feet on the riverbank as we grasp the boats, heave them out onto the river and leap in before the water pulls them away. Water splashes on our faces and furs, sending cold shivers down our backs and we laugh. The drops of morning dew catch the light of the sun rising over the mountain above us.

I take one last look at Carraig. The soft outlines of buildings bathe in the early morning light and people around the fire at the Cistin wave to us. I blink back tears as we push away from the shoreline and focus on our journey ahead. Bres and Gormley are in a bigger boat with me and Shula, while Neasa and Murta follow us in a smaller boat.

My hands grasp the paddles as the currents push and pull, and my arms move back and forth in time with my breathing. The river is unruly; it moves in all directions as the currents crisscross. I glance at Gormley's strong body, as muscles shift with the pump of his arms, and I miss a beat of the oar. The boat lurches and grates against the riverbed. A quick push from Bres brings it back into the current that carries us downstream. My face flushes as I lower my head and focus on the movement.

The river picks up speed, and we move with fast rhythmic paddles. I press my feet against the beam at the bottom of the boat and push my arms to move faster. The cool, damp breeze caresses my face, and the thick, earthy smell of gushing water fills my nostrils. Soon we are downriver, surrounded by trees. Bres pauses his paddling, and we drift in silence. The sun is high in the sky when the river changes pace, and the slow, deep current shifts to rippling surfaces. The river is shallow yet moves along faster; it pushes the boats in jerky movements from side to side.

"I see a waterfall," Shula shouts with a big smile on her face.

"Yes, up ahead," Bres calls.

"My vision is right again!" Shula exclaims and laughs in her bubbly way, and we all laugh with her.

"We bring the boat ashore and carry it downhill to the foot of the waterfall," Bres shouts. A sudden current catches the boat. "*Quick!* Go to the bank!"

He steers the boat towards the bank. Ahead the waters narrow and rush along with strong currents. We tug the boat over to the left; it crunches across the riverbed and grinds to a stop at the bank. The river disappears over an edge ahead of us. We jump out - and Murta's boat hurtles past.

"No." Gormley throws himself into the water and wades towards Murta's boat, but he is too slow; he stands soaked as the boat plunges over the edge. We run towards the edge, but Bres holds out a hand. We stop - he has been on this journey many times.

"It's too dangerous with the rocky ravine!" Exclaims Bres.

"But we *have* to save them!" Shula cries, her eyes wide with fear.

"Gormley, go!" Bres shouts, pointing toward the edge.

Gormley shivers with cold, but he sets off close to the riverbank and soon disappears over the edge. I stand, unsure what to do, and take hold of Shula's hand. Her face is white.

"Hurry, carry the boat to the edge of the waterfall!" Bres urges.

"What will happen to them?" I ask.

"Wait and see."

My heart beats faster at these words. We need to get down to Murta and Neasa quickly. We move as fast as possible. Shula and I stand on each side of the boat with Bres at the back and heave it onto our shoulders. It is hard to keep our balance on the rocks, tufts of grass and reeds. At last, the path shifts downward in a gentle slope. Shula and I quicken our pace.

"*Stop!*" Bres shouts.

We halt on the edge of a small ravine above the river. Water cascades down from a height, bare rocks stick out from a gully wall, and here and there, trees sprout. Loud gushing sounds as water pounds the rocks below, spraying everywhere, then surging forward. My mouth goes dry - at the base of the waterfall are the smashed remains of a boat. Murta and Neasa lie on the ground by the riverbank with Gormley kneeling beside them.

"I climb down, you lower the boat," Bres says as he scrambles down the side and catches the boat as we lower it over the edge with two ropes and guide it to the ground. We hurry down just in time to see Neasa sit up, a big gash on her forehead. She is pale but her eyes are clear. Tears stream down her face as she grasps Gormley's hand.

Murta lies unmoving on the ground. Surely it is not time for Murta to go to the Otherworld like my mother. I run over, kneel beside him and put my hands on his body. It is cold and quiet, but his chest still rises and falls. We hunker in a circle around him. Shula places her hands on each side of his head.

"Gormley - hold his feet," Bres tells him, looking around. "We need a healing stone."

"Briona knows stones," Shula says.

I jump up, pause, and look around. Maybe someone else knows more. But no one moves, they are waiting for me.

"*Quick!*" Bres urges me.

He puts his hands on Murta's chest and pumps up and down. I stand, mouth dry, a quiver in my chest, unsure how to find a stone.

"Hurry, or we won't save him." Bres looks up at me. But I'm still not able to move. I stand there, stuck, with tears in my eyes. I blink them away. If Beo leaves Murta's body, he loses his life. I need to find a stone to bring Beo back into his body.

"*Briona!*" shouts Shula to me as she hits the ground with her fist. "*Come here!* Put your feet on the ground. Glan."

I go and stand beside Shula. She puts her hands on my feet and presses them into the ground. Breathe. I move away step by step towards the bank of the river, eyes half open. A healing stone is waiting there, but I must go slow so that I can feel the pulse of the earth and sense the stone. I scan the ground, looking for a stone that shines.

A light pulls me; I bend and there is a white stone on the ground. I pick it up, yes, it is solid with a soft throb. I hold it in my hands to warm it and run to Murta. I place the stone on his belly to let its heat enter his body. I take a deep breath and call on Beo to flow through my hands into his body.

We all breathe Beo together, slowly, in and out, bringing it through our hands and into Murta's body. As we breathe and press, his cold body shifts to cool. We keep our hands in place and wait. At last, Murta opens his eyes. I touch his cheek.

"Murta..." Bres says gently and touches his arm.

"I tried to pull the boat to the left," says Murta with a hoarse voice.

"That's why you and Neasa are alive," Bres says.

"Is Neasa...?" asks Murta as he struggles to sit up.

"She's sitting up. You're hurt!"

With all our eyes on Murta, we forgot about Neasa, but she has a big gash – she's not alright. Gormley goes to put his arm around her, while we keep our hands on Murta's body. I put his hands on the healing stone; he smiles and tries to sit up.

"Stay," Bres says and presses his shoulder.

We sit for a long time with our hands on his body until Murta's breath is steady and his body warms. At last Murta gets to his feet, but his leg is swollen. We stand in a circle with our arms around our shoulders and give thanks for the lack of broken bones.

"We need to make a fire," Bres says.

He leaves the group and walks over to a cave dug out of the side of the ravine. A circle of stones marks a fire pit beside it. He beckons us to come over, but we want to stay with Murta, and Neasa is still shaking. Gormley holds her in a close embrace.

"This is a stopping place for travellers, we use what we need and then replace it," calls Bres. "We can stay here tonight. Thank Spirit we have food for one night."

He takes firewood out of the cave and lights a fire with his firestick, then walks over and picks up broken bits of the boat to use in the fire. Murta's face goes pale again and he shivers. We bring him over to the fire where Gormley and Neasa sit, colour back in her face.

The fire warms us all. We get shelters and beds ready for a night in the cave and hope the fire keeps the cold out. Bres hands out bread and nuts and dried meat. It is odd to eat familiar food in a strange place. The food and fire soothe us.

"That was a joyful Imbolc celebration," Neasa says.

"And we're all Seekers now!" Gormley exclaims, his eyes shining in the firelight.

I beam with excitement – we are beginning Turas together. We exchange smiles, but we are worn from the long day and don't have much to say. Soon people lie down to sleep, bodies side by side covered in furs. I lie on my back. Mona said there will be tests on Turas and it will happen on the first day. I thank Shula in my head, for helping me with Glan, so I could find a stone to help Murta.

The next morning, I wake up from a very long sleep. The damp air is cool on my face and the smell of mist fills my nostrils.

"We can't see enough to go on the river." I hear Bres' voice. "We need to stay here today and go to Cill Dara tomorrow."

"We can climb up to the forest and collect food and wood," Gormley responds.

"And we can make a net and catch some fish," Bres adds.

Beside me, Murta opens his eyes.

"I hurt everywhere," he murmurs, his voice weak.

Shula and I help Murta to get up and he limps outside.

"It's good to move," Shula says gently.

Murta sits as we do our daily movements. Neasa is well enough to move with us. We stand silently and attune to the stars. The movements bring heat through our bodies and help tensions flow out. Bres doesn't join in, he just watches, but even he seems calm and peaceful when we finish. We are ready to go and look for food and wood for the fire.

I climb up the side of the ravine into the forest with Shula. We fan out in different directions, moving slowly, staying close to the trees, and making noise to keep animals away. We move carefully as we gather up firewood in this strange forest, bring armloads back and toss them over the side. We don't know what animals are out there, or where the forest ends. It is different from the times at home with Dori when we talked and laughed as we carried the wood through the forest to the Cistin so that Gara could use it to bake bread.

We meet at the edge and then turn back into the forest again. Shula digs up roots and I look for nuts that animals hide. The rain keeps our faces cold and soon we are back to warm ourselves at the fire. I sit close to Murta, and he smiles at me and squeezes my hand, the colour back in his face. Bres and Gormley sit by a net stretched out over the river, woven from reeds with worms attached. We stoke the fire. Soon Bres and Gormley have enough fish for us all. They are pleased as they prepare the fish for cooking. We have roots and nuts and with Shula's tasty plants from the forest, we have enough for a lovely meal.

We gather by the fire before dark. Bres, Gormley, Neasa, Murta - but not Shula, where is she? She is not in the cave or down by the river. We call her name and there is no response. We run to climb the ravine; we must find her before the light fades. I scramble straight up the bank with Bres as Gormley goes around and climbs up the side.

"Shula! Shula!" We yell her name.

We scan the forest with eyes and ears, calling out her name. The forest is eerily quiet as we wait for a sound.

"*Shula!*" Bres bellows.

He stretches out his arms, I grasp his hand, Gormley takes the other hand, and we stand together to reach out to her. Nothing. As we hold a picture of Shula in our heads, we reach out through the trees, calling her name. A breeze ripples from the forest. A picture of her caught in some mist comes into my head, but I don't know the direction. We strengthen our reach and fix on a spot in the direction of sunset. We focus as hard as we can to draw her back to the river. Slowly we feel her move in our direction. As she gets closer, we call her name again. A wave of relief washes over us as we hear her answering cry. Soon she appears out of the forest and runs to us, words tumbling out, eyes wide.

"I wandered into a clearing in the forest and was unable to find my way out." Shula looks back at the forest as she speaks. "There was a Hawthorne tree, dancing lights and some sweet sounds. A mist came out of nowhere, filling the clearing and making the world fade away. It made me want to stay. Then I heard your shouts. I still couldn't move. But then you got stronger, I felt you, but I didn't know what direction to go in. I couldn't see any gaps in the clearing. I kept going around and around in circles."

Bres touches her shoulder.

"Have you got a message? Did you have a vision?" he asks gently.

Shula pauses and lowers her eyes.

"Sometimes I can't see, the visions aren't always right," she says in a low voice.

"I *love* to hear your visions, they always help," I say, trying to comfort her.

Shula shrugs and looks down, hunching her shoulders.

"We must get back, it's getting dark," Bres says.

He steps forward, taking Shula's arm and helps her back down the bank. Shula has the gift of second sight; she sometimes wanders off to follow a vision. But it is not safe for her to do that here; she can get lost in the forest, where a wolf or boar might get her.

We walk over to the fire where Murta and Neasa sit. Murta's face brightens when he sees us with Shula. Bres continues to hold onto Shula's arm. She is in a daze, she is drawn to stay with the forest spirits, and we need to get her back with us. The Moon peers through the mist above. The air is still damp, but the fire dries our clothes and warms our bodies. I want Shula to tell me more, but nobody talks, we are all hungry and ready to eat.

"In the forest," Shula says slowly after we finish the meal, "I sensed some nettles and walked that way. The mist came and grew denser, and a big old Hawthorne tree reached out and pulled me over."

She starts to sing a beautiful melody. My head tingles and longing fills me - I want to go back with her to the forest. Shula's voice fades and she looks around with joy in her eyes. We are silent as the spell of the melody holds us.

"You know that big tree is a Wishing Tree," Bres points out, not happy. He looks around at the group. We are quiet. The strong force of a Wishing Tree can take people away.

"Bres is right," Murta says. "You must not go there alone."

Shula raises her shoulders and looks away, eyes closed.

"Stay with the group, it's not safe to be alone in the forest," Bres says in a gentle voice with his eyes on Shula.

We sit in silence until Gormley starts a song about forest spirits, and we join in. Pitch dark surrounds us, as the fire lights up our faces and warms my body. A picture of Gormley's strong body on the boat flashes into my head, sending tingles throughout my body. I look at him and our eyes meet - there is that spark again! I want to snuggle up with him. But Bres says something and Gormley looks away. The spark fades, maybe it is not so strong, or the time is wrong. Or maybe he is with Neasa. They are close but I don't see a spark between them.

"Time to sleep. Let's hope we can travel tomorrow," Bres says as he settles the fire.

I lie back with Shula beside me. She is quiet. Bres is right, no one goes to the forest alone when it is cold and dark, it is too dangerous.

Shula's melody rings in my head when I wake up the next morning. Joy seeps through my body, like in the Labyrinth when I held my birthstone, though it is not as strong. I shake Shula and we get up and walk along the river to the waterfall. Shula seems only half awake, her head still somewhere in a dream. We stand and watch sunlight dance on the water through the trees.

We move through our attunements together, but the sound of water gushing by fills my head with questions. What if I can't sense stones enough to be a Keeper of Stones? I feel unsure about Shula. What if she wanders off and gets lost in visions again? At the end of our movements, we stand close together, uneasy about what lies ahead. Already Turas challenges us - first, the accident, where I was slow to find a healing stone, and now Shula got lost in the mist and is unsure about her vision. I fear we may have more challenges on Turas.

"Time to go!" Bres shouts.

We go back and help rake out the fire and put leftover firewood in the cave. Bres and Gormley pull the boat down to the river and we all scramble in. Murta and Neasa squeeze into the middle; they are still sore and stiff, leaving just enough room for the rest of us at either end.

The rush of water from the waterfall rocks the boat, it is hard to keep it balanced, but soon the river is calm and deep. We settle into a steady rhythm, paddling faster and picking up speed. Trees streak by, it is exciting to travel so fast in a boat. I keep pace with Bres, as I breathe and paddle, breathe and paddle. We pass a gap in the trees, maybe a settlement like ours, but there is no time to look. We paddle together for a long time with our bodies swaying, sweat flowing, our arms moving up and down, back and forth, back and forth until we are one.

When Bres slows the pace of the boat, I look up to see a big open space ahead. We slow further and approach the riverbank. The forest is cleared far back and a huge plain of green grass stretches along and up from the river - the Plain of Cill Dara! Roofs of buildings peek across the horizon. Rows and rows of boats of different shapes and sizes line the river - long narrow canoes and barges, round basket boats for fishing and stargazing. Bres and Gormley steer the boat over and pull up beside a wooden pier built out into the river.

"Welcome to Cill Dara," Bres declares as he turns towards Shula and holds out a hand.

- 5 -

The Temple at Cill Dara

Bres helps Shula onto the wooden pier, and they stand for a moment as Shula gazes around, wide-eyed. I step forward to join her, but Murta stumbles as he rises. I hurry to steady him and with help from Neasa and Gormley, we step onto the pier. Bres points to the first longhouse close to the river.

"That's where you stay tonight, there are also other Seekers who are here on their journey to Brú," Bres says. "Tomorrow morning you go to the Temple of the Bright One and leave your birthstones there for Imbolc."

Mona lived at the Temple for many years before she came back to Carraig. She says it is wonderful, full of beautiful art, jewellery and pottery, a magical place of joy and healing.

"My leg still hurts from the accident," Murta says, grimacing.

"Gormley, Neasa, take Murta to the Labyrinth," Bres says, and points to a pathway.

"I want to go too," I say and look to Murta.

"No, you need to stay with the Seekers, you have to be ready for the Temple," Bres replies firmly.

I turn and take Murta's arm; I want to stay close to him and help him to heal. But Murta squeezes my hand gently.

"Stay with the Seekers, we all need to rest," he says, his voice softer now.

"But I don't know where you're going!"

I look around at the immense plain of green that undulates into the distance. Clusters of buildings stretch in all directions, with rows of longhouses where many people come and go while big groups of children play and a huge fire blazes in the centre. The roof of a large, curved building peeps over the gentle swell of the land, maybe the Temple of the Bright One.

"Go with Shula and meet other Seekers," Murta repeats. He puts an arm around me and turns me to face the big fire. "See, the Cistin is by the fire, we can meet there." Pain flashes across his face as he steps away. I turn to Shula, but she is already walking ahead with Bres. Their hands brush as she looks back and beckons me along.

We enter the longhouse to the familiar sight of candles along the walls with a fire in the centre. There is a hum of conversation and people scattered around. They look like our clan, but their clothes are different. They wear tunics, shirts of wool and jackets of animal skin, with plenty of headbands but not many feathers, and necklaces of animal bone and stone.

"Here are two Seekers from Carraig, from beside the river up in the mountains. Briona and Shula," Bres says, waving us over to the fire where a group of people sit together. Friendly faces look up. "Meet the Seekers who live here in Cill Dara."

He turns to us. How can there be so many with Bright Star Return here, and only two of us in Carraig? I barely hear as Bres tells us their names. They smile at us as we take off our furs and sit down.

Neasa and Gormley come into the longhouse and join the group.

"Is Murta feeling better?" I ask, worried.

"Yes, he's getting help," Gormley replies, smiles at us and then sweeps his arms around the group. "Welcome to Cill Dara. We can help you settle."

He holds my gaze, and I smile back. Shula sits beside me, she senses the connection with Gormley, she presses her arm against me and leans in with a small raise of eyebrows. I smile and nod to Bres, raising my eyebrows at her. Gormley gestures to the group and they each repeat their names. Another group comes into the longhouse - more Seekers. They arrive from further downriver. Thirteen Seekers. So many new people all at once.

There are piles of food - bread and spreads, nuts and seeds, dried meat, milk - and we gather around the fire to eat. I sit quietly and listen to the talk about the Imbolc festival. Like us, they heard that Voyagers may come to our island later this year. I lean in to hear more.

"Áine travels with them. She left here to go to their land, now she's coming back," someone says.

"She left from Cill Dara? When did she go?" another asks.

"Many years ago. We had a farewell ceremony for her."

"Is she bringing them here?"

"We're not sure when they arrive. She may go with them to Brú for Winter Sun Standstill," the first speaker replies. She talks smoothly as if she knows Áine. But then Shula's vision outside the Dreamhouse at Carraig comes into my head - someone missing at Brú. I wonder if we can all get to Brú and enter the chamber of Newgrange. I look around at the new faces. There are many moons before Winter Sun Standstill. How will we all work together until then? They all grew up together, they have the Temple of the Bright One and a huge farm. Shula and I may get lost in this big place.

Someone begins to play drums, and we get to our feet to dance, glad to move after the long journey. We scatter through the longhouse dancing and skipping, twirling and smiling. The energy sweeps away questions - this year can be fun.

Gormley comes towards me, his blue eyes full of light. He is taller than me, his leggings of dark brown animal skin make his legs look long and solid. A blue wool shirt covers his broad chest, and he wears a necklace of deer bones with markings that look like stars. Around his head is a red band with small crystals that sparkle in the firelight. I sway in rhythm with him, and we hold each other's gaze with big smiles on our faces. We take each other's hands and twirl around. His hands feel warm and gentle. Warmth spreads through my body and sparks rise as his body brushes mine when we move together. Then someone else grabs Gormley's arm and twirls him away. The spark fades - I hope it grows stronger.

Cill Dara is so much bigger, but maybe things are not so different after all. I weave around Bres and Shula as they sway together. Bres is almost a head taller, but Shula looks strong and sturdy beside his long frame. She sways in front of me, catches my hands and twirls me around. She raises eyebrows at me and then draws them together. We dance until people drift off to the sides of the longhouse to settle for sleep.

I wake up to a dark morning. Shula is beside me; she wants to go outside. I follow her out.

"Do you like Gormley?" she asks, standing to face me, her hands on her hips.

"Maybe."

"What about Dori?" Shula presses, her tone shifting slightly. As Dori's sister, she is protective.

"I don't know. It's too soon." I answer.

I turn to go back inside, but Shula presses forward.

"Do you have *feelings* for Dori?"

"*How* can you ask that?"

"You have *a lot of sparks*, Briona," she remarks.

"You danced with Bres," I answer back.

Why is Shula talking to me like this?

"Bres danced with you too," Shula points out sharply. She is right. But everyone danced together. "Sparks come and go for you, *you don't care.*"

"I don't *look* for sparks," I answer, frustrated.

"But you *always* follow them."

"*No,* that's not right. We all have sparks we don't follow," I respond.

"You follow sparks and forget about Dori."

"*I love Dori!*"

My legs twitch, I want to stop this talk.

"Dori loves you, and now you have a spark with Gormley and even Bres."

"Not *Bres,*" I snap.

Is this why Shula is angry? I saw him look at Shula, hold her hand, and Shula's beam when they danced together. I have sparks with Bres, but I am not drawn to him.

"And Gormley and Neasa, *what about them?* Maybe they're together," Shula says. I open my mouth to answer, but I don't know what to say about them. "Dori, Gormley, Bres, *you want everyone!*"

She stares into my eyes.

"You don't *know* what I want," I say, my voice shaking.

"*You draw people in*, you have many sparks, but you don't stop to think about how people feel!" Shula says, her voice rising as she takes a step back.

"You follow sparks too…"

"I don't leave someone behind! *Dori loves you!*"

"You follow your visions, you go off to the forest, you leave us. How can we know you'll stay with us?" I ask. Shula stares blankly at me. "Shula! How can we know?"

Shula's eyes snap wide.

"Briona, you know I want to stay."

"You go into the forest, and you follow the call of a Wishing Tree," I continue. Blood rushes through my body at the picture of us at the top of the ridge, full of fear that she is gone. "Can you be *sure* your visions are always right?"

"It was hard for you to find a stone to heal Murta," she states as tears well in her eyes and she kicks a stone with her foot.

We stand facing each other, hands tight and faces red. Footsteps approach, interrupting the moment.

"Tension often rises between Seekers," someone says. A Keeper in a long, deep blue robe with a green band around short auburn hair stands there and looks at us with arms crossed. We glance at each other and shift uneasily. We are silent, even Shula does not question the new Keeper. "Do your attunements, when we go to the Temple you must be clear."

We stand in silence, eyes down, breathing fast. We don't look at each other as we shift from one foot to the other. The Keeper waits with a calm face. Shula sighs and holds out a hand, but I am stung by her words. He looks from me to Shula and back. I take her hand. We are in this together, I hope we stay together.

We follow the Keeper to the longhouse where Seekers stand outside in a cluster ready for attunements. I'm unsure if I can do the movements when there is so much tension between Shula and me, but I go through the motions. We face east with our feet firm on the ground, just as the sun peeps over the horizon. We raise arms to greet it, then turn south and welcome the warmth of fire, then west to the flow of water and north for our grounding in the earth. Energy circulates through my body and the tension sinks into the ground. Even with so many new people in the group, we can do familiar movements in harmony. We finish the movements and stand to face the Keeper.

"My name is Coll," the Keeper introduces himself as he claps hands, calling us to listen. "Welcome to every Seeker who has arrived over the last two days as you start on Turas, your journey to Brú. I hope you all had a chance to get to know each other."

"Oh yes," somebody says, and laughter ripples through the group, even with a Keeper standing there. Although Coll does not smile, he has a kind look on his face.

Shula and I stand apart, the eight Seekers from Cill Dara stand in a cluster, and the three Seekers from downriver also stand together. They dress more like us, in furs and woven tunics.

"Follow me to the Cistin and then to the Temple of the Bright One to offer your birthstones. Stay together," Coll says, looking to each of us.

We hurry into the longhouse and take the boxes with birthstones from our packs, then follow Coll outside. A big group of people in the central area between the Longhouses are doing daily attunements. They all move together gracefully, like a flock of birds. They finish the movements and people drift off, some over the crest of the hill or down to the river, others to big barns made of wood that stand beside rows of stone and wooden fences where farm animals live.

We enter the Cistin, it is huge, and many people bustle around. Long rows of shelves hold jars of nuts and seeds. Two people grind wheat into bowls and hand them over to a table where people make dough for bread, while another group feeds wood into four big clay ovens. My mouth waters, I want to explore every corner. Gormley stops beside me. I smile at him, and he smiles back as he hands me a slab of bread and his fingers brush my palm. I want to stay with him, but Coll moves us along. I take handfuls of nuts and seeds - I hope we come back for a big meal in the middle of the day like at home and I can see Murta then. We leave the Cistin and follow a path through more longhouses.

"This is the Temple of the Bright One," Coll says.

He gestures at a round roof that peeks over a curve in the land, the same roof that we saw when we arrived. The building comes into view, and we stop.

"It's *beautiful*, its shape is like a flower," someone says.

"*It's alive!* Like a dancing body!" Shula exclaims.

She beams at us all as we gaze at the undulating wall. It is painted in beautiful earth red with lighter and darker shades. A round roof made of thatch rises from the edges to the centre with many colours of sparkling stones woven through. Lights, shades and sparkles dance in the low sunlight. It calls me to enter, and I quickly move forward.

"The Temple holds the stillness of Imbolc - we need to enter slowly," Coll says as he holds up a hand to stop me. I press my lips together and Neasa raises her eyebrows at me. "You'll see the wheel of the year unfold through eight tapestries. We see the Sun Standstills of Summer and Winter and the Sun Balances of Spring and Autumn. In between are times of shifts in energy - Imbolc, Bealtaine, Lúnasa, and Samhain. As you know, each brings its own form of joy that comes to us at our celebrations."

Coll's familiar words about the wheel of the year soothe me. We are just at Imbolc; we have plenty of time until Winter Sun Standstill.

I follow the group into a square chamber big enough to hold us all. Shula touches my hand and stands beside me in front of Coll.

"This is the Haven," Coll explains. "You'll come here for lessons with me and other Keepers. You can come to me for help. Most of you will need it!"

He smiles - Keepers don't often make jokes. Coll is different, he is warm and funny, but we all do what he says. He stands at the top of the room and raises his hands. We stand in rows and breathe together for a long time, air moving in and out until tension fades from my body and I feel like a tree rooted in the forest with other trees beside me. A gong sounds.

We follow Coll along a pathway that brings us to a round stone wall.

"This well gives us precious water of life that we use in the Temple," Coll says as he picks up a cup. He leans in to fill the cup, then passes the cup for each of us to take a drink.

The Temple doors open and we glide through. Waves of colour wash over us. All around us are beautiful tapestries, pottery, jewellery, carved wood, bones, stones - a dazzling display of artistry. A shiver runs down my back and my hair prickles all over my body. Mona is right, this fills me with awe. In the centre a big tree runs from floor to roof. The cycle of the seasons unfolds on the tapestries in the alcoves that surround us - the sun and moon shift from dark to light across a starry sky while the earth awakens, blossoms and settles back. The soft light and sense of peace hold the stillness for wonderful energy to unfold.

The Keepers stop at the alcove for Imbolc, and we stand in front of the beautiful tapestry that shows a backdrop of a starry indigo night sky with the crescent moon, a white band of stars and the sun peeking. In the forest little buds are still closed, and green shoots peep up from the ground, while birds perch on branches, awakening from Winter. Wheels woven from reeds sit on the ground with bursts of colour from feathers and bits of dyed cloth woven in. An image of Mona at the stone circle in the forest fills my head. Carraig feels so far away already.

Next is the alcove for the Sun Balance of Spring, when night and day are equal. The tapestry shows a backdrop of the night sky with one-half of the sun showing above the horizon. Small animals - rabbits and moles - scurry across the forest floor. Birds' nests are full of eggs and blossoms and buds are everywhere. Rows of small pottery bowls painted with spirals and wavy lines contain seeds for sowing. My heart sinks - we may not be at home in Carraig for Sun Balance this year.

The alcove for Bealtaine, when clans come together at Cloch Mhór to share sparks and charge the earth, brings joy. Mona, Dori and others from Carraig may come for the Bealtaine festival and meet us there. Now the tapestry backdrop shifts to daylight with the full sun above the horizon. Warmth rises in my body as the orange yellow of the sun catches the colours of a huge fire burning in the middle of the tapestry and people dance beneath the full moon.

The Summer Sun Standstill alcove bursts with bright oranges from a blazing sun in the centre of the tapestry, with many figures dancing in a double spiral for the longest day of the year. At the edge of the tapestry are trees in beautiful shades of green. I want to jump in and join the dance. I wonder what new energy the Voyagers may bring.

My head spins as we move to the next alcove, vivid with yellows and oranges of Lúnasa, when energies let loose with fun and games before the harvest. Who knows where we all may be by then? The sun is still full in the centre of the tapestry and the full moon beams from the sky. Woven through the sun is a huge ribbon of fields with bright yellow plants growing in waves, with rows of people, some bent over and some with their arms raised to the sky.

The colours fade on the leaves in the forest on the tapestry for the Sun Balance of Autumn, with one-half of the sun below the horizon against the night sky. I smile at the image of the people beaming from the harvest gathering. They fill boats as they return home, their bags brimming with roots and greens, wheat, apples, berries and nuts.

Then comes the alcove for Samhain and the turn to Winter's darkness, when the weave between our world and the Otherworld stretches and ancestors can visit. The tapestry shows a dark night sky and bare trees in the forest with dolmens and cairns in the distance. A huge cauldron sits on a fire and around it is a circle of people in robes with white faces. My heart beats for my mother. I don't have a picture of her in my head, I was too young when she left this world, but we speak her name every year at Samhain.

In the alcove for Winter Sun Standstill, a huge cairn covered in white stones shines in the centre. Swans glide on the wide river below the cairn, with bare trees to the sides. Beams of orange light shine into the entrance of the cairn from the sun that rises above the horizon against the night sky - it is Newgrange, the great mound at Brú. My eyes widen at the huge spirals and diamonds that leap out. I put a hand to my box with my birthstone and turn to see Shula touch hers. When we lay our birthstones on the mound, our energy spirals with earth, sea and sky, with our ancestors and all life to come. Shula trembles beside me. Our eyes meet, full of joy.

We turn to face the centre of the temple. A huge rug lies on the ground in earth colours of green and brown. We stand in a circle around the large tree that rises through a hole in the rug with roots that sink into the earth and branches that reach up to a curved roof with a painted sky. Carved fruits and berries weave around the branches. The animals carved into the trunk - salmon, wolf, eagle, raven, bear, deer, forest birds, dog, cows and sheep - come alive as we circle them.

A gong sounds and we lie on the ground with our heads in the direction of the tree. Above our heads, spirals, circles, wavy lines, and diamonds and half diamonds dance. The sound of a pipe drifts into the temple, a long, slow note that rises and falls. It fills the space with a beautiful sound and sets my hair on end and my skin prickling. Soon I am floating and bobbing on waves of sound. The music grows louder, it sweeps up and down, with long and short notes, loud and soft. It holds us in rapture as it sweeps to higher notes. Dazzling white light fills my head and body. My birthstone throbs as a vision comes to my head.

A boat glides upriver and arrives at a cavern filled with white light. At the back of the cavern, gentle streams of water flow down the walls. In the centre, a woman in robes sits on a big round chair. She glows, she is the source of white light, so bright that I can't see the colour of her robes. She gazes out with beaming eyes and smiling lips.

This is the Bright One, Source of life! She who gives me my name. Waves of love for our tribe wash over me. Bliss flows through my head and my body feels like it is floating in a warm pool of water. The music goes lower, holds, and then lowers again. The energy flows out, down my arms and legs and back into the earth as the vision fades. The pipe slows down and then stops. My eyes open.

We rise and leave the temple slowly, step by step, down the corridor back to the Haven. We stand in front of Coll and breathe together. Beautiful pictures fill my head, and I beam with joy as Coll leads us in slow movements that keep us calm.

"Glan is good from Imbolc, the Temple of the Bright One brings great joy," Coll comments.

A Keeper in a deep blue robe with an indigo headband enters the room. She is tall with a thin face and sharp eyes.

"This is Sorcha, Keeper of Stones," Coll introduces her as he turns to her. Her eyes sweep over us. "Now we take your birthstones to keep in the Temple until you leave for Summer Sun Standstill."

Coll waves us over to Sorcha one by one. I reach into my pouch and take out the box. I don't want to hand over my birthstone. The Seekers from Cill Dara each hand Sorcha the box with their birthstone. Then Coll gestures to me.

"Are you from Carraig?" Sorcha asks. I nod. She leans forward and murmurs in my ear. "Mona is soft. We will test you here."

My face goes white, and my mouth goes dry. How can she say that? We never hear a Keeper speak badly about another Keeper. Surely, she knows Mona, they are the same age and Mona spent time here when she was young. Maybe she does not like Mona, but I'm not sure why she brings that into this ceremony. I hold my box tightly as pictures of Mona in the Labyrinth go through my head.

Sorcha holds out her hand for the box. My hand does not move. She stares into my eyes. Her look is so powerful that my hand moves forward and gives the box to her. My hand feels bare without it. She looks away and I move back to the other Seekers, my mouth dry, and my body shaking.

Shula steps forward and hand her box to Sorcha. There are no words between them. We wait in silence as the last few Seekers move forward. Coll says we can go to the Cistin and enjoy the rest of the day, tomorrow we will start training.

I stumble out with tears in my eyes, all joy and love gone from my body. My stomach churns, and my face is flushed. Did I do something wrong? Can Sorcha block me from Glan, or even stop me from going to Brú? Shula comes and embraces me, holds me close, the tension between us gone for now. I tell her of Sorcha's words. We don't know why she said this to me. We walk down to the Cistin together in silence. The big meal is finished but there is plenty of food left. I eat in a daze.

-6-

Sparking

That night I toss and turn. My head is too busy. What kind of tests did Sorcha mean? I don't know why she would call Mona soft, she is strong and clear. Here there are so many people, no one knows us. I hope Murta is getting healing. I long for Mona and Dori, I miss my people, and I miss home. What if I am not able to read stones? Questions go around and round until sleep falls.

In the morning Coll comes and says it is time to go to the Haven. We do daily attunements, enter the Haven and sit on the ground in rows.

"It's time to find your path," Coll says as he stands at the top of the room. "Some of you can work with stones, some with plants, some will go stargazing. Now, select a stone, one you are drawn to, and hold it against your belly."

Coll points to the wall where baskets filled with stones are laid out. I kneel and run my hands over the stones. One stone tingles in my hand and I pick it up.

"Now sit and focus," Coll says, sitting down.

We sit for a long time with a stone in our hands. Heat from my body enters the stone and I hold it against my belly and breathe in its warm glow.

"Those who sense heat in the stone stay here." Coll stands up as he speaks. "You'll train here in the Haven, sometimes at the Labyrinth. Every morning there are different stones, there is much to learn."

"What if we don't sense heat?" someone asks.

"You go to the star mounds or the gardens, everyone has a gift."

"How do we know what our gift is?" Another person asks.

"When you have Glan, when your body is clear for Beo to flow, you'll know," Coll assures us and looks at each person. "Some of you find it easier to have Glan, the position of the stars at your birth gives an easy flow. Others have stars that cross and bring blocks to Beo. That is why we do our daily movements - they help us attune to earth and sky and sense when the stars bring dense energy to our bodies that can block the flow of Beo."

Coll gestures to the door and people get up to leave.

"Do we all come here every day?" Somebody asks.

"Yes," affirms Coll, "you come here first. In the middle of the day, everyone eats and then helps at the farmland, which keeps us connected with each other and with the earth."

A burst of talk fills the room as people go to put their stones back in the baskets.

"Did you sense the heat of the stone?" Neasa asks as she turns to me with sharp green eyes.

She has a small frown on her face. I hesitate. I feel a glow from the stone - is that heat?

"Yes, my stone glows," I say.

"My stone throbs with heat," she responds and then pauses. "You're a stone reader?"

"I'm not sure - I hope so," I reply.

"Sorcha is my father's sister, we have the gift of stone," she says in a strong voice. "And my father is a Keeper of Herbs."

"Sorcha teaches you about stones?" I ask, interested in this connection.

"Yes, she teaches us all, and she tests birthstones for Brú."

Neasa tilts her head and raises her eyebrows at me.

"Mona, the Keeper of Charts at Carraig, says my birthstone is strong," I say.

"Maybe, for Carraig. Cill Dara is big; it has the Temple of the Bright One and lots of farmland."

Small trembles rise in my belly.

"Carraig may be small, but the white stones that cover the mounds at Brú came from near our settlement," I say to Neasa, I want her to know that Carraig has its own connection to Brú.

"That was a long time ago."

"Mona brings a special stone from Carraig every year to the Summer Festival," I continue, but Neasa turns away.

"Sorcha will test us and tell us whether we can go to Brú," she says firmly.

Heat rises in my body, my eyes blink fast. What if Sorcha says I can't go to Brú?

I turn to look at Coll.

"This year is special, you'll learn what you need," he says.

He leans forward and places a finger on his lips just as Sorcha enters the room. My stomach lurches. She wears a dark blue robe and an indigo band around her head. No feathers or crystals brighten her robe. Her eyes look over us. Suddenly I long for Mona's bright clothes and warm hugs. Coll glances at her then smiles at us and leaves. Only three Seekers are left - Neasa, me and Felim.

Felim comes from a small settlement further downriver and wears a band around their head that says they are Flowing Star, able to flow between the energies of women and men.

Sorcha picks up the baskets of stones and places one in front of each of us. She holds out headbands and tells us to put them around our heads and over our eyes. She smiles as she hands headbands to Neasa and Felim. Then she turns to me. I hold my breath as I look at her face. Her eyes flicker. It seems she does not know me. I take the band and put it around my head so that I am not able to see.

"Pick up the stones from the basket, see if each is different, place similar stones in a pile," she instructs us.

I hear the other two pick up stones and put them down. I focus on the stones in the basket in front of me, hold them in my hand one by one, and take my time to sense if they are the same or different. Sometimes I'm sure, sometimes I'm not so sure. What if my sense of stones is not enough? Over and over I pick up the stones until the basket is empty. It is so hard to tell the difference between them. Maybe I will fail this test, not go to Brú, not be a healer or a Keeper of Stones. I try to keep tears from my eyes and focus on the sense of the stones.

"Open your eyes," Sorcha says. I look at the two piles of stones in front of me, they look similar. "All the stones are the same."

Silence. I drop my head down as my face goes red, then look at Neasa. Nearly all her stones are in one pile. Felim is like me, with a small pile and a big pile.

"This is your first lesson," continues Sorcha. "Don't always listen to a Keeper, or anyone else. Learn to listen to your body." I clench my hands for a moment. She told us to see if the stones were different, but now I see she did not say that they were. I was too keen on the task I wanted to please her. "Take the time to sense in your body, your body is the channel. Take your time. That is the most important lesson."

Sorcha stands up to leave and we follow.

Outside Coll stands beside Ollie, one of the Seekers from Cill Dara. She stands in a brown robe and dark fur with her shoulders down and arms at her side. Her black hair is pushed back and her brown eyes are dark.

"Ollie's energy is blocked, she needs Sos," Coll says to Sorcha.

"I can't focus!" Ollie sobs, her eyes glistening with tears.

"Everyone gets blocks," reassures Coll as he pats her arm.

Ollie shrugs his arm away.

"*Why* was I born with a clash of stars? Glan is so *hard* for me. I've too many blocks," she complains.

"Do your daily movements and go to the Labyrinth," Sorcha says.

"I do that, but I'm still blocked."

Ollie's face is dark.

"I can help at the Labyrinth," I say, stepping forward.

"Briona, surely you know, Seekers don't help at the Labyrinth," Sorcha says to me in a sharp tone.

I look down. Why did Mona take me to the Labyrinth before Turas? Maybe it is best not to tell her of the balancing back home.

"Have you been to the Labyrinth?" Sorcha asks, her piercing eyes holding my gaze.

"Yes, I was in the Labyrinth for Sos," I say slowly.

"You needed Sos?" Sorcha asks.

"I helped with Sos."

"Mona allowed *you* do Sos?" asks Sorcha, raising her eyebrows.

"Yes."

There is a long silence.

"Why you?" she finally asks.

"She said my birth moon was in a good place."

A long silence follows again. Sorcha stands with her eyes closed. I think about Mona. Shula questioned why Mona chose me. Now

Sorcha thinks she is wrong. Maybe Mona does not always know what is good for us.

"There is no Sos before Turas," states Sorcha firmly. "But in a small place like Carraig, there aren't enough people."

I try to quell the flash of anger that rises in my chest. I want to stand up for Mona.

"She says I have the gift of stone," I assert, raising my head.

Sorcha frowns and draws her lips together to suck in air. Neasa and Felim shuffle.

"A gift is *not* enough, Briona, you have much to learn," Sorcha speaks with flashing eyes. My cheeks flush. Sorcha turns to Coll and Ollie. "Let us go to the labyrinth and clear that dense energy."

She walks away and Coll and Ollie follow.

"Mona asked you to help with Sos?" Neasa asks, turning to me.

"Yes, at Imbolc."

"But you're too young."

"Mona had her reasons," I affirm, pressing my lips together.

Neasa stands for a moment. Then she asks me about Sos. She listens as I tell of the pulses in the stones, the humming and the different flows of energy.

"Sorcha is right, no Sos before Turas," she states, ending the conversation.

She frowns and walks away. Anger, fear and confusion rise in my body. Why does Sorcha speak to me so harshly? And does Neasa know much more than me? Shula says Mona chooses me, now it looks like Sorcha chooses Neasa. My belly churns.

"They don't understand small settlements!" Felim exclaims as they stand beside me. We smile, we both come from small settlements by the same river, An Life. "The Keepers at home say we must be strong for Cill Dara, it's so much bigger. That's why I did the Flowing Spirit ceremony before Turas."

"Who did the ceremony?" I ask.

"My father, he's a Keeper of Charts."

"Oh, like Mona," I point out. We smile at each other. "How did you feel after the ceremony?"

"It was very moving, I felt sure of my path after it brought the strength of ancestors," Felim explains and shows me the hare fur and the weave of hazel that is special to Flowing Spirits. "So now people say 'they' when they talk about me."

"My friend Dori, who lives in Carraig is Flowing Spirit."

"Did they do their ceremony?"

"Not yet, they're not sure. They'll know in time."

"And you work with stones?"

"Yes, I still have much to learn. But maybe not from Sorcha!"

We both laugh. Felim's warm energy helps to calm me as we walk towards the Cistin. But Sorcha's words sting, and Neasa seems to know so much. I wish I could talk to Mona. I'm unsure if I can talk to Shula about this, she often questions Mona and says that she treats me differently. Murta can help - he said to meet him at the Cistin. I look for him, but there is no sign of him. We take some food and sit with Ollie, Neasa and Gormley.

"Are you looking for Shula?" Gormley asks.

"No, Murta, I want to see him," I reply.

"I can take you to the Labyrinth, he's still there."

Gormley stands up. Just then Shula arrives.

"I can go with you," she tells us.

We follow Gormley through rows of longhouses, there are so many, and they all look alike. He says people come and go from the longhouses. They are busy at Sun Balance when people come to help with planting and looking after animals. Then people leave for the Summer Festival and return to help with the harvest. We turn at the edge of the forest. Gormley points to rows of pits and says that is where to empty body waste. Further into the forest, huts are scattered as far as we can see.

"You can find a hut to use any time, and make a small fire if you want," he says.

His blue eyes catch mine; a smile plays on his mouth. An urge to lean into his strong body takes me by surprise.

"Here's the Labyrinth!" he exclaims.

He points at a building that has the shape of three curved domes like the Labyrinth at home, but the walls are built of wattle and daub with a thatched roof. A big dolmen looms on a hill beyond the Labyrinth, beyond the forest. It is much bigger than our dolmen. Three boulders stand taller than Gormley and the slab on top is big enough for two or three bodies.

"Murta may be here," says Gormley, pointing to a longhouse nearby and when we enter, Murta is sitting by a fire. He jumps up with a big beam on his face when he sees me and limps as he moves to embrace me.

"Briona. Shula."

The tension in my body seeps out into the ground as we give him a big hug.

"Murta, my father, is a stargazer," I say to Gormley and his face lights up.

"You too?" Murta asks with a smile on his face.

"And my mother before me. I learn so much from her," Gormley explains as he smiles back.

"Your healers are very good here, soon I can go back to Carraig," Murta says.

"But your leg isn't healed, you need more rest," I say with concern as I look into his eyes.

"It's good enough. I can heal more at Carraig," Murta replies.

I blink back tears; I don't want Murta to leave.

"We met Sorcha, she doesn't like Mona," I burst out.

"She's hard on Briona," adds Shula.

"Sorcha wants everyone to always have good Glan. She was born with stars across from each other, she had to go to the Labyrinth many times growing up. Now she has strong Beo," Murta says.

I catch Shula's eyes, surprised to hear this.

"She and Neasa said Carraig is small," I say.

"It may be small, but you know it has the strong energy of white stones," Murta says softly and puts his hands together. "It's part of the web of life, like all of us here."

I smile at the familiar words.

"Does Mona know Sorcha?" I ask.

"Yes, they stayed here together when the Shining One, Áine, was at the Temple."

We wait for Murta to say more about Mona and Sorcha, but he lowers his eyes.

"Why did Mona leave?" Gormley asks.

"Briona's mother fell and hit her head. She went to the Otherworld. Mona came back to Carraig to take care of Briona," Murta says, his eyes filling with tears as he looks at me.

"Maybe it was hard for her to leave," I say.

Everyone wants to be near a Shining One, they bring the beautiful energy of Buí, the Source of Life. I hang my head as I speak. It was because of me that Mona had to leave Cill Dara. She often spoke of Cill Dara, but I never asked her about leaving.

"Mona rushed back to Carraig, she longed to hold you in her arms," Murta says and smiles at me as he tilts my face and runs his fingers through my hair. "Sorcha wanted her to stay, Mona was born with an easy flow of stars, she has many gifts."

"Was Mona sad to leave here?" I ask.

"She loves the Temple of the Bright One, that's what she misses. Have you been there?"

"Yes... Beautiful white light," Shula murmurs.

"Dazzling," I say.

"That shows your stars are in a strong place, you have good Glan," Murta assures us as he squeezes our hands and beams at us. "This is a good place for you."

Shula's face lights up as she stands, ready to leave. We say goodbye to Murta and leave the longhouse.

Outside Gormley wants to show us where the stargazers go. He brings us to four small cairns - mounds of earth and stone with a round cover of grass - and stops in front of one of them.

"The passageway leads into an inner chamber," explains Gormley. "Stargazers go inside and look out. The direction of the passageway - north, south, east, west - focuses them on a particular part of the sky. They draw birth charts and track the stars."

His eyes shine as he speaks, that is what he wants to do. He makes the signs for the stars with his hands, which are strong and supple. Then he points to a patchwork of fields with woven fences that we can just see on the other side of the longhouses.

"That's where we grow plants and herbs, and further are the big fields for wheat and barley," he says.

Shula's eyes light up when she sees the gardens.

"Plants and herbs for healing?" she asks.

"And cooking! We often thank plants for the taste they bring to food!"

We all laugh.

"Maybe I have a feel for plants that can heal, like you have for stones," Shula exclaims.

She smiles and I beam at her. We all have gifts; Turas helps us find the strongest one.

The patter of rain starts just as we walk past the Temple. It spatters in little dots and bubbles on the roof and walls. Even in the grey light the temple glistens and undulates. A picture of the wonderful white light in the temple flashes through my head and I turn to smile at Gormley. He puts a hand on my back, a calm, strong touch. A smile between us brings a tingle through my body.

The rain comes down faster. Gormley brings us back to the Cistin and we take food to the longhouse. A warm fire lights the inside. We tell stories, sing songs and settle in. Shula goes out and comes back later with a big smile on her face.

"I have big sparks with Bres," she says as she sits beside me.

We sit close, I am happy for her. Felim makes us laugh with jokes about Keepers and tests. But my stomach sinks as I watch Neasa and Gormley. They are close, they sit side by side and Neasa links his arm.

The moon gets bigger each night. We have fun at the fire in the evening, and we start to feel at home. Each day we go to the Haven, sometimes with a big group, sometimes with a small group. Sorcha watches us closely. I stay with Neasa and Felim for stone-reading. I often struggle to sense the stones and sometimes my face flushes. Once I even froze like I did when I was looking for a stone by the river for Murta. Sorcha just sits and waits as I struggle, sweat on my face, until my breath calms and I sense my body on the ground - then I can sense the stone. Neasa knows about stones, she senses their energy, and she knows what stones to use.

Sparks with Gormley grow. Does Neasa have a spark with him too? I don't want to cross her; I want her help with Sorcha. But as I see them by the fire, I know they are friends since they were children, like Dori and me. I don't see a spark between them, they don't go to the forest. A smile grows on my face as I think of Dori. We grew up together, we love each other, and we had our first kiss together. Maybe Dori is too familiar. I have a lot of love for Dori, but Dori is not here. There is a spark with Gormley, why not go with that?

On the night of the full moon, we gather around the fire at the centre of Cill Dara. We huddle in groups and talk easily. Shula and Bres are side by side. Gormley comes over and sits beside me and sparks flicker between us. He is warm and has a big smile on his face. He is wearing a wool shirt and a necklace with a deer bone. His eyes light up when he looks at me and asks about Carraig. The full moon shines and stars twinkle in the sky. We sing and dance and share food. Gormley hardly takes his eyes off me as we sit by the fire, hold hands, and lean into each other, a warm glow between us. He touches my face and says how much he likes my curly black hair. I admire his long and sturdy legs.

"Come to the forest," he says.

We take hands and wander slowly towards the forest. We wear furs, but the cold air chills me as soon as we leave the fire. Occasional chirpings of birds break the silence. We pause at a huge oak tree that is hollow in the centre of its trunk and lean against it. We kiss and press into each other. Lips tingle, warm mouths open, and pleasure seeps through my body. Gormley's fingers trace the line of my neck down to my chest, gently caressing my breast and sending tingles down my body.

"We can go to a hut, there are furs and blankets there," Gormley whispers in my ear.

We walk hand in hand to a hut and Gormley opens the door. We lie down and pull layers on top of us. We are back to kissing, our hands moving up and down our bodies. Our clothes come off, our hands touch and stroke smooth skin. My breath deepens as the rhythmic stroking pushes waves of pleasure through me, from head to toe. I close my eyes and sink into ripples of joy, lulled by the heat of our bodies and the warm layers of fur and wool. We share more hugs and kisses before we dress. I enjoy the feel of his body; he is strong and tender. We smile at each other and step outside to a chill that makes us shiver.

The Bards Arrive at Sun Balance

Days crawl or sometimes fly by. It is still cold and dark, there is often rain, sometimes frost, then a beautiful day bursts open and tells us Spring has arrived. The earth opens, leaves and blossoms grow, and little ones are born. Our bodies grow more alive and alert. Then a sharp wind and frost came again, more days of wind and cloud when we huddle close to the fire in the Haven or in the longhouse.

The crescent moon brings a big wind that sweeps through the forest and the farmlands. Around the fire, we hear murmurs and talk of the Voyagers from people who come to Cill Dara to help get the fields ready for planting and sowing. We hear that Bards may visit at Sun Balance with news of the Voyagers. I'm excited to hear this as Bards never come to Carraig, it is too far up the mountain. Gormley and other stargazers watch the shadow on the stone dial get shorter and shorter as the sun creeps to a balance of day and night.

The winds are clear, and a blue sky welcomes the day of Sun Balance. Big groups gather wood and build a fire near the bank of the river. We lay out food at the Cistin - we have nuts and seeds, and bread made of grains from the store in the Cistin, along with dried meat and milk and cheese from the farm animals. People trap rabbits and deer and catch fish further down the river. Later we help each other polish jewellery, gather feathers and stones, and clean amulets. Shula and I take out our special shawls from Carraig and hang them out. Excitement builds as the sun climbs through the sky until the sound of oars tells us that a group of boats are on the river.

"The Bards are here!" I exclaim, pointing to the boats.

We hurry down to the river and join the crowd milling around as the visitors get out of the boats and pause on the pier to raise their hands in greeting. They wear long, dark cloaks that swing around, and colourful bands around their heads. One has long white hair, another carries a big bundle in their arms. A surge of warmth rises and cheers erupt from the crowd. There is talk all around about what they look like, how they dress, what is in the bundle, and what stories they bring.

And then a rainbow appears in the sky right above the Bards. We gasp at the beautiful sight. Then a full double rainbow appears. The bands of colour are so clear they shimmer, each band shines bright in the sunlight. The arc rises from the river over the heads of the Bards and comes to rest near the fire. The Bards halt and raise their arms to the double rainbow as it hovers for a moment. Then the rainbow disappears. The Bards bow from their waist and sweep their arms out to the setting sun. A huge cheer rises from the crowd; we clap and call out as the Bards proceed up the pathway. I love the bright colours and feathers in their clothes and the way they walk in slow steps. Sorcha, Coll and other Keepers bring them into a small hut, and they disappear from view.

We drift towards a big platform beside the river with rows and rows of benches that are spread out in a half circle on the slope in front of the platform. At the back of the benches, small fires burn, with stacks of wood to keep them going. Gormley waves me over to the Cistin to get platters of food and cups of mead or juice to bring back to the benches. We sit together and share food with the other Seekers. Shula and Bres come to sit behind us, and I smile as Shula leans forward and presses her face to mine. The glow from the fires behind us keeps the sharp cold of the evening air away. All around us are clusters of people from different settlements as well as those who live all year at Cill Dara. Talk and laughter surround us and bring a smile to my face - Cill Dara feels more like home now.

The Sun goes down and the light fades to deep blue. A drum booms out to the right as a procession emerges from the hut. My heart opens at the burst of colour. At the front are Sorcha and Coll, wearing the deep blue robes of Keepers and carrying burning wooden torches. Next is the Bard with white hair, in a long green robe that is covered in feathers - white, blue, black, yellow - and more feathers rise from the band around their head. They shift and float like a big bird with each step that the Bard takes. Another Bard follows with long dark hair wearing a blue robe with crystals and many feathers in their hair. Next, in a light blue robe, someone carries a harp, it is beautiful.

Behind them comes a woman in a bright yellow robe, like the colour of the morning sun with a purple shawl. Other Keepers from Cill Dara follow. We stand to clap and cheer as the Bards walk onto the platform. The harp rings out.

"*Welcome!*" Coll calls, his voice reaching out to all of us as he steps forward. We smile and cheer back to him. "Welcome to Finn and Mara." The two Bards bow to more cheering. "We're full of joy to have Áine back here in Éire, she who travelled away long ago."

The woman in the yellow robe comes forward and people from Cill Dara leap up. Áine holds out her arms and smiles in every direction. She is my height, with long hair the colour of the sun that matches her yellow gown. Around her hair is a simple purple band, the same colour as her shawl, decorated with yellow spirals. Now I see why people cheer - she glows with the light of a Shining One.

Finn moves to the front with his arms outstretched.

"Let us invoke the spirits of this land, of trees, plants, animals, birds, rain, of sun, moon and stars." Finn speaks with a booming voice and drums roll. "Let us celebrate this turn in the wheel of the year, the time of equal day and night. Let the sun grow stronger, the earth grows warm, and let water feed our seeds and plants and animals."

Drums beat out to the familiar words of Sun Balance, and I beam as a picture of people around the fire at Carraig comes into my head - I'm sure they are also celebrating Sun Balance.

"The Voyagers have landed on our island, as our prophecies foretell. Let us hear how they arrived at Sligeach," Finn continues, then, he turns. "Mara…"

Mara steps forward. Her gown dances in the glow of firelight and her feathers sway as she swings her long white hair and speaks.

"*It is the start of Imbolc,*
Of nights that are long and dark.
And days that are short and always cold,
Though often bright and sunny.
Earth yields and stirs as the wheel turns.
Our dreams see that a boat arrives.
On a hilltop we stand to watch,
Our eyes scanning across the bay.

A small boat heads for shore.
Six hooded figures in cloaks
Wield oars with steady hands.
And then the boat disappears,
As if swallowed by nine waves or more.
Time ticks by slowly.
We see a thick cloud of dark smoke,
And then the sun goes down to night."

The crowd stirs uneasily at the words 'dark smoke'. But it is just like the dream at Imbolc that morning in Carraig! My head fills with a picture of six figures in a boat. Mona and the Dreamers are right after all, their dreams showed the Voyagers arriving just like this. Mara looks out over our heads.

"At sunrise we take our boats
And cross the bay to find them.
We pull our boats ashore.
Wind swirls and mist rolls in.
We cannot see.
We look for shelter for the night.
Hoping to find the Voyagers in first light.
But still the mist stays heavy.
We sit and wait and watch and hope.
Even on the third day the mist still holds.
We wait and then we start a hum."

Mara pauses and looks out over the group. There is silence as we hang on every word. Finn stands beside Mara and starts to hum. He signals to us all to join. Many different sounds, low, high, short, long, ragged, rise and blend. Energy gathers as the hum grows louder and my body quivers to pulses that connect me with the people around me - it is my first time to be in a group so big and hear a hum so loud. Finn stands with arms outstretched and waits for the moment when the hum comes together in one long harmonious sound. He holds his palms out to us, and we pause. The sound hangs in the air above. Finn stands back and Mara continues.

"Suddenly six figures appear through the mist.
The Voyagers come here to Éire from Melita,

*An island of great temples
That sits in the Middle Sea,
Across the big lands to the south.
Two of them, Arzu and Mata,
Are Lanas, just like our Keepers.
Three can read sea and night sky,
Gora, Saleem and Hendri.
One of them is Áine.
Áine left here long ago,
She travelled across land and sea
To their island of great Temples."*

Áine steps to the front of the stage. Cheers and murmurs rise from the crowd and some people stand up. She beams and then holds out her arms.

"It is a joy to be back here in my land after many years in Melita, an island to the south baked by sun, an island of vast temples with alters and chambers and great statues. Statues that are bigger than us, strong statues that hold the energy of the Source of Life," she says.

Finn places a bundle covered with a cloth on the stage. Áine and Finn lift the cover. The crowd gasps at the sight of the huge clay figure of a big woman sitting on her haunches with full bare breasts. A skirt of many colours covers her curved hips and big thighs. Even though sitting, she is up to Finn's chest. The harp rings out, trills up and down the scale and joy surges through me. This figure embraces us all with the strength of Buí, our Great Spirit. Áine turns and bows to the figure.

"They love the Spirit of their land just as we do," continues Áine. "They have their own ways of attuning to the web of life, some are like ours, and some are different. People come from north and south and east and west to learn their ways. For they sleep and dream in a special way and their dreamers see what is to come."

Mara hands Áine a small item and Áine walks along the front of the stage holding it up so that we can all see it. It is a figure of a woman, the same shape as the huge statue, but very small and delicate with beautiful curves. She lies on her side, head resting on her arm, breasts visible. A skirt covers her big hips. I take a deep breath - her figure holds the peace of deep sleep and brings calm to my heart.

"They heard of our wonderful island on the edge of the ocean, they know about our temple by the river where sunbeams fill the chamber at Winter Sun Standstill," Áine speaks again.

Drums roll again. Coll and another Keeper step forward. They unroll the beautiful tapestry of Newgrange that comes from the Temple of the Bright One.

The wide blue water of the river winds through the middle and the huge green mound rises from the banks. It sparkles with a white band of stones. I glance around and wonder how many know that the white stones come from the mountains near Carraig. Stones as big as people stand in front of the mound, carved with images of the earth, sea and sky - spirals, wavy lines, circles and diamonds. The Seekers huddle together as we gaze at the tapestry. Shula squeezes my shoulder, and I turn to catch her eye - we may place our birthstones there at the end of Turas!

As Áine gestures to the picture of Newgrange, it seems to glow and shimmer in the torchlight.

"Our island is a perfect spot to channel the energy of the Grand Cross that comes at Winter Sun Standstill," Áine resumes. "The Voyagers want that energy in their crystals. They asked me to guide them here. So, we set sail across the ocean with their precious stones in a special cauldron, wrapped in a woven cloth."

Mara makes a loud swishing noise, blowing through her mouth to sound like wind. We join in, smiling and swaying back and forth. A picture of a big boat bobbing on water comes into my head, starry nights, full moons, wind and rain.

"They want our help," continues Áine. "For in their land, far away, there is a big change in energy. Winds and clouds come from the east and make it hard to grow food. Different people want their land. They may have to close their temples and move to another place. They need the life force, Beo, from this land to give them strength."

Some people go silent, there are shuffles and murmurs, and unease grows in me. On the one hand, our land is full of Beo, we can share it with others. On the other hand, what if these big changes come here? What if clouds come for longer and longer, and we are not able to find food?

"This island, Éire, our home, is special," says Áine as she reaches out to the group. "It is far away on the edge of the ocean. Let me tell you how it looks from far out at sea, for I can still see that sight. Shimmering greens and soft rolling hills with trees and rivers, mountains and lakes rise from the ocean. The island glistens with water from the rain that comes endlessly, so unlike the burnt baked yellow of Melita. From our ship, we see a beautiful mountain with a breast on top, a resting place for our Great Spirit. We gather together as Spirit beckons us to land."

Gentle harp music plays. Is it the end of the story? There is silence. Everyone leans forward, wanting more.

"This land is rich," she carries on, "it teems with life - Beo, its life force, is strong! The Voyagers are right - the power of love throbs in this land where the rich mixture of earth, plant and animal resonates with the beats of nearby stars. We can share Beo with them and help them with these changes."

Áine's voice rises and her arms reach out to us all as she comes to an end.

Finn and Mara stand beside Áine and all three raise their arms. Drums and pipes ring out. Everyone jumps up, clapping and cheering, stamping their feet. On and on we cheer. We are filled with love for this land, this beautiful island. We can share this with the Voyagers. The harp trills up and down and shivers run through my body. Maybe they will take our food. Can they take Beo away? How can we help? Áine turns and walks toward the Temple and the Bards follow. The moon hovers on the horizon and stars shine brightly above us, the canopy of the sky sparkling in the cool night. Áine fills us with love for our land, bountiful and rich. I push away questions and doubts about the Voyagers.

When we go to the longhouse that night the Seekers sit in a group. None of us knows Áine. Gormley tells us she went away a long time ago. Neasa says she is a Shining One, that special energy from the Great Spirit flows through her. We are all in awe of the Shining Ones, we hear many stories of their special gifts to channel Beo, to heal people, and to have dreams and visions. Questions start around the room about the Voyagers.

"Can the Voyagers *harm us?*" Ollie asks.

"Where is the big boat they travel on?" Someone else demands.

"Do they have magic that we don't know?" Ollie says, worried.

"We have more to learn about our journey to Brú," Shula states.

She catches my eye and a picture of us in the labyrinth with Mona comes into my head. I wonder why she did not say more about the need to leave Carraig early.

"Áine is right, our land is full of Beo, we can help the Voyagers," Gormley speaks to the group in a firm voice, his blue eyes serious as he looks from one to the next.

"We can be strong channels at Winter Sun Standstill, even if the Voyagers are there," Neasa adds.

She looks small and slight beside Gormley, but her strong voice and sharp green eyes hold everyone's attention.

"Shula and I shared a dream of the Voyagers arriving when we were in Carraig, maybe we'll dream tonight," I suggest.

"Tomorrow we can ask Coll to tell us more," Felim says, calming the group.

We settle as it is time to sleep. I go to get a stone to help me dream and lie down for the night.

The next morning a surge of heat in my belly jolts me awake. A vivid picture fills my head.

Six Voyagers stand rooted to the earth at the edge of the forest around a small cauldron. The cauldron sits in the middle of a small circle of stones surrounded by another circle and another to make three circles. They join hands. A beam of white light shoots from the cauldron up through their hands and into their bodies.

The dream shows me the intense focus on their faces, the dark colour of their skin and curly hair. I place the dreamstone on top of my belly. It does not feel like the energy of the Labyrinth or of the Source or the Temple. It is a new kind of energy that connects me to the Voyagers - it tells me I can help the Voyagers. Heat burns in my body. I want to jump up and go and find them.

Just then Shula sits up, she also has a dream. We step outside towards the Dreamhouse, arms linked. We smile; it is a long time since we walked to the Dreamhouse back in Carraig. Longing for home still washes over me, especially after Murta went back. I miss time with Shula. We laugh together and sometimes walk in the forest, but when she is not in the Haven or at the herb gardens, she wants to be with Bres.

Soon we see the low dome building of the Dreamhouse with the door closed. No one waits to enter; there is no sound of drums. Maybe we are too late. A quick look between us says - let's do daily movements. The sun is already up in the sky, not yet warm, it shines on us as we turn. Just as we finish the door opens and there is Sorcha, winter furs around her tall, thin body.

"Do you have a dream to share?" she asks.

We nod and she brings us inside. It is just like the Dreamhouse of Carraig with a fire in the centre and colourful rugs along the walls.

"Do you have a dreamstone?" Sorcha requests, and we both nod. She takes the dreamstone from Shula but doesn't take mine. She always tests me. Heat rises in my body, but I know this anger is not good for sharing dreams, so I push it away. She holds Shula's stone in her hand for a long time, then gestures for us to lie down.

I lie on the solid earth and breathe slowly. I don't know how to do what dreamers do; they send dreams into the heads of people in the room. I drift with a picture of the Voyagers gathered around the cauldron. The strong, hot energy of the dream slowly returns to my body. The Voyagers call me; I want to meet them soon.

A gong sounds.

"The dreams show the Voyagers drawing white light from their crystals," Sorcha speaks as people sit up.

"The crystals they bring to Brú," someone adds.

"The cauldron holds strong energy," says another voice.

We sit in silence with the other dreamers until Sorcha sounds a gong. She steps to the door, and we all follow her out, some going off in different directions. When I glance at Shula her face looks ruffled. She stands beside me with her eyes closed and a small tremble in her body. She blinks many times and then gazes with a sheen in her eyes. Her red hair shimmers as she shakes her head.

"I see a big boat out on the sea," Shula says, raising her arms. "Many people travel on the boat; it's coming to our island." She turns and clutches my arm. "Big sails, strong wind, all goes dark."

The joy of the dream leaves my body as I see her fear.

"Shula, there are always boats on the sea with many people," Sorcha remarks. "You must take care with your visions. Learn what's important." Tears come to Shula's eyes. She drops my arm and looks down with a flush on her face. Sorcha's eyes stay fixed on her. "Come, let's go to the Haven," she says and walks quickly towards the Haven. I pause for a moment to give Shula a hug and we follow.

Coll and the other Seekers are already at the Haven when we arrive.

"Shula and Briona dream of the Voyagers," Sorcha says to the group. "They bring powerful energy and new ways with them. We must take care. No matter what, we must stay attuned to the wheel of the year and keep our bodies clear for Beo."

Sorcha's words bring a strange unease. My dream feels good; it connects me to the Voyagers. But now Sorcha seems to say something may happen that is not so good. And Shula's vision shows that maybe there is danger ahead.

"Shula, share your dream," Sorcha instructs Shula. She gives us a clear picture of the cauldron with crystals but does not tell us of her vision of the boat.

"The dream shows we have a good connection with the Voyagers," explains Sorcha, then turns to the group.

"How can we know they want to help us?" Shula asks.

"We know. Áine and Mara said so."

Sorcha's lips press together.

"They want to share the Beo of this land," Coll says, joining in.

"How can we share Beo?" I ask.

"We channel it into stones, stones that can hold Beo," answers Sorcha.

"But maybe their energy is different," Shula speaks up. Tension simmers as Sorcha seems unsure for a moment. Shula's face goes dark and the lines on her forehead deepen. Maybe her vision shows more than she says. "I see -"

"Shula, we know how to place stones to give us strength," Sorcha raises her voice across Shula's and gazes at her with a stern look.

Coll steps forward.

"We all have questions," he says.

Sorcha turns to him and raises her eyebrows. Tension rises in the room as they stand and face each other. Coll drops his eyes and turns to the group.

"Áine lived with the Voyagers for a long time, she knows their ways," explains Coll.

Áine's name brings calm to the group.

"When may we meet the Voyagers?" Ollie asks in a low voice.

We lean forward, eager to know.

"The stars decide when we meet them," Sorcha responds.

The group falls back; this does not tell us anything.

"Mona told us we will meet them at the Summer Festival," I say.

Sorcha's eyes narrow.

"The stars decide," she repeats.

I lower my eyes. Sorcha always wants to settle things her way.

"Time to go to the Cistin," Coll speaks firmly as he holds out his hands. "Sun Balance has passed, Beo is rising in the earth, the sun grows stronger. Another moon cycle brings us to Bealtaine."

He and Sorcha gather us for daily attunements, they lead us over and over until the group moves in harmony.

There are still questions when we go to the Cistin and bring food to the fire. We see Coll and Sorcha talk with Áine. The Bards and other Keepers cluster around them and people nearby lean in to listen. Sorcha and Coll talk back and forth, their eyes flashing and hands making gestures and signs. Áine places her hands on their arms and speaks to both of them. Another Keeper taps Sorcha on her shoulder. Keepers move to stand around Coll and Sorcha, blocking our view. They huddle together, talking, and then they all stand up and move away towards the Temple.

We sit and watch and glance at each other – it is strange to see Keepers disagree or show tension between them. There is talk all around of the Bards and the Voyagers and Áine's journey. Most people seem excited to hear of the island across the sea with its big statues and temples. In my head I wonder if the Keepers are telling us all they know. I turn to Shula, maybe we can go somewhere and talk about her vision. We stand up just as Coll returns and asks us to follow him back to the Haven.

When we arrive, the fire is lit at the centre with seats all around, and we sit down. Coll's face shines as he looks to the door. He says that he grew up with Áine and that she had a calling to travel across the sea and learn new ways of healing and prophecy. There is a rustle in the room - Áine enters. She glows like no one else. It is hard to breathe so close to her, she radiates beautiful energy.

"Áine can tell us more about the Voyagers," says Coll.

Áine smiles at us.

"They come from Melita, an island in the east of the Middle Sea, so much warmer, where the sun shines every day- not like here!" She laughs and catches each of our eyes. Questions leave my head as I listen. "They're smaller than us, they have dark skin and brown eyes and very black hair. They wear beautiful colourful clothes. It's colder here, the people in Sligeach had to give us warm winter furs when we arrived." She laughs again. Our eyes shine as we listen to her every word. "They come here for the Grand Cross. They dream of Brú na Bóinne, of Newgrange, our temple covered in earth and stone that lines up exactly with Sun Standstill at Winter so that the sun lights up the inner chamber."

"Are their temples like ours?" Felim asks.

They love to hear about lineups of stones and stars.

"They have big open temples. I went there to learn a special method called incubation."

"In-cu-bation," I say the word slowly out loud.

Áine nods at me.

"They go into underground caves and take plants that put them in a trance, like sleep, for a long while, maybe days, maybe a moon cycle. Their dreams tell them what's happening here on earth and in the sky. They can bring messages from ancestors," she continues.

We listen intently.

"What about food when they're in a trance?" Shula asks her.

"They have Lanas, like our Keepers, who look after us. Incubation takes time. We go to a special temple built into the ground. We focus on a question. Lanas knows what plants to take and for how long. We lie in chambers in a trance for a long time, and when we wake, we share our dreams."

"You had these dreams?" Shula asks, intrigued.

"Yes, I dreamt like them. There are many places where there are temples covered by earth and stone, but our dreams told us that this island is a special place for the Grand Cross."

Áine pauses, her voice rich with excitement.

"Do you know about the Grand Cross? Stars in the sky line up with each other in a cross and the Bright Star shines strong," she asks us.

"That's why you Seekers are training so much this year," Coll joins in.

A ripple runs through the group.

We know of our Bright Star Return, it marks the start of Turas, our passage to being an adult, but now we see the link to the Grand Cross. That is why things are different this year, why we are here in Cill Dara for so long, and why they teach us so much.

"Our temples line up with the earth and with the stars, which makes good energy for incubation," explains Áine. "We think that stone-sensing and incubation can be powerful together." We sit in silence. Áine closes her eyes, she seems far away. "The Voyagers want to channel the energies of the Grand Cross at Winter Sun Standstill into their crystals to take back to their land. That can help with the big changes where they live."

"How can we help?" Gormley asks.

Áine opens her eyes and beams at us, it feels like the energy of the Temple running through us.

"For you," she says, "just practice good Glan, so that you're an open channel for the Winter Sun Standstill at Brú." She stands up and raises her arms and beams at us. "We need you all with your birthstones at Brú."

Coll leaves with her. Several Seekers let out big sighs.

"I hope she visits again," says Felim.

There is a murmur of agreement. Áine leaves us all with excitement about the Voyagers and longing to learn more about their ways. My head is filled with pictures of the big statue and the sleeping woman. I want to learn more about incubation, I want to meet the Voyagers and hear more about where they come from.

After that Cill Dara settles into a busy time with the farmland. Every day we go to the Haven in the morning and work in the fields after the meal in the Cistin. Some Seekers get tired of being in the Haven, they don't like working with stones or plants or stargazing, and they are weary of being in the group, daily attunements, and tests of what we know. They say they don't want to go to Brú; they want to work on the farm and just go to Tara and join in the Summer Festival. They leave the Seeker Longhouse and the group becomes smaller.

The sun shines stronger, and the moon gets bigger in the sky. We sit out at night around the fire and listen to singing and drumming. People from Cill Dara know our faces, they like to see us laugh. It is getting close to Bealtaine, the time when we have a fire dance at the big standing stone. After that is the Summer Festival when Mona says we will meet the Voyagers. Sometimes I wake with the dream of the Voyagers in my head and a flash of their energy rises in my body, but it fades away with daily attunements and lessons in the Haven.

One night when the moon is bright, strong sparks rise with Gormley. We hurry to the forest and stop at our tree to kiss. The hot kisses make us laugh and we run to the hut. I shiver as we plunge under the warm furs. We press our bodies together, holding each other tight. We rub and stroke each other until waves break, roll over, laugh, talk and go again. I like Gormley. I like his strong body and his firm heart; it is easy to be with him. He is like me, we both want to develop our gifts, we go to the Haven every day to practice, and he loves stargazing.

We don't have wood for a fire, so we leave the hut to go back to the big fire. We can see in moonlight as we walk back through the forest, our arms wrapped around our bodies. As we come close to our tree, Gormley stiffens. I look over - there are Neasa and Ailbe standing against the tree, kissing.

"That's our tree!" I exclaim, the words out of my mouth before I can stop.

Gormley moves along quickly.

"Do you and Neasa go to that tree?" I ask, my voice full of curiosity.

He nods.

"Only with Neasa?" I press.

"Not just Neasa."

This is the first time we talk about other sparks.

"Do you have many sparks?" I ask, hoping I can keep the conversation light.

"I like sparks," he says with a shrug.

"Do you still have sparks with Neasa?" I ask.

"Sparks come and go with Neasa, but we're friends now."

There is tension in Gormley's body, maybe he is not so easy about Neasa. We walk for a while in silence.

"Do you always follow your sparks?" I ask, I really want to know.

"*Do you?*" he counters, not answering my question.

Heat fills my body. For now, I feel unsure if I want to follow other sparks.

"Maybe I just follow my spark for you," I say quietly, holding my breath as the words leave my mouth.

"Maybe," he responds softly.

We arrive back at the fire. It is busy tonight, many people sit in groups, some sing. We sit with Felim and Ollie as people come and go. There is no sign of Shula. My shoulders sink. Gormley did not tell me what he wants. Maybe I need to watch my heart.

-8-

The Bealtaine Fire Dance

When the moon almost fills the sky, it is time to travel to Cloch Mhór for the Bealtaine Festival. We clean our tunics and jewellery, brush skins and furs, and load baskets with food for the festival onto boats, along with poles and skins for shelter. We cram into the boats for a quick paddle downriver and soon we see rows of boats at the side of the riverbank. Many people travel for the festival; it is a big gathering of clans from all around. We mix our energies and share pleasure; it is a special time when fire takes us and brings us together.

"There!" Shula exclaims and points to boats from Carraig. Soon we will see who is here from home! "They're here already!" Shula longs to see Gara and Teelin, her mother and father. I want to see Mona and Murta and Dori. It has been so long since we were together, and I hope it is easy between Dori and me. We steer the boat to the bank and lift the basket out of the boat to carry it down the trail into the forest.

The forest rings with voices as people greet each other. Birds chirp and dart above our heads and sunlight dances through the canopy of greens. My feet spring on the soft moistness of earth until we come to a big, wide field with trees - oak, birch, hazel, elm - all around. A tall thin stone, the height of 2 or 3 people, stands in the centre with piles of firewood beside it.

"Look!" Shula cries out as she points to Teelin and Murta, who sit by a small group of shelters.

We run across the field, hug and kiss and beam at each other. Teelin is not in his Keeper gown. He is older than Coll, but he has the same warmth. Murta still has a limp from the boat accident.

"Murta, is your leg healing?" I ask.

"Better every day," he affirms and beams at me. "Are things good at Cill Dara - with Sorcha?"

"I know her better now."

A picture of early days in the temple flashes through my head, when I was still unsure of her way of teaching. I am more at ease with her now, but still, there is little warmth between us.

"Who is here for the festival?" Shula asks.

"Gara and Dori are coming later with a group from Slaney." Teelin answers.

"Mona isn't coming, she's busy with a birth," Murta tells us. I long for Mona's warm arms, I want to tell her all my stories, want her to help with Sorcha, with stones, talk about the Voyagers. Murta hands us a pouch. "She sends you this, she may stop and see you at Cill Dara on her way to Tara for Summer Sun Standstill."

Inside is a bone with wavy lines and a small spiral, it tells us to keep clear. I look at Shula and we laugh, Mona says that so often.

Teelin and Murta tell us news from Carraig - one birth and two new people who want to live there. They heard that our settlement has special stones like the ones that went to Brú long ago. They built a new hut in the forest and want to stay. They know how to carve stones and grow wheat and plants in the ground. Everyone is pleased. Teelin leans forward with a gleam in his eyes and tells us there is more news. We crowd around him, calling out for him to tell us now. He smiles and says we will hear about it later when he gives us the story of Uisneach.

Around us, more and more people are coming to the field. The air is full of greetings. People build little shelters of poles and skins and dig small fire pits. Soon shelters fill the edges of the field as people gather, walk around, call names and sit to talk.

"Time for fun!" Shula declares as she pulls me over to a group with Gormley, Neasa and other Seekers from Cill Dara. The spark with Gormley stirs, we smile and joke, he touches my face. I flush as pictures of our bodies together in the forest flash through my head.

Shula catches my eyes and tilts her head. I turn. Dori stands there, looking from me to Gormley. I run over.

"*You found someone else.*" Dori's eyes flash.

"Dori, sparks come and go with people."

"You're *always* looking for more sparks," Dori snaps back, voice tight with a mix of hurt and frustration.

"I go with the energy…" I explain carefully.

"It's *easy* for you."

"Sometimes it is. Dori, *we grew up together.* There is no one like you. There's still a spark with you, too," I gently say and reach to hug Dori.

"I'm not like you; I don't follow sparks. It hurts when you do."

Dori's eyes glaze with tears. Pain fills my chest. We stand there; bodies tense.

"Come to the forest," I say, reaching out to link arms.

"Then *what*, Briona?"

"The festival is open; we can be with who we like!" I exclaim.

"So, you want to be with *me*, then with *him*?"

"We follow the sparks of Bealtaine," I answer softly.

Dori knows this - at Bealtaine, we dance and follow sparks wherever they go

"*Do what you want!*" Dori says, shrugging my arm off.

"Dori, the tension between us *isn't good.*"

But Dori walks off, over to the firepit beside the shelters from Carraig. I stand and watch. I feel stung. I want to be free to follow sparks. People are different; some follow sparks, and some don't. Now the warmth of my special feelings for Dori slips away. I look over at Gormley. Why is Dori not easy like that? Sadness fills my chest.

"*Briona!*" Shula calls my name. "Walk to the forest with me." She links my arm. "Dori loves you."

My mouth tightens. How can I talk of all this to Shula? She is Dori's sister. And she is so sure about Bres.

"And I love Dori - but it's different now."

"But you grew up with Dori, you spend so much time together."

"We're special to each other," I confirm. "But we're so *young.*"

"You always want what's next!" Shula declares, her voice sharp in my ears.

"I like Gormley."

"Yet you aren't close with Gormley," Shula pushes. I don't like it, but she is right.

"Not as close as Dori, not like you and Bres," I speak in slow words.

Often, I see they are so close, they spend so much time together, they are not open to other sparks.

"I have so much love for Bres."

Shula's face glows.

"And other sparks?" I ask.

"I'm not open to other sparks, we're together," she affirms.

"But at Bealtaine we follow sparks."

"I just want to be with Bres," Shula says in a fierce voice, and I stop for a moment.

I don't have strong feelings like that for Dori or Gormley. I love to go to the forest with Gormley, but we don't often speak from our hearts. He always wants to be with the group and join in conversations. Sometimes I drift off to sleep with longing for something, but unsure of what.

"I'm unsure about Gormley," I finally say.

"Briona, why do you *always* look for more?" Shula asks as she pulls back.

"Maybe I want the same as *you*," I reply. I look into her eyes, I want her to see that I long for love, not just to follow sparks. "It's hard to get close to Gormley." Shula softens. "We have a good spark but not a strong heart bond."

"So, you don't want to be with Dori or Gormley, you want someone new?"

Shula laughs and touches my shoulder. My mouth opens, I am not ready for someone new, but she shushes me with a finger on my mouth, and we both laugh. I forget how Shula teases.

A big oak tree with a hollow at its base calls us over. All this confusion can get in the way of Bealtaine sparks. All over the island, people gather for the full moon to dance and share pleasure. Fire energy roars, but tension brings blocks that can drag it down. I often see people looking for help to get Glan before the fire dance. Now here I am, full of tension about Gormley and Dori that I need to clear. I sit with my back to the tree beside Shula. The bark of the tree presses on my back. Its roots go deep into the earth, connect to other trees and plants, to water.

Back in the field, we go to help with firewood. People with axes chop branches off trees and cut them into smaller pieces. We bring them to the pile at the centre fire, where we gather before the fire-dance. The huge Standing Stone is surrounded by small firepits filled with wood, ready for the fire-dance. As I walk back and forth, I wonder - maybe Shula is right, there may be Bealtaine sparks with someone new!

We return to the shelters as the sun starts to fade and share food with people from home. Gara and Shula sit side by side with Teelin. It is so lovely to sit together. Gara has a bag of long spindles with different colours, and we sit in a circle and weave Bealtaine garlands. We hear more news from home; we hum and sing songs. My hand brushes Dori's. I feel surprised as a warm spark runs through me. Our eyes meet for a moment, I'm unsure if Dori senses it too. My tension is gone for now and the glow of Bealtaine fills the group. Teelin sits forward to tell us a story.

"Long ago," Teelin starts, "when this island was covered in snow and ice, no one was able to live here. But at last, it melted and out of the beautiful land grew trees and shrubs with rivers full of fish and forests of nuts and berries." Teelin's words are full of love for the land we live in. "Soon after, the first people came. They travelled across many lands and seas to get here. They walked the land and followed the lines of earth and water and at last, they found the place where north and south and east and west all come together. There lies a great stone, a big curly wedge on the ground that looks like the place on the belly where the baby cord comes out. They knew they had found the centre of the island, a place of peace. They called it Uisneach."

We lean in to hear Teelin's words.

"They built a strong wall around the Stone and after many days and nights Great Spirit, Buí, came to them, for here is the belly of the Great Mother, a cord between earth and sky. She placed her staff on the ground and told them they could live here, but each year they have to come and ask her if they can stay. On the full moon after Sun Balance, they must light a huge fire. They know they can stay when the moon shows her face above the hill and smiles at them. No one goes hungry as long as we treat the land with love and care, as we treat our mother. For then we have plenty."

"And that is the Stone of Uisneach." Murta continues the story. "And so ever since we light the fires of Bealtaine. Keepers gather at Uisneach and prepare the ground all around the Stone. They cleanse themselves with fire and then crawl through the belly of the Stone. If they can do that, they can be Keepers of Stone at Uisneach. That gives them special powers to see lines of earth energy and use stones for prophecy and healing."

"We have good news!" Teelin resumes in a strong voice as he spreads his arms. "Keepers at Uisneach asked Ciara to go there. She is at Uisneach now."

My eyes widen. Ciara is there tonight!

"Is she going to live there?" I ask.

"She'll go back to Carraig, then return to Uisneach for the next Bealtaine," Teelin answers, and then continues the story. "At Bealtaine on the night of the full moon when the moon shows her face, the Keepers at Uisneach light a big fire. On the high hills all around people wait in darkness until they see the flare of the Uisneach fire. Then they light their fires. The people on hilltops further away see these fires and so light their own fires. This continues until the people on the cliffs at the very edge of the ocean light their fires. All these fires warm the land and animals and people so that seeds grow, and young ones are born." Teelin stands up and holds out his arms. "We all connect together as the fires light."

Excitement ripples through the group - time to go to the fire ceremony.

We walk together and join people at the Standing Stone. People walk around on the path between the Standing Stone and the firewood placed in a ring around the Stone, ready for lighting. The evening grows dark. Music and singing begin. I love to stand with people squeezed beside me and more behind, bodies brushing as we huddle and then change places. Sparks rise, flare and fade. There are smiles all around as eyes connect and energies rise and fall with different songs. Drummers and pipers join in as we sway and clap, and people get up to dance, their bodies weaving in the glow of torches. The night is bright and starry; we know the moon is ready to show her face. We are charged, humming, ready for the fire dance.

Drummers and pipers stand and pause. The crowd parts to make a pathway as a procession of Keepers with baskets and torches moves to the fire and stands around it. They are all dressed in the deep blue robes of Keepers. The Bealtaine chant rings out.

Let fires of Bealtaine light.
Let us charge earth,
Let earth charge us,
May seeds sprout,
May young ones thrive.
Let us all thrive.

The words are so familiar. We hear them every year at the Bealtaine celebration in Carraig. Now we chant the words over and over, louder and louder. Heads hum with the sound of voices, deep and high, strong and quiet. Faces lit by torches are full of joy, smiling and beaming. A high-pitched gong sounds. The chant fades as the song of Bealtaine begins. Keepers step between us and hand each of us a stone from their baskets. My stone is warm to the touch, and I hold it tight. As we sing, Teelin comes and stands beside me, his body vibrating. He pulls Dori over to his other side and puts his arms around both of us. Heat crackles from Teelin's arms as Dori and I cross arms along his shoulders. I want to shout and leap around, but we hold onto that energy for the fire-dance.

Drums boom out. Horns sound. Excitement surges, it is time to light our Bealtaine fire. Lights flare, colours of garlands, feathers and jewellery swirl. Drums tinkle, tap and boom, pipes sweep high and low as the soft edge of the full moon pushes up over the horizon.

Around us fires flare on hilltops, telling us that the fire at Uisneach is alight. The full moon rises high, big and strong, its pale white light beaming down. Keepers step forward and ignite the piles of wood that surround the Standing Stone. Whoosh! Bright flames crackle and spark, burn into the base of the fires, lick up the sides and climb to the sky until the big Stone stands amid a circle of fire.

Drums and pipes burst into rhythm. We are in motion. Joy surges through my body as we dance around the Standing Stone. We make two circles and face each other going in different directions. Around and around, we dance. Somebody falls and is quickly scooped up. Dancing bodies flash in front of me, our eyes gleam.

Faster and faster, we dance. Breaths quicken, sweat glistens, mouths water. Dance and breathe, dance and breathe. Swirling, whirling, we begin to hum. Heat rises from between my hips, my breasts tingle, hands glide over bodies, rub, nuzzle and cuddle, as the sparks of Bealtaine flare. Currents of heat and pleasure run through us, and love flows between us.

Boom, boom, boom.

Loud drums ring out. Waves of sound crash over our heads. Time to cast our stones over the fire to the base of the Standing Stone. A familiar body stops beside me - Dori. Our eyes meet and joy sweeps through me. We cling to each other, swaying, as pleasure flows between us. We turn to the Standing Stone, to the sounds of clicks and thuds as people stand together arm in arm and cast their stones to the base. I click stones with Dori, and we cast them. The drums beat a steady rhythm as we run to the forest. My body tingles from my feet up through my chest to my mouth. My love for Dori surges. We stand by a willow tree and push our bodies together, kissing and laughing at sounds all around of fun and pleasure. Tension with Dori melts away as we kiss and touch all over and then return to the fire to dance all night.

At the fire in the morning everyone is bright with joy. Warmth for Dori fills me, our connection is so strong. Too soon everyone is busy packing up shelters and clearing the field. Dori and I cling together as we say goodbye. I stand with Shula and watch people from Carraig get into boats to go home. I hope that we may meet again at the Summer Festival.

"There were many sparks at Bealtaine," Shula says as we stand and watch them leave.

"I had a good time," I say, with a big smile.

"And Dori?"

"I love Dori."

"And?"

"And what?"

I don't want Shula to look for answers.

"You look happy," Shula says with a question in her voice.

"Bealtaine sparks," I respond, laughter in my voice. Who knows what is next.

"Dori is happy."

"We had fun."

"It's more than just fun with Dori," Shula says in a sharp voice, and I press my lips together.

Before Bealtaine I had big sparks with Gormley. So why did I go with Dori? A picture of Teelin at the fire before the dance comes into my head. He brought Dori and me together; he pulled us in and raised energy between us. He didn't want tension between us at the Bealtaine Festival. Anger rises in my body. Teelin pushed us together and now Dori may think we can stay together. I try to tell Shula how Teelin channelled energy between us, but she doesn't listen. She looks away. Tears come to my eyes and my belly churns.

"Shula, I have so many feelings," I say, my voice shaking.

Tears flow down my cheeks. I want Shula to hug me, but she stands away.

"Dori told me it's time for their Flowing Spirit ceremony," she reveals.

My head fills with questions. Dori was born with Flowing Spirit in the stars but was still unsure of what path to take when Shula and I left Carraig. We often talked about when to do the ceremony. Why did Dori not say this to me?

"Dori didn't say that to me…" I speak in a low voice as I turn to Shula, surprised.

"They wanted to, but they saw you with Gormley and later we were all so busy."

"But… we had a lovely time in the forest."

"Now you say that was because Teelin brought you together," Shula points out.

"Maybe," I respond.

"I want you to be sure of your feelings when Dori next visits."

I know Shula is right, but how can I be sure?

Shouts from the river tell us our boats are ready to leave for Cill Dara. On our return we gather at the fire and tell those who stayed behind about the festival. They were happy to light their fire at Cill Dara when they saw the fires light up on hills and mountain-tops around. The evening at the fire is full of fun and banter about clicking stones and weaving garlands, fire and forest and sparks flying. Gormley sits beside me, and we talk of the fire dance.

"Who were you with?" Gormley asks, curious.

"Dori, from Carraig."

"Is Dori special?"

"I have love in my heart, but I'm not sure about sparks," I answer.

"Yes, it's the same with Neasa. Sparks come and go," he says with a soft look.

I laugh - I say that to Shula so often, now I hear it from Gormley. He beams into my eyes and takes my hand.

"Are you ready for the forest?" he asks.

My face flushes and I look around. Shula sits near us and she gets up and comes over. Gormley drops my hand. Why is Shula doing this? I jump up and walk off. Gormley does not follow. I walk away quickly, down to the river and sit and watch the water flow by. There was so much energy at Bealtaine. Now feelings churn in my body. I don't want to hurt Dori after a lovely time in the forest, but so much has changed since I left Carraig. I want to stay on Turas, meet the Voyagers, and bring my birthstone to Brú. How can I be with Dori and still follow the path to Brú? I'm not sure about Gormley either; sometimes he holds me tight and other times he keeps away. Maybe it is best not to follow sparks for now, better to let things settle.

Soon after the next moon, there is a big surprise. A familiar boat pulls up - it is from Carraig. We run down, there is Murta, and Dori wearing a flowing robe. We hug; I love Murta's warm arms and Dori's squeeze.

Dori's eyes shine as the words burst out.

"I had my Flowing Spirit ceremony," they say.

They beam at me, we laugh together, and I touch their hair.

"Tell me about it," I ask.

"After Bealtaine I was ready. Teelin did the ceremony in the Labyrinth." Dori describes the ceremony, how they went to the Labyrinth with Mona and Teelin, they gave Dori a blue and yellow robe and asked them to lie on the ground with crystals. Dori's eyes shine as they recount their vision of white light that flowed through them. Teelin gave Dori a special stone wrapped in woven hazel to wear around their neck.

"Do you feel different?" I ask.

"Stronger."

"You look stronger."

We laugh and Dori pulls me close. We go to the fire - we want to hear more about Dori's ceremony. Everyone is pleased, there are many hugs and smiles. Murta beams and tells us how people at Carraig celebrated with Dori. Felim gives Dori a big hug and tells them that soon they may find their gift.

Later, we all go to the Visitor's Longhouse to sleep. Dori walks beside me, still happy with the celebration.

"Come to the forest," Dori invites me.

They link my arm and draw me away, but I hesitate.

"Do we still have sparks?" Dori asks.

"Our heart bond is very strong, maybe sparks aren't so strong."

I try to hug Dori, I want them close, but Dori shrugs me off. Their arms drop to their side as their whole body slumps.

"We had sparks at Bealtaine. *Why* don't we have them *now?*" Dori asks and lifts their head sharply. "There's someone else - Gormley."

"I do have sparks with Gormley, but I'm not sure about him."

"Do you still have sparks for me?"

"Yes, but...not always," I admit.

"Is it because of Flowing Spirit?"

"You know that's not why."

"We were together at Bealtaine. How can things change *that much?*" Dori asks as tears gleam in their eyes.

"There's so much here at Cill Dara, I've been here a long time," I say then pause, unsure whether I should tell Dori about Teelin. "At Bealtaine, the fire dance carried us along."

Dori gives a half smile and reaches towards me.

"We have so much love for each other," they affirm.

We hug each other, but Dori feels the tension in my body, and they draw back.

"Are you with Gormley?"

"I said, I'm unsure about Gormley."

"The *why* can't we just go to the forest?"

"The spark doesn't feel the same," I answer.

"Then it *is* Flowing Spirit," Dori states as they walk off.

I stand there, stomach-churning and thoughts racing. Why can't I just be with Dori? Our spark is still there. Maybe Dori is right, maybe Flowing Spirit has changed things? No, Flowing Spirit is special, and I am happy that Dori had their ceremony. A picture of Gormley flashes through my head. That is it. I want to be with Gormley, I don't want to follow sparks with Dori.

The next morning Murta is at the Cistin, getting ready to leave.

"We're going back to Carraig, Dori's at the boat. They don't want to see you," Murta tells me then sits beside me and holds me close. "Energy stirs at Bealtaine, we don't always know why things happen."

"I'm unsure about everything," I admit, confusion clouding my head.

"All Seekers have questions and challenges."

"I hurt Dori," I whisper, feeling heavy in my chest.

"You love Dori, they know that. You have good friends here now."

"When you go, there will only be Shula."

Murta stands up.

"And other Seekers, and Coll," Murta reminds me. "Things will change. Mona wants to visit you on her way to Tara for the Summer Festival. And you will see other people from Carraig at Tara."

We hug goodbye and I stand there on my own and watch as he leaves, his limp slowing him down. An ache rises in my chest. I miss Carraig, and now I hurt Dori, and Shula is angry.

When Murta goes, Shula comes over. There is a chill between us.

"Dori left. *What happened?*" Shula asks, angrily.

"They didn't want to talk. I tried to talk, and they walked off."

"They're *hurt,* Briona. You ruined their celebration of Flowing Spirit."

"I told Dori - I've changed, it's not about Flowing Spirit," I say.

"You didn't tell them about Gormley, now Dori thinks it *is* about Flowing Spirit."

"I was *unsure* about Gormley."

"If you keep quiet, *how* can Dori know how you feel?"

Now my face is red, I don't want to look at her. Dori does not know how I feel and that hurts them more. Maybe it is easy to hide and say nothing, but that leaves tension and blocks. A big sigh comes from my chest.

"It's hard to know what I want," I finally say.

It is easy for her, she knows she wants Bres.

"You want Gormley."

"Maybe, but I am closer to Dori."

"So talk to Dori about Gormley. *It's better if you tell them,*" she advises.

But how does she know how Dori or Gormley or anyone feels when I speak to them about my feelings? Maybe telling them hurts just as much as not telling them.

"I feel sad about Dori, I wish we spoke more," I say and turn to her, my eyes full of tears.

Shula is right - it is better to speak even if Dori is angry at me and turns away. Shula knows me, she knows I have many sparks and conflicts. I hope she sees the different feelings that swirl inside me. But she stands with her arms by her side and her mouth in a straight line. I want us all to be close like we were at Carraig, but Dori is gone, and Shula wants to be with Bres; she has little time for me.

Soon after, I talk to Neasa. She and Ailbe often go to the forest, and she doesn't sit so close to Gormley. We are always together in the Haven with Felim to learn about stones. We help each other when it is difficult or when we are unsure about Sorcha. Even Neasa has a hard time with Sorcha sometimes. I tell her I have strong sparks with Gormley and that my feelings grow warmer. Neasa laughs and tells me it is the same for Gormley.

"Did Gormley say something?" I ask.

"No, but I know him, I see how he looks at you," Neasa tells me.

I beam; there may be a strong bond growing with Gormley.

That evening, Gormley sits beside me at the fire. I lean into his strong body and soon sparks rise. He puts an arm around me and squeezes me close; we smile at each other. We get up and wander into the forest. I like him now, he is fun and steady, strong, and he is clear that he wants to go to Brú. He helps keep the Seekers together. We laugh and smile when we stop by our tree for long kisses. The familiar touch of our bodies under the furs in the hut brings joy. We take our time to kiss and hold each other. Our hands travel over our bodies, as our sparks spread slowly and then turn to currents of pleasure that ripple through us, making us laugh with joy.

After that Gormley and I go to the forest often - it is still almost a full moon cycle until we leave for the Summer Festival. We bring food from the Cistin and look for eggs and greens to bring to the hut. We collect branches and stones and sit there and carve spirals and arrows. We light fires and cook food and talk about Carraig and Cill Dara and watch the sky - when the new Moon arrives, it will be time to leave Cill Dara.

One morning when the moon's tiny crescent is barely visible on the horizon, Bres comes and tells Shula and me that we have visitors from Carraig. Mona is here; she is on her way to Tara for the Summer festival. She stands with her arms open and her face beaming. My face lights up as my body fills with joy. We run to embrace each other, and she holds me tight. I lean into her; I don't have a love like this with anyone in Cill Dara.

We go to the Cistin, find a quiet bench and sit together. We want to tell Mona everything, hear news of Carraig, and ask her questions about the Voyagers. We talk about our journey down the river, the beautiful Temple, the visit from the Bards, Áine and the Voyagers. But she doesn't want to talk about the big changes or the help that the Voyagers want. She tells us we will hear more when we meet the Voyagers at Tara. She wants to go to the Haven.

In the Haven, she lights some candles and rattles in the four directions. We sit on benches while she opens her pack, takes out a pouch and lays a cloth woven with spirals and circles on the ground. She takes deer bones out of the pouch.

"Here are your birth charts," Mona tells us, "the bones where we marked the pattern of stars at your birth." She hands a bone to me and one to Shula, and then gives us another long, thin deer bone and a small piece of flint with a sharp edge. "Copy your chart onto this piece of bone."

I look at the bone she hands me. There is a pattern on the bone of stars with lines between them.

"Briona, see, you have a starburst in your chart that gives you a richness of different energies and you have many sparks that draw people to you, but sometimes you change too easily. You can be good with Glan. Your chart tells us your Geis, what destiny says you must avoid. Your Geis - never take mushrooms, they destroy Glan," she explains.

"Is this Geis just for me?"

"Everyone has a Geis, this one is yours. And your chart tells us your gift - you have the gift of stone. Do your attunements every day and continue to work with stones."

Mona points at the Bright Star in my chart.

"This year you'll meet a special one to love before Samhain. And the Further Star gives you a choice about your destiny," she says. My eyes widen. Turas brings answers about our destiny. Now Mona tells us it may bring love as well. "The stars bring very strong energy this year. If Glan is good, you'll know who it is."

I want her to tell me more about this special person, who they are, when I will meet them. Does she know? Or maybe she knows but does not say.

Mona turns to Shula and picks up her chart.

"Shula, here are four stars that cluster very close together. You have the gift of Sight. You must be careful. What you see is sometimes wrong. Your Geis - never reveal if you see death in a vision."

I feel surprised at Mona's words. I always listen when Shula tells me her visions, but I don't ask if they are right.

"How can I be open to visions and prophecies and think they aren't true?" Shula exclaims, confused.

"You'll learn with time to look more deeply at what your visions mean."

"But the visions come so quickly!" Shula says.

"You'll learn to slow down," replies Mona. Shula's eyes flash; she doesn't want to hear Mona's words, and she doesn't want more doubts about her visions. Mona points to Shula's chart. "The stars show someone to love."

Mona smiles as Shula's eyes widen and her face beams.

"I love Bres, I want to be with him!"

Mona hugs Shula then turns to me with a big smile and pulls me in.

"You two have strong gifts," Mona says, then places her finger on her lips. "Now copy your charts onto the bone and see if you can sense the patterns."

We take the bones and trace the carvings of dots and lines and little circles with our fingers. A dot with lines coming out is the sign for the sun. The crescent beside it is the Moon. Opposite them is an arrow for the Swan Stars. I pick up the bone and flint and start with the sun, it is easy to scratch on the bone. I mark the lines between the stars slowly. A picture of the night sky full of stars fills my head and a glow fills my body. I want to be a Keeper of Stones like Ciara or Sorcha. They can bring a pulse from stones through their body to heal. And I want a love like Shula and Bres.

"You're born with these patterns. Learn how they work through you. Remember we all play our part in the web of life." Mona repeats the familiar words.

Shula leans forward.

"I found a Wishing Tree in the forest on the way here," she says slowly in a low voice.

"And did you get a message?"

"These visions aren't always right," Shula admits, then pauses. The words rush out of her mouth. "The sight is too much, I don't know what is real. I don't want to go to Brú; I want to stay at Cill Dara."

How can Shula say this? How can she not go to Brú? My breath stops, my body freezes. We are always so busy. She is with Bres, and we don't talk as much. She does not tell the group at Cill Dara when she has visions - not since the vision of the boat after the Bards arrived. Maybe Sorcha's sharp words keep her quiet. I see now that she has been quiet for a long time, not just with me.

"Shula, we need you at Brú, we need your birthstone for the Grand Cross," Mona says.

"I fear the visions at Brú."

"You'll get stronger with time on Turas."

"I may not go," Shula repeats.

Mona leans forward, takes Shula's hands and gazes into her eyes.

"Go to Tara, that is the next step. There is strong energy at Tara, you'll meet the Voyagers there, they have new ways to see visions."

"Maybe I don't want new ways..." Shula murmurs and lowers her eyes.

"We all need new ways for the changes that are coming. We need you with your gifts, we need your birthstone at Brú."

Mona keeps her eyes on Shula and squeezes her hands. I feel uneasy at the strength of her words. Maybe Shula has more to tell.

Shula laughs and straightens her shoulders.

"You're right," Shula replies. Mona drops her hands and smiles. Shula turns to me with a big smile and slaps me on the arm. "I will go to Tara."

I let out a big breath and hold her eyes - why did she not tell me of her questions about Turas, or that she wants to stay at Cill Dara? Now is not the time to ask.

"It's good to tell us of your doubts," Mona tells her and smiles.

Shula nods.

I lean forward; I want to tell Mona about my dreams.

"I dreamt of the Voyagers. I felt a surge of heat from their crystals. Sorcha says I have a strong connection with the Voyagers," I say.

The energy from the dream surges in my body as I speak, and I sense a pull so strong, I want to jump up and go straight to the river, to Tara, and find them.

A frown crosses Mona's face, but then she gives a big smile and stands up.

"The Voyagers bring strong energy. That is why you must practice good Glan," she reminds us. Shula and I laugh, she says that so often. Mona shifts her gaze from my face to Shula's. "You must both be at Brú; your people need you."

She hugs us both and leaves to go to the Temple.

I turn to talk to Shula about her doubts, but she hurries away to be with Bres. I feel sad as I watch her walk away. She glows when she is with Bres, but some of the brightness that she gets from visions has faded since the time in the forest on the journey to Cill Dara, and Sorcha's sharp words. I hope with all of my heart that she comes to Brú.

The next morning at the Haven, Coll stands in front of us and raises his arms.

"It's time to collect your birthstones!" he says. "Today you will start the journey to Tara for the Summer Sun Standstill."

Six boxes with birthstones sit in a row - for Shula and me, Gormley, Ollie, and Neasa from Cill Dara, and Felim. My heart eases to see Shula stand firm, she smiles at me, she seems ready for the journey. We all have good Glan now after a long time at Cill Dara doing our daily attunements and sensing when blocks may come so that we can clear them with stones or plants or time in the Labyrinth.

A gong sounds and Sorcha enters the room. She gazes out over our heads, she's not warm like Mona. She has little time for questions and confusion.

"Listen to your body," she always says.

By now I know she is right, the answer always comes from my body, but first, my body needs Glan. After Sorcha, Mona enters in a Keeper gown with a band of feathers in her hair. Áine follows, dressed in yellow. Ripples run through the room. Mona is so warm, and Áine shines with bright light.

We stand with our eyes closed as the Keepers move around each of us to rattle up and down our bodies. Even though our eyes are closed, I can sense each energy - Sorcha is cool and still, while Mona radiates warmth, Áine is like a light breeze, and Coll is steady and strong. The gong sounds and we open our eyes. Coll hands each Seeker the box with their birthstone, places his hands on either shoulder and gazes into their eyes. I take the box with my birthstone into my hand and sense its gentle glow. A smile lights my face as his hands press my shoulders - I am ready for the next step on Turas. Shula takes her box after me, our eyes meet in a steady beam as she comes to stand beside me.

The Keepers rattle again and Áine steps forward.

"Here we end your stay at Cill Dara," Áine states. "This is a special year - the Voyagers are here, and the Grand Cross brings many changes. We need you to be strong and clear, keep good Glan, protect your birthstone until you can lay it on the great mound of Newgrange at Brú na Bóinne." Our bodies brace at her words. "Each stone has its place in the energy field at Brú."

Coll steps forward.

"Tomorrow, you travel to Tara to learn more of your destiny. First, we'll go to the Cistin, and then you can return to your longhouse and prepare your packs. Keep your birthstone close to your body," he reminds us.

The Journey to Tara

The longhouse fills with talk and laughter as we gather light summer clothes to wear to Tara and prepare packs with furs, tunics, jewellery and birthstones. Coll drums outside until we are all ready to go. We gather in a circle to give thanks for the training and care we received, then move down to the river where boats and rafts are lined up. Tears fill my eyes to see kin gathering to give hugs to Gormley, Neasa and Ollie. I look around for Mona as I stand with Shula and Felim. We say goodbye to all the people we met at Cill Dara.

Soon I see Mona walk over with a big smile on her face. She hugs me and says it is just a few days before Tara, where we will meet again. Excitement fills the air - we are on the next step of Turas; at Tara we may learn more of our destiny. Maybe I will meet the special person that Mona saw in my chart. And Mona said the Voyagers will be there, with their own energy. People travel from far and wide for the Summer Festival at Tara. They bring goods for the big market, play music and tell stories, show different ways to weave and carve, and make clothes and jewellery and pots.

Coll and Bres wave us onto the boats, they are ready to travel downriver with us. There is a lot of bustle as people come and go with goods for boats or stand around talking and smiling as they wait.

"We'll travel down the river to Claona and then walk through the forest to Troim, on the banks of An Bhóinn. From there we will take a boat to Tara," Bres informs us about the journey ahead.

Our eyes brighten when we hear An Bhóinn - the river that brings us to Brú for Winter Sun Standstill. Felim beams - Claona is their home, they tell us it is always busy with travellers moving between the two rivers, An Life and An Bhóinn.

Bres guides us to different boats, and we step on, placing our packs carefully to keep the boat balanced. The river flows smoothly and moves us along at a fast pace. The smells of damp leaves and mud, reeds and earth fill my nostrils. The forest flashes by, but clouds gather overhead, and we hurry to get to Claona. We move at a steady pace and round a bend where we see a clearing on the riverbank. We pull our boats over to the side, gather our packs and follow others along a short pathway until we come to a big clearing in the forest.

"Claona!" Felim exclaims, running towards the big fire at the centre of the settlement next to the Cistin that is surrounded by a group who hug and kiss them, it is a joy to see so much love for them.

Tears prickle my eyes as I look around - Claona feels more like home. It is a small settlement, no bigger than Carraig, and the people look like our people, they wear furs and woven tunics with colourful bands around their heads. At the Cistin people gather to greet us - they smile as Bres places a huge slab of meat on a table for roasting later.

"You can sleep in a longhouse or find a hut in the forest," Felim suggests.

I turn to Shula.

"Let's find a hut in the forest," I say, and she hesitates. "It's too long since we spent time together in the forest," I add.

"Let's go now," she says, linking my arm.

We walk into the forest, now rich with green leaves and moss and flowers. Birds dart above our heads and animals rustle around full of summer energy. We soon find a hut. We make a little wood pile for fire and clear out the hut, then collect reeds and bark from the forest to make a soft bed on the floor. We laugh and tease, full of joy at the two of us together in the forest, like back in Carraig.

A drum sounds from the settlement, and we hasten back to the Cistin. People gather around the fire, with meat roasting on top. My mouth waters. On a table nearby are pots of soup, honey, bread, plates of eggs, nuts, seeds, and green leaves. Everyone is pleased with the visitors from Cill Dara, as we brought plenty of food from the farm. One of them steps forward and welcomes us, she wears a green band around her short black hair. She holds a staff in her hand, carved with spirals.

"Each year, Seekers come here on their journey to Brú. This gathering is our gift to you for Turas," she explains as she bows and everyone claps.

"Thank you, Keelin," Coll says.

We sit around the fire under the evening sky with the forest all around, so different from the huge space of Cill Dara. Here we are in a small circle by the fire, happy to sit and enjoy the food. Keelin, Felim's mother, tells us about the Hill of Tara, where the earth takes heat from the summer sun and spreads it across the island, and the big standing stone, Lia Fáil, shows us our destiny. Stories and singing follow until people move away, readying for the journey the following day. Felim takes me to meet their father, Cian. They are alike, with blue eyes and curly brown hair.

"Briona wants to be a Keeper of Stones," Felim says.

"Ah, like you! That's a wonderful path, full of healing," Cian says, and his face lights up.

"We know more now about how different stones can bring healing," Felim affirms.

"Good, and soon you'll learn about how the stones and stars line up," Cian exclaims.

"Tell us more," I ask him as I lean towards him.

"At different times on the wheel of the year, the stars bring energy that we can channel with standing stones and cairns. That's why Lia Fáil, the stone at Tara, pulses at Summer Sun Standstill, and Newgrange, the big cairn at Brú, vibrates at the Winter Sun Standstill."

Ripples run down my back as I listen. Mona said that the stars lined up to bring joyful energy to my body when she gave me my birthstone. Now Cian gives us a bigger picture.

"Oh, so the standing stones and cairns amplify the energy?" Felim asks.

"Yes. And this year your birthstones at Brú help us and the earth to have strong Beo."

"We better get to Brú then!" Felim exclaims.

Felim smiles and I smile back. The tapestry of Newgrange from the Temple at Cill Dara comes into my head and a thrill courses through my body. It seems that the energy there will be even stronger than the beautiful energy of the Temple. Other people join in to talk about Summer Sun Standstill and the celebrations at Tara.

"Briona!" Shula calls, and I get up to go with her to our hut.

I'm excited as I talk about what Cian has said. We light a fire in front of the hut. Small fires glow all around us in the forest and murmurs of conversations drift by. We sit together, look at each other, smile and sigh. Shula's auburn hair glistens, her eyes are clear, she is happy and content.

"Where's Bres?" I ask her.

"With Coll. They're staying in the settlement."

"How are you two?"

"I love him more every day. There is so much love and pleasure with him, he's like no one else…" she says, a dreamy look in her eyes.

Words gush out of Shula's mouth. I beam, glad to see her happy.

"Are you staying together?"

"Yes. And we may mate soon."

"*Mate? Now?*"

"Yes - we're nearly at Brú."

"But there is no mating before Turas!" I exclaim.

Even as I say the words, it seems not so simple. Before Turas we share pleasure as we follow our sparks. Sometimes sparks just bring pleasure and other times they build into a heart connection, a bond.

"That's *just* a guide. If we bond, we can mate," she asserts.

Maybe Shula is right. She knows she loves Bres. But Bres wants a child more than Shula does, he is older, and he wants to settle.

"It may hurt your body if you bear a child too soon!" I try to convince her

The Keepers say no mating before Turas; we are too young for children before then.

"*I'm ready*. Bres and I are happy together!"

I listen to Shula, her eyes shine, and her face lights up as she talks about Bres. She knows she wants to be with him. Still, I feel uneasy. I don't want to mate with Gormley, I am not ready for children. But I look at Shula full of love for Bres and a longing fills me.

"What about you and Gormley?" Shula asks, turning to me.

"I have fun with Gormley," I say, trying to keep things light.

"Do you want to mate?"

"Not now," I answer, shifting slightly.

"Do you think he's the special one that Mona sees?"

"I'm not sure…"

"Briona, *not again*…" Shula flares up at me. "Gormley is lovely and kind. Why don't you want to stay together?"

"I'm not ready, I want to stay open to other sparks."

"But you have sparks with Gormley."

"Sparks are strong," I say, my voice faltering slightly, "but it's not like you and Bres."

"It can get stronger."

"Who knows?"

"Briona, *you always move on*," Shula accuses me as her face flushes, her voice rises. "Now you may hurt Gormley as well."

She looks down as colour rises in her chest and face.

"Gormley feels like I do," I say. "The stars brought you and Bres together; it's not my time yet."

"Mona is right, the stars bring strong love for me…" Shula says.

I am glad to see Shula smile when she says Mona's name.

"But Mona didn't see my questions," Shula adds, and her shoulders hunch. She jumps up. "Look at the sky…" She pulls me away from the fire and gazes up. Bursts of stars sweep across the dark blue night sky. Shula points to the Swan Star in the middle of the White Band of stars that arcs across the sky. "That points to Brú, it will be right above us when we get there."

I smile to hear Shula speak in a firm voice about Brú.

We wake to forest sounds - the birds singing a wonderful chorus. I lie there listening as the morning light brightens. After morning attunements we go to the clearing where people gather and get ready to travel. The morning is bright but clouds hover in the sky. Bres says we need to leave before the rain starts. We eat quickly and gather at the fire.

"Stay together everyone," Bres tells us. "Animals are our friends, but there may be some boars in the forest. No one leaves the group or goes off on their own. We can stop along the way for a break."

"What about water?" Someone asks.

"There are many streams on the way," Bres replies.

We set out along the path and settle into a good stride. The path is well used. Trees are cut down and thistles and ivy are cleared. Low-lying branches are cut back, in some uneven places, a handrail of posts helps us along the way and pine branches sit on the ground for benches. Deeper into the forest the clouds darken and the light fades. It gets harder to see but Bres knows the path to Troim.

I walk beside Gormley. We are full of excitement for the journey ahead. Our hands touch as we walk, and tingles run up and down my body. Pictures of our times in the forest go through my head. We come to a big clearing with the remains of a firepit and a longhouse that almost blends into the forest, and we stop for food. All kinds of forest goods appear; some are new to me.

I squeeze Gormley's hand, and we slip into the forest. We find a little clearing and lean against a tree. Our kisses are long and warm, our mouths are hot for each other, and we slip our hands under our clothes, stroking pleasure through our bodies. Then we hurry back to the group.

"There are good sparks between us," I say and look at him as we walk along.

"You have many sparks," he responds.

"You too…"

I want to tell him I like him more, but the words don't come. There is silence between us. We are on a journey to Tara now, who knows what can happen next.

"Have you been with anyone else?" Gormley asks.

He looks at me with blue eyes slightly narrowed. Suddenly I feel like I don't know him.

"Have you?" I ask.

"Neasa, at Bealtaine."

"That's different, it's like Dori, we follow sparks at Bealtaine," I state. "Do you have *other sparks?*"

"Sometimes…" Gormley speaks slowly.

"And you go to the forest?" I ask and my eyes widen as Gormley pauses.

"With Aran."

I pull away and stand to face him.

"Do you share pleasure with Aran?"

"Sometimes," Gormley replies, not looking at me.

How do I not know this?

"You didn't tell me…"

But as the words leave my mouth, I hear Shula's voice. She was angry at me because I did not tell Dori about Gormley. I shake my head. It is hard to know when and how to speak.

"Briona, we're young, it's time to have fun!" Gormley exclaims. He stands in front of me and raises his eyebrows, making faces and trying to make me laugh. "There is no one else like you, we have strong sparks." I turn and stalk on through the forest. He catches up. "Tension between us now isn't good, we're on the way to Tara."

"Briona! Gormley!" Bres shouts our names, and we hasten to join him. "Stay with the group."

Anger churns through me as we walk along. How can Gormley do that and not tell me? And then I think of Dori, I did that to Dori. Shula is right, it hurts more not knowing. And why am I so angry with Gormley? We didn't talk about staying together. I enjoy pleasure with him, but I often find myself wishing for more. Tears prickle my eyes, and hot anger churns in my belly. I want to stamp my foot into the ground with each step. It is a long way to Troim, and I walk in time with the group, step by step, with my head down and try to walk the anger off.

"This is Troim," shouts Bres.

A big river flows in front of us - An Bhóinn. It stretches out, deep and wide, with strong ripples and currents. Shivers run down my back as my eyes follow its flow - it will take us to Tara, and after that to Brú. It was good to have that talk with Gormley, it cleared my head and now I am ready for the next steps on Turas.

"At Troim we grow healing plants in these gardens, with different colours and smells," Bres explains, pointing at the fences.

Rich odours waft over - so many, some I don't know, but I recognise dandelions and nettles. Splashes of colours - purples, yellows, deep blues, greens - rise from the gardens. Butterflies hover over us and further down are clusters of beehives.

We stop and gaze in wonder at the beautiful tapestry in front of us, the patchwork of fields, people moving around easily, a sense of calm and restfulness. Boats, rafts and barges are scattered along the riverbank and longhouses line up from the river beside rows of fences and walls. Bres is pleased at the surprise on our faces.

"Troim is a healing centre, people come from all over for baths, special plants, body touch, and stone healing," he continues.

"This is where I want to live!" Shula exclaims. She stands there, her face lit up with a huge smile, eyes shining. "This is it, I want to stay here!"

Everyone laughs at her joy.

"We stop here for a few days and then we travel to Tara," Bres says.

A wave of excitement runs through the group at the mention of Tara.

"And we meet the Voyagers at Tara!" I add.

"The Voyagers are on their way to Sliabh na Caillí, close to here."

"When do they come to Tara?" I ask.

"They stay there until after Samhain," affirms Bres.

What does Bres mean? Samhain is many moons after Summer Sun Standstill.

"But the Voyagers are coming to Tara for Summer Sun Standstill," I say.

"No," Bres says.

"But Mona just said they'll be at Tara!" Shula steps in.

"No. They're travelling to Sliabh na Caillí, we won't see them at Tara," Bres says firmly.

My mouth goes dry. Surely Bres is wrong.

"But the dreamers saw... and stargazers and stone-readers!" Shula exclaims.

"No Voyagers at Tara," Bres repeats.

He gestures at us to follow him and the other Seekers move away.

"Mona said many times we'll meet the Voyagers at Tara," Shula asserts as she stands with her hands clenched. I stand still as my stomach sinks. There are no words, and my head is full of questions. I never thought that Dreamers or Keepers could be wrong. I always accepted what they said. "Why did we do so much training for Tara?" Shula looks at me. Doubt and confusion grow as the ground shifts beneath our feet. I want to get in a boat and go straight to Tara, to find answers to these questions. Shula folds her arms across her chest.

"I had doubts. Now, I'm sure. I'm not going to Tara or Brú. No more daily practices, or attunements, clearing blocks, always working for the group. No more. I'm staying here. With Bres."

"Shula we all..." I start and put my hands to my head.

"*I don't care!*" Shula interrupts, her voice sharp.

"Shula, *we need you...*" I search for strong words.

"I want to stay here and learn more about plants. They are good for me; they help me with my visions."

"Take the plants to Brú," I suggest.

"There are too many visions. The Wishing Tree warned me. But Mona told me to keep going."

"You can learn more on Turas," I try again.

"Mona pushed me, *she didn't listen!*"

Shula puts her hands on her hips.

"But come to Brú. People say it is wonderful, even more with the Grand Cross of stars and the Voyagers..."

My voice trails off as I hear the words from my mouth. I sound like Mona as she pressed Shula to go to Brú.

"How can we know what to believe? The Voyagers are not at Tara like Mona said. Maybe they won't be at Brú!" Shula exclaims as her eyes flash.

"The Bards said they're here..." I struggle to answer.

"*Stop, Briona.* You have questions too. The Keepers don't tell us everything. How can you know?" Shula challenges me.

"Let's focus on Glan."

But questions rise even as I say the words.

"I'm tired of that, always change... always clear... always something!" Shula cries out as she throws her hands up.

A sudden surge of anger at Mona rises in my body. She was so sure about the Voyagers at Tara. Now we may not see them until Samhain.

"If Mona is wrong about this, is she wrong about the special person that the stars show for me?" I question and stamp my foot. "You are right Shula. Mona isn't always right."

"Don't speak like that about Mona, Briona!"

Shula surprises me.

"You can't stop me," I snap back.

"Why are *you* so angry?" Shula asks.

"You're angry too. Mona is wrong about the Voyagers, and she was wrong to push you. She knows more than she says. She wants us at Brú, but maybe she does not know what is good for us."

Unease about Mona churns in my stomach.

Shula plants her two feet on the ground.

"I am not going to Tara. I am staying here. This is what I saw under the Wishing Tree," she says.

I stand, my eyes on her. Silence. Is she staying here? Tears rise in my eyes. Shula's mouth sets. I shift from one foot to the other. People move around us and the sound of boats drifts from the river. There is no sign of the other Seekers. I feel lost, unsure of my place. I am unsure how to get back to Cill Dara or get home to Carraig.

"Shula, *don't leave us*, we...."

"*Stop it, Briona*. I made my choice." Shula interrupts as she stands there straight and firm, her eyes clear. She has decided.

"Briona. Shula." Gormley and Bres come back. "The storm is here, come to the longhouse."

We follow them to the longhouse.

"I'm not going to Tara," Shula bursts out just before we go in.

"You *aren't* going?" Gormley asks.

"There are too many questions, nothing is sure."

Shula is red in the face.

"We know where the stars are," Gormley says.

"But how do we know what the stars say?" Shula asks.

Gormley and Bres look at each other with raised eyebrows.

"The stars and stones guide us, they bring us energy," Bres speaks slowly.

"How can we be sure?" I ask.

The dark clouds gather above our heads as the tension grows in the group.

"The Keepers tell us," Gormley affirms and turns towards me.

"Mona said the Voyagers are at Tara, but Bres tells us they are staying at Sliabh na Caillí," I say back at him.

Gormley's eyes flash.

"Mona got it wrong," Gormley says firmly.

The words sting. Gormley knows I have special feelings for Mona. The distance between us grows.

"They need you at Brú for Sun Standstill," Bres says to Shula.

"They don't need me."

Shula presses her lips together.

"Mona said our birthstones fit the energy at Brú, that could be wrong too," I say.

Shula gazes at me with eyebrows raised, a small smile on her face. Are the other Keepers wrong as well? Maybe they do not care, they just want us at Brú for the energy of our birthstones. Questions spin around my head, I don't know what to believe. Gormley went with someone else, Shula refuses to go to Tara, Mona did not tell us all she knew, and she was wrong about the Voyagers. Who can give us answers? Longing to be back home at Carraig fills me - to sit with Murta, to listen to his stories, to hear him talk of the stars and help him with trapping and fishing.

A sudden gust of wind tells us that rain is close. It swirls around and ruffles our clothes. A clap of thunder sends everyone running. We turn to enter the longhouse just as big, heavy drops of rain fall on our heads and crackles of lightning flash in the distance.

-10-

Summer Sun Standstill at Tara

Shula is firm, she is not going to Tara. This is my first time seeing Shula this way. We talk and talk, but nothing works. We hope she changes before we leave and comes with us for the Summer Festival. Most of all, we want her to come to Brú. She says she sees fields of plants in her visions, and this is what she wants. I ask if she is staying for Bres, and she just shrugs. She does not want to talk about her visions. How can I leave Shula behind?

The day is warm and bright when we leave. The other Seekers know that I don't want to leave Shula behind. They surround me with hugs and tell me we are so close to Tara. But I am sad about Shula, and about Mona too, and how she is wrong about the Voyagers. I want to believe Mona is right, that she loves us all, but now I feel unsure. I wonder if she is looking out for the Tribe and not for me. I don't know who can understand my feelings for Mona - no one from Carraig is here to calm me.

I look back at the longhouse where Shula stands at the door, and I pause. The quiet gushing of the river pulls me towards the boat. I put my hand to the box that holds my birthstone, I want to bring it to Brú. I turn and step onto the boat.

Soon we are in the midst of a stream of boats moving downriver towards Tara. Big ones for traders carry heavy goods like animal skins, carved stone and wood, smaller ones carry lighter bundles of jewellery, woven cloths and rugs, dyes and plants. Some boats carry food, plants and food from the forest.

Along both sides of the river streams of people journey on foot carrying packs and bundles. All around us, we hear singing, humming, banter and greetings between boats and people walking along the bank. The river is broad and deep; it meanders through a flat plain with trees on either side. Gormley, Neasa, Felim and Ollie are bright with joy, they laugh and joke, slap water with their hands and splash each other. I want to join in, but I miss Shula. The gentle flow of the river eases me and the good humour and hope for fun at Tara brighten me. After some time, the forest thins, and we see a long stretch where trees are cleared back from the riverbank and boats are piled up.

"Welcome to Tara," Coll calls.

We jump out of the boats and stand close together on the bank, eyes and ears full of the sounds and sights around us. Faces beam to see the bright colours of summer clothes - light tunics, shirts and short leggings - as people mill about. They talk and greet each other with hugs, moving back and forth from boats, walking up and down, looking for a place to set up camp. The bustle washes over us and fills us with energy for the Summer Festival.

Coll points to rows and rows of poles that lie on the ground along the riverbank.

"These are for shelters, they store them here for the winter and take them out for the Summer Festival," he says.

We follow Coll past people as they lift the poles and cover them with skins, leaving their packs underneath.

He pauses in front of a huge Cistin laid out with tables and shelves. All around us people unload food from boats in a relay. Big sacks of fruit, nuts, vegetables, greens and plants are passed up to the Cistin. Another group lays food out on shelves.

"Everyone helps to unload food for the Summer Festival when they arrive. We have enough food for a moon cycle. You have Bright Star Return, so this year you don't do that," he explains.

"As long as we can eat!" Felim jokes.

We laugh. So much activity, so many people - like all of Cill Dara together on the riverbank. Past the Cistin are rows of big square frames of wood with light thatched roofs and open sides.

"That's the market. It's very busy, people come and go from many places for the festival," Coll explains.

Already people are placing wares on tables - pottery, jewellery, skins, furs, tools, weaves, dyes, carved wood, stones and crystals.

"Briona!"

I smile at the familiar voices - Teelin and Dori walk over. Dori hugs me but does not look me in the eye.

"Where's Shula?" Teelin asks.

"She's staying at Troim," I answer. Teelin raises his eyebrows, his face lined with concern. "She has a vision of fields of healing plants; she wants to stay there."

"But she's going to Brú?"

"I hope so."

"We'll find her after the festival. The stars say she goes to Brú," affirms Teelin.

"Is Murta here?" I ask.

Teelin tells me Murta stayed at Carraig, his leg is not strong enough for the journey to Tara. He hands me a bone with a carving of stars.

"Murta sees the stars are watching over you," he finishes.

I am happy to hear the words of love from Murta. Teelin moves away and leaves Dori and me together. I don't want anger and tension between us. Maybe I can try to tell Dori about Gormley.

"You look good," I finally say, feeling unsure.

I admire the colourful gown of Flowing Spirit that Dori wears and the woven hazel around their neck.

"I hope to meet more Flowing Spirit people here," Dori says, still avoiding my gaze.

"At Cill Dara, I was with Gormley," I burst out, and Dori turns to face me. "But I'm not sure about him. Sorry, I didn't say anything when you came to Cill Dara."

"You said you love *me*, but why did you not tell me about your feelings for Gormley." Dori's words sting, sharp and raw.

"Dori, I love you and *always* will," I say, my voice trembling. "But I was confused, there were too many people, and so much happening at Cill Dara."

Even as I say this, I know Dori has been through changes too. They have had their Flowing Spirit Ceremony and soon they will start their Turas. Maybe after a while we will be easy with each other.

"I was right, *you moved on*."

"You and I always have a strong connection."

"Just not *enough*," they murmur.

Dori moves away. I pull on their arm, I want them close.

"We grew up with each other, we had so much fun, but we're too young to stay together!" I exclaim.

I look at them, wanting them to hug me, wanting the warmth of their body. My head fills with pictures from Carraig and the fun that I had with Dori and Shula. We helped each other, we looked after each other.

Dori looks at their feet, shifting from one to the other.

"Flowing Spirit was hard at first, but I feel strong now. Briona, *you didn't help.*"

"I know," I whisper and lower my head.

"Are you happy with Gormley?"

The question takes me by surprise.

"We're just friends."

Dori looks over at Gormley and back at me.

"So, you haven't bonded?"

"No," I answer softly, my throat tight. "Gormley likes to follow sparks."

My lips shake, and tears fill my eyes.

"So, you won't move on so *quickly?*"

"I know now that it can hurt other people when we follow sparks," I reply.

Dori smiles at my words and I blink away tears.

"Briona, *you hurt my heart.*" Dori says with a sigh.

"I'm sorry. My love for you is like the oak tree - *always there.*"

Dori steps up to me and holds me in their embrace, body to body. I hold them tight, breathing in their scent. Dori tosses their auburn hair, their brown eyes gazing into mine. Dori knows me, I hope they see that I can change, that we can always love each other.

"Briona!" Coll calls and points to a trail marked by bright yellow ribbons attached to trees. I hug Dori goodbye and hope to see them after Sun Standstill.

"This is the path from the festival area to the Hill of Tara for the day of the Sun Standstill Celebration," Coll says.

We step forward onto the trail. Sunlight brings speckles to our faces as we walk through the trees and arrive at a clearing.

"We now enter the Hill of Tara," Coll says, turning to us, "it holds the Spirit of this island. It stores the bright energy of the sun and charges the earth and waterways." A vast, round hill covered in grass rises in front of us as we move along. My body stretches at the big, wide curve of green. Towards the top of the Hill, a huge circle of wooden posts sweeps around with space between each for one person to stand. "These posts surround Cnoc Beo, it's where we celebrate the strength of the sun on the longest day. Let's stand here now with our feet on the ground."

I dig my feet into the earth and gaze through the posts. Two peaks rise from the ground like two breasts. On the ground between the peaks lies a small cairn. A big sturdy stone, shoulder height, with a rounded top, stands in front of it. The grass caresses my feet, and the soft, warm throb of the earth rises into my body until my belly glows. We laugh and beam at each other - at last, we are here at Tara, ready to celebrate after the long days at Cill Dara.

Coll leads us away from the hill until we come to a fence that curves around.

"Welcome to the Grove," he says.

He leads us through a gate. The Grove is like a little Carraig, with a big hearth at the centre and benches laid out, a Cistin with shelves of food and a stove with wood piled up. The longhouses and huts sit in a circle around the hearth and Cistin. The peace of the Grove settles in my belly and my breath eases.

"The Keepers and Seekers stay here until Sun Standstill. It's a special time for all," Coll adds.

A tall woman comes over in bright clothes that hang loose on her frame, wearing a Keeper's band around her head. Her blue eyes beam from a smiling face.

"Welcome, my name is Gráinne. You must be from Cill Dara, you are the first Seekers to arrive, we expect others over the next day or two." Her voice is warm and inviting as she leads us to the fire pit. "We stay here and practice to keep Glan for the Sun Standstill Ceremony." She smiles at us all. "You look as if you need some food - sit down!"

We move to the benches, tired now after the long day. Gormley sits beside me and turns to me.

"You still love Dori," he says, his voice low.

"I grew up with Dori."

"You don't have that for me?"
I shake my head.
"Maybe we just have sparks," I suggest.
"Sorry, I didn't tell you about Aran."
"I didn't tell Dori about you," I say.
We smile. I know now that friendship suits us better.
"We both learn that it's better to tell someone," Gormley says.
"There is so much to learn on this journey!"
I had a lot of fun and pleasure with Gormley, but we are not close like Dori and me, and we don't have a bond like Shula and Bres.
"We can be friends?" he asks. I nod. I want to know that we can stay strong together on the journey to Brú. He smiles, then rubs my back with the palm of his hand. "Shula isn't here, but you have us."
The warmth of Gormley's touch eases me. I look around at the smiling faces sitting beside us.
"I miss Shula," I say.
My lips tremble, and they cluster around me.
"We're together for many moon cycles, she is one of us," Neasa says, smiling.
"We talked a lot. I often felt that I didn't want to keep going, but Shula helped me. I wanted to stay with her at Troim," Ollie tells us.
Tears prick my eyes at her words - why did Shula not talk to me?
"She's sure to join us again," Felim says and touches my arm.
"We all miss her," Gormley adds.
Neasa and Gormley gesture for us all to stand with arms around our shoulders.
"We stay together, we keep Glan for the ceremony," Gormley affirms.
Low murmurs from everyone say that is what we want.
Another group of Seekers comes to join us. Some of them are from Ard Mhacha, where there is a temple for Great Spirit, and others are from An Uaimh. When they hear that we are from Cill Dara they tell us that An Uaimh is like Cill Dara - a big farmland that gives food for Tara and Brú, where two rivers meet, one that comes from Sliabh na Caillí and one that goes to Brú na Bóinne. We are excited when they tell us that Brú is just a short journey downriver from An Uaimh,

where we will go for the harvest after Summer Sun Standstill. We are getting so close to Brú.

"I came for the festival last year, we stayed by the river, danced and sang, went to the market, ate different food and met visitors from other places," a Seeker from An Uaimh beams at us all.

"Gráinne says the Seekers stay in the Grove," Neasa responds.

"So, no fun for us at this Summer festival!"

"Conor, fun is all you want!" another Seeker exclaims, then laughs.

Just then, Gráinne and Coll come back to light the fire and bring food. We sit and eat, hungry after the journey. Gráinne stretches out her arms to the group. Excitement rises.

"This year is special for you," Gráinne states. "The Bright Star returns to the place in the sky where it was at your birth, your birthstones are charged, and you have good Glan from many moons of practice. At sunrise on Summer Sun Standstill, the morning of the longest day, you may learn your destiny. Lia Fáil, the stone on top of the Hill of Tara, may give you a vision that reveals your place in the tribe and shows your path. This vision is part of Turas, your passage to becoming an adult."

"Do we all get a vision and know what it means?" Conor asks.

"If you stay clear and practice Glan you will understand the vision when you get it," Gráinne speaks in a strong voice, and we all listen.

It is time to put tensions that block Glan out of our bodies. I miss Shula but I hope to see her soon. I push away my questions about Mona, about the Voyagers, and the Keepers. I want to get a clear vision at Lia Fáil.

"When is Sun Standstill?" Ollie asks.

"It's in three days. You stay here, we show you a special dance, and you'll practice it each day. Each of you will wear a light blue gown for the Ceremony. You can decorate the gown while you are here. So, you'll all be busy until Sun Standstill!" Gráinne explains, laughing. She begins to sing. We sit quietly as someone drums along. We listen and when she finishes, we drift off to bed in the longhouse. It is late, even though it is barely dark, and I fall asleep instantly.

The next morning, we gather for our daily attunements. There is a bustle at the gate as we finish - a new group of people arrives. They wear colourful robes and the headbands of Keepers - Mona is among them. She looks bright, she is glowing. She is wearing a long, dark blue cloak dotted with crystals and an indigo band around her hair. My stomach lurches and a rush of heat runs through my body with a mix of feelings. Questions fill my head, but my mouth goes dry when I try to think of words. How did she get it wrong about the Voyagers? Why did she push Shula?

I step forward but I'm unable to speak in front of the group. Tears well behind my eyes, and I swallow. Gormley and Neasa move over, and I follow. Mona's warmth sweeps over me as she hugs me. She glances into my eyes and then moves to hug someone else. I close my eyes to hide the tears and confusion.

We are all busy for the rest of the day and I focus on keeping my breath calm. People come and go, greet each other, sit by the fire, and help with food. The Keepers move around in bright robes, take charge, and settle themselves and everybody else. Mona constantly has people around her, or she moves from one person to the next. When doubts and confusion about Mona arise, I take Murta's carving and push feelings away. I don't want to speak out now, ask questions or have tension in my body that can bring blocks. I want to focus on Glan for the Summer Standstill celebration, do attunements, laugh, and join the group.

Two days go by in a gentle rhythm. We wake to the dawn chorus and do attunements. The Keepers spend the afternoon doing body movements with us, practising a special dance that takes us time to learn. We form two circles that dance round and around. We then take turns to step from one circle to the other so that the two circles form a double spiral. It is hard not to trip up as we move between circles. We learn the steps in rhythm, so it is easy for dancers to cross in front of each other - it keeps our body and head focused. Later we sit to decorate our Seeker gowns that are the colour of the morning sky. I sit at the fire pit and listen to the Keepers tell us more about stars and stones. I give over to the rhythm and flow and blend into the group until the day of Summer Sun Standstill.

Just before dawn on the morning of Sun Standstill Keepers set torches alight. The orange glow of the flames dances off our light blue robes that we've decorated with dyes and feathers. Jewellery sparkles around our necks and arms. Gráinne, the Keeper of Tara, stands surrounded by Keepers and holds a small cauldron painted a deep red with white spirals. Her beautiful robe with weaves of many colours shimmers in the torchlight and flowers and feathers dance in her headband. Mona glows as the light catches the small white stones stitched into her gown. She carries a beautiful, deep brown box carved with double spirals that holds the special white stone she brings from Carraig. Feathers in Coll's headband sway as he catches our eyes, one by one, and smiles. We beam back - after days in the Grove, tensions and blocks are gone, we are ready for the next step in Turas, to learn our destiny from Lia Fáil.

The Keepers raise their arms to the sky. The words of Summer Sun Standstill ring out.

"May the sun blaze
May waters flow
May the earth glow
May winds blow."

Gráinne leads us out of the Grove towards the beautiful green expanse of the Hill. My body glows as the steady stream of people joins us in waiting for the sun to rise over the horizon. Warm smiles follow us up the Hill to the huge circle of wooden posts, where an arch carved with beautiful spirals, circles and long wavy lines lies open. The Keepers turn to us with beaming faces and stretch out their arms to make a passageway. We step through the arch towards the two soft peaks that rise gently, with a cairn nestled between them and the standing stone, Lia Fáil, arising in front of it. A strong pulse draws us to the front of the cairn. The Keepers hum as Gráinne steps forward, raises the cauldron and enters the cairn, followed by Mona, who holds the precious box aloft. We open our throats to join the hum of the other Keepers as a low note from the cairn echoes our hum. My belly and chest open and close like a bellow, like a string plucked to the perfect note.

The hum fades and Gráinne and Mona step out of the cairn. We follow the Keepers through the morning attunements that charge our bodies for the glorious day ahead. We move as one through the four directions and sense the pulse of the earth through our bare feet on the ground. Earth stills as we wait for the moment of sunrise. The sky is completely clear - the Stargazers are right, today the sun shines in all its glory. Bright Star glistens on the edge of the horizon. Energy ripples from the movements of the big crowd outside. Already we are in a beautiful spiral.

A low drumbeat begins as Gráinne places her hands on the crown of Lia Fáil. Her deep blue gown sparkles and her golden hair glows as she circles three times, then turns away towards the east. Other Keepers move forward and circle Lia three times with their hands on top. We move forward step by step to circle Lia and follow others around the brow of the hill. Gormley's face lights up as he places his hands on top of Lia, next is Neasa and I follow her.

Sizzling currents run straight through my arms and fill my belly as soon as my hands touch the stone. The energy in my body grows as it travels to my hips, legs and feet. I circle three times, just me and Lia and the sky above and the earth below. I'm unsure where my body ends and the stone begins as we blend into one current of bright sparkling energy spiralling out to the stars that swirl above and the earth that dissolves into warm liquid beneath. White lines flow out from the stone and travel across the island. A picture lights up my head - I stand in gleaming white light, dressed in a deep blue Keeper robe in front of a huge cairn facing a big group of people. My body stretches open to fill with Beo.

The picture is suddenly gone, as if Lia let go of my hands. I step away, the earth feels instantly solid beneath my feet again and each foot moves forward step by step to follow Neasa. The vision is clear. My path is to be a Keeper of Stones, to understand and channel the energies of stones and earth lines, to bring healing to my people, to be part of the great balance between earth and sky that keeps us all alive and full of joy.

My body tingles from head to toe as we dance to the east around the first crest, come back to cross over at Lia, and then move to the second crest and return. The deep and light blues of the gowns of Keepers and Seekers sway to the rhythm of the low drumbeat. All I see are beaming faces as we dance past each other and cross over at Lia again and again until we blend into a spiral, spinning and whirling.

The drumbeats slow. It's time to greet the sun as it rises over the horizon. Gráinne leads us towards the circle of wooden posts and steps between two of them to face out over the Hill, followed by the other Keepers. Gormley steps into a space between two posts, Neasa fills the space beside that, I step into the next space, Felim and Ollie come next. We all face out to the people on the Hill. My feet grip the ground, and my breath quickens at the sight of the huge gathering of people that fills the Hill. They wait in silence with their arms outstretched and palms facing out to where the sun rises. My breath slows as I stand, the energy from my body spiralling into the ground. We wait together until the sun's rim peaks above the horizon and sends rays sparkling in every direction.

Boom! Boom! Boom!

Huge drumbeats ring out to the glow of yellow sunlight. Joyous cheers rise over and over from the crowd. The golden globe rises slowly, first an arc, then a half ball, and finally the full sun. We cheer and cheer until the low rim of the sun clears the horizon, basking in its warm vibrations.

"Cara." Gráinne calls someone's name.

Time for the people on the Hill to enter through the wooden arch and touch Lia Fáil. Cara moves forward and calls another name and so it goes. Each person calls the name of someone else as they step through the arch. Once inside the circle of posts, they walk around Lia three times with their hands on top. Then they are off to dance around the two peaks and back to the Hill outside. Everyone has a turn at Lia, to feel connected with earth and sky, to dance the spiral dance.

Drummers, pipers and bone clickers start a fast rhythm. The Seekers and Keepers stay between the posts, swaying to the drumbeats. Inside the circle of posts people wait in line to join the dance. Outside the posts, people move everywhere, dancing how and where they like.

The energy rises higher and higher, faces beam, and bodies are awash with love and joy. Drums continue the loud boom boom of the Summer Sun Standstill celebration. The deep drums give a rhythm for other drums of all kinds - large and small, deep and bright, high and low. Rattles made from shells and seeds join in. People clack bones, pipes rise and fall, sweep up and down, sometimes play together, sometimes not connected. Horns blast out as the sun rises higher in the sky. Drummers form a circle and beat out a wonderful dancing rhythm. Another group starts a new rhythm. One after another people dance through the arch, circle Lia then spiral around the hillcrests and go back to join the crowd outside. And on we go, dancing and drumming. Feet thud on the earth, we jump, skip, shout and sing, roar at the sun as it rises close to the highest point in the sky just as the last people circle Lia.

Boom! Boom! Boom!

We begin pounding with our feet on the earth, building to a crescendo. Our hands and feet tingle as our soles hit the ground in rhythm with the beat of drums. A deep rhythm gathers pace but is still not settled. We lighten the beat of our feet on the ground, our ears and bodies strain on full alert, as we allow the rhythm to settle. It gathers, and all we need is to stay together until the rhythm hits its stride. We are ready for the moment when we rise together. Odd notes fade, and all we hear is the harmonised rhythmic pounding of feet and beating of drums. Hold it, hold it, we keep to the central rhythm, hang on, wait, let it gather. We grow stronger, we connect and flow, and we let the rhythm take over, swelling and rolling, taking us with it.

Our feet let go and we dance as one with the drums as joy gathers and rises. We glisten, our eyes shine, our nostrils flare, our hands and feet tingle, our throats are ready. Our breathing gets deeper; our mouths open and ragged murmurs begin that quickly become single tones. Now we are heaving, pounding, toning, immersed in beautiful, ecstatic energy. We rush along to a crescendo, entire bodies tingling and faces beaming. As the rhythms break, we are barely aware of bodies but only of sweeping energy crashing and breaking over us as we abandon our flow, jumping, shouting, screaming, singing, clapping then hugging and embracing. Bliss flows through me, better than ever before. I revel in waves of pleasure, elation, love, catch shining faces and sparkling eyes, share the glory of the moment.

Boom! Boom! Boom!

We fall to the ground and press our vibrating bodies into the earth. I push my nose into the grass as my body pulses and my skin tingles and becomes one with earth. I lie there breathing into the earth, sensing the grass breathe. I turn on my back and absorb the heat of the sun, panting and laughing. New rhythms bring us back onto our feet, back to dancing as groups form and dissolve. We dance as long as we like. People move off through the forest to the festival area for food and fun, continuing to dance into the night.

Full of love and joy, the Seekers skip back to the Grove. The Keepers gather us in a half circle at the entrance to give thanks to the sun. It shimmers through bands of orange and yellow that stretch out across the sky. The colours fade into wisps of clouds that hover above us. The deep indigo blue of the sky forms a canopy around us, reaching down to touch the tops of the trees that encircle us. We stretch out our arms and sing together until the sun sinks below the horizon. As it dips out of sight, the earth seems to stand still, and a beautiful, calm silence falls around us. We are one with earth and sky, we are charged with love and gratitude. Then the peep of small birds begins and a breeze whispers through the trees. Earth is alive, we are alive, and we are ready for the next step on the path through the year.

We go to get food and gather around the hearth with much bustle, milling, hugging and embracing, eager to share our visions from Lia. The light barely fades as we sit by the fire pit, there is no need for a fire tonight as the sun returns soon. I look around at the shining faces, some I know, some are from further away. I love to hear the stories. Some see children, others see stargazing, some healing with plants. So many different visions - cooking, fishing, trapping, working on the farm, looking after cairns, carrying the ashes of the dead to Sliabh na Caillí, carving stones at Brú.

"In my vision, I'm singing in a big group in the Temple at Cill Dara, surrounded by beautiful tapestries," Neasa says.

"I'm carving wavy lines on a huge stone on a hilltop where we are building a cairn," Felim reports as their eyes sparkle.

"I saw a Keeper of Stones in front of a cairn with a big group at the front!" I exclaim and beam at the faces around me, grateful that Glan is good enough for a clear vision.

"I have a daughter by my side and I'm gazing at the stars!" Ollie says and her face shines.

"I have a daughter too, I'm in the Labyrinth in Cill Dara carving stars on her birth chart," Gormley adds with tears in his eyes.

The stories go on - everyone is pleased with their visions. We love this land that gives us so much, where Beo flows and seasons come and go, where we work together for food, build homes for shelter, tend to the tribe, and gather for festivals. I listen to the visions, and a picture of the island and all that we share grows. Neasa sings us the song from her vision. The Keepers join in, it is a song they know, passed on from their ancestors. We sit in a circle, our world dancing around us.

-11-

Looking for Adventure

Everyone is full of joy for days after the celebration. People wake with smiles on their faces and walk with a spring in their steps. I tried so hard before the Standstill to put questions and sadness away so that I could have good Glan for the ceremony, but after a while, my heart felt heavy in my chest. Mona is here, but I'm not sure how I can talk to her with so many questions. Whenever Mona hugs me, I know she loves me. But for days after the celebration, I am unsure, I don't know what to say or how to speak to her. My belly grows uneasy, and my body tenses.

I stand outside the longhouse, step towards the Cistin, then step back. Neasa comes over.

"Briona, what is it?" she asks.

Tears roll down my cheeks, the tension is too much. My face is red, and my breathing is fast. Anger, confusion and fear swirl around my head. I struggle for words.

"Mona..." I finally say, my voice shaking.

"*What?* Did something happen?"

"She said that the Voyagers will come to Tara, but they *aren't here!*" Neasa looks in surprise.

"*That's all?*" she asks, her voice flat.

She does not see that Mona is special to me.

"I can't talk to her," I admit, my confusion creeping into my tone. "She doesn't listen to my questions."

My voice rises, heat gathers in my body.

"Briona, the stars change, energies shift," Neasa says firmly. Her face flushes and her eyes widen. "You have all this in your body? Maybe you didn't have Glan for the Sun Standstill ceremony?"

How can Neasa say I was not clear for Sun Standstill? I stare back at her. Does she think I brought blocks to the Sun Standstill Celebration?

"I had a beautiful vision!" I snap back.

Neasa blows through her lips.

"You're heavy and stuck, you need to go to the Labyrinth," she says, looking straight at me, her eyes sharp, and steps back.

She doesn't want anger and confusion.

"I just want to go to Mona and tell her all this," I murmur.

Neasa steps further away as I speak.

"Go to the Labyrinth and get help. We need Glan."

She turns and walks away. It is hard to see her turn her back on me. What I said about Mona sounds small. I sit down on a nearby bench, I can hardly sense my body. People come out of the longhouses and gather for daily attunements. I don't feel able to get up and join in. I want to move my body, my feet on the ground, but I sit there with my head down.

"Briona," Coll calls me and sits beside me. He senses my unease; he keeps his eyes on my face and his body still. "What's happening?"

Tears well in my eyes again. I want arms around me to help me settle.

"I have so many questions," I say with a shake in my voice.

"Briona, you should go to the Labyrinth."

He senses my energies but does not know what they mean. Do the other Seekers have questions? I look over to the Cistin, everyone looks calm, their eyes shine as they gaze at someone - Mona. She beams at them as they listen to her every word. I stay stuck to the bench, swirling inside.

"You're blocked," he adds. "You need to get clear at the Labyrinth if you want to read stones."

But we may be able to tune into stones even when we are blocked. How can we know if we sense the right energies, get the right messages, who knows what is right?

Coll shifts on the bench, he too wants to get away. I want him to hug me, but he moves further away.

"Find a way to the Labyrinth today. This energy isn't good for Lúnasa."

Lúnasa is like Bealtaine, with high energy, dancing, music, and fun. It is open when all the different energies are let loose, there are no rules or ceremonies and there is no need for Glan. So, what does it matter how my energy is by then? My questions and tensions may go away with time. Stories of Lúnasa in my head, of swirling and whirling on a hillside, lift me. I can wait, there is no need to go to the Labyrinth now.

"Thank you, Coll. I feel better now."

"That's not enough Briona. I speak as a Keeper and a friend. You need clearing at the Labyrinth. You must have good Glan for Brú. Let's walk over."

Coll stands and holds out his hand.

"I can go later," I blurt out.

I said no to a Keeper. Fear rushes through me. Can Coll ask me to leave? Will he go to Mona or Sorcha and tell them I am not clear to go to Brú?

"Briona, Keepers are advisers and wise ones. That is all. We have experience and gifts to sense energy. We cannot make you do something. That doesn't work, energy needs…"

The sound of a gong interrupts Coll. It is time for our daily practice.

We stand and walk over to the hearth, join the circle and begin to move in the four directions. But Mona leads and I am unable to focus. Everyone else has their eyes on Mona. Her eyes slide over me as she scans the group. I move with the motions and try to stop the questions that run through my head.

When the practice ends, everyone goes to prepare food and do the tasks of the day. Nobody speaks to me as we go to collect wood in the forest. Coll helped to calm me. His words go around my head - Keepers only advise, everyone makes their own choice. So, no one is right. We do what we want, what we think is good. That is what Shula did - she made her own choice even when Mona pushed her. Maybe I listen to the Keepers too much. At the evening meal I stay quiet by the fire.

I lie awake in the longhouse that night. I don't want to toss and turn as people sleep. I try to tune in to the quiet chatting and humming of people by the fire. I reach with my ears beyond the Grove to the sound of drumming in the distance, a deep, slow rhythm that is carried on the night air. The sounds of voices, singing, and a party at the river drift by. A picture comes into my head of fires and people gathering, playing drums, laughing, singing, dancing, and having fun.

I long to dance and sing and join in the merriment. The Keepers tell us we must keep Glan, stay in the Grove, but Coll says that Keepers only advise. So, I can go to the party and then I can go to the labyrinth. Or the party may clear my energy - I just need some fun.

I slip out of bed. A half-moon hangs in the sky, but the clouds obscure it, and as the light fades, it becomes hard to see. I take each step slowly along the fence to the gates of the Grove. They are shut, and I can see no way to open them. I creep along the fence, checking for gaps, and find a loose post. It seems that other Seekers have come and gone like this. I push easily through the gap. Outside it is quiet and I pause. It may be hard to get back in.

The sound of laughter rings out into the night air and draws me to trees that lead to the river. I want to keep moving so I set off towards the trees, straining to hear the voices, scanning for signs of fire or people moving. They are all on the other side of the trees, near the river where the shelters and market stalls and the Cistin are. In the dim light, I see a pathway stretching in front of me, but the moonlight fades as soon as I step into the trees. I move forward as my eyes adjust. Soon, I am surrounded by trees, shadows and shapes loom, I don't know which direction to go in or where the river is. The trees crowd together as I turn towards the sound of drums. My ears stay alert to sounds on the ground as animals move around, then prick up at a crackling sound of movement through the trees. My hair stands on end, and I stop beside a tree. A person comes into view, a man, tall with long hair. He may know the path to the river. I step forward.

"Hello," I say.

"Who are you?" he asks casually.

"Briona."

"I'm Croom. You're in the forest alone?"

I like his name, the rich sound of his voice.

"I like to look at the night sky."

"It's hard to see the night sky in the forest," Croom points out as he laughs.

He tilts his head and smiles at me.

"I heard drums."

"The drums are nearby, at the Hollow," he explains, his voice steady.

"What is the Hollow?" I ask, I haven't heard of it.

"I can show you the way."

Croom takes my arm and continues along the path. His touch brings a strange feeling in my body - unease, yet there are sparks between us. My skin prickles. I am drawn to him, but he is a stranger. He links my arm, and warmth rises in my body. The sounds of talking, drums, music get louder. Maybe the stars brought me to Croom, and he is the special one that Mona saw in my chart.

We arrive at the edge of the forest, and there is a big fire in a dip of the hill. Flames cast an orange glow on groups of people. Some talk in small groups, others sit silently gazing at the flames or standing around. They wear leggings made from animal skins, or tunics, with scarves around their necks. Some have long hair, many have beards. They look like they have been travelling for a long time. Drummers stand here and there around the fire, some in groups, one is alone. There is no sign of other fires, of shelters or longhouses or a Cistin. I'm not sure how to approach this fire with many scattered groups and drums beating different rhythms. I wonder who these people are - are they part of the festival, where do they come from? They seem very calm - this is not what I expected. I was hoping for a party, with singing and dancing.

Croom puts an arm around my waist and guides me towards the fire. Some people wave us over and we sit down. Sudden silence falls as Croom says my name.

"This is Briona, she's on her way to Brú."

How does Croom know this?

"You're not the first Seeker to find us!" Croom exclaims.

Chuckles rise from others in the group, and I look down - they recognise my Seeker's gown. It is strange to wear it outside the Grove. I don't know how to respond, unsure if this is a welcome, or if they are laughing at me. I sit down. Food and drink are passed around. Bread comes my way, nuts and seeds, strange-tasting buns. Croom hands a cup to me and I take a sip - it is mead. I enjoy the taste and warmth as I swallow. Croom keeps an arm around me, and a warm tingle starts. Our bodies press together, but my shoulders hunch.

More people arrive. They wave over to Croom and make another group. Croom gets up and goes over, leaving me alone. Sparks leave my body and my heart sinks. I know nobody, I don't know how to get back to the Grove. I catch the eye of a woman in the group who stares at me, her eyes shift from Croom to me and back. She gets up and moves away. Soon people fill the seats around me, so I go and join Croom. He pulls me into the conversation.

"The Voyagers bring change," someone says, their voice heavy.

"And what do the stars tell us?" Croom asks, turning to me.

"The Grand Cross peaks at Winter Sun Standstill," I respond.

"That means conflict and change," a small man adds.

He talks like someone from across the sea.

"We're ready for that," I say, trying to sound clear as I look back at him.

"I mean big changes, bigger than expected," he explains and looks around at the group.

"You've heard of the Voyagers?" Croom asks me.

"Yes," I reply. "They're coming with crystals to channel Beo."

"Briona, they closed their temples and moved away," Croom says, his voice low as his eyes flash.

"That's not what they say at Cill Dara," I reply, pressing my hands together.

"Brodi, tell her what you heard," Croom demands sharply.

"Their land went dry, not enough rain," Brodi says.

"That can never happen here," I say quickly.

Even Croom laughs at that.

"Too much rain, dark clouds, plants and crops don't grow," Brodi continues. "This is what the Grand Cross brings."

Surely this is not possible here. We get many clouds, but they always blow away, and the sun comes back.

"We keep Glan, that's good for Beo, for rain and sun," I state.

"Briona, Glan isn't enough," Brodi says with regret.

Croom looks at me, and I shift in my seat. Energies of Beo help everything - heal Murta after the accident, heal people who are sick, make the earth strong and help things grow.

"There are big changes ahead," Brodi speaks again. "In my land we're preparing."

"We're prepared," I answer, more firmly than I feel. "We've a big gathering at Brú."

"Beo isn't enough, stones aren't enough," Croom repeats.

"Beo is all anyone has," another voice breaks in.

More people are listening.

"They have new spears and knives, hard and shiny, easy to drive people off their land," Brodi says.

My stomach sinks and shivers run through my body. It's hard to see people attacking other people and taking their land.

"They may *attack us?*" I ask.

"With spears and knives."

"We have spears and knives. And the energy of stones that can stop them," I say.

"Our spears are just made of wood and stone, theirs are stronger, harder. They come in big numbers; they kill and hurt people."

"But *why?*" someone asks.

"There are too many people on their lands," Brodi answers, his eyes darkening.

"Where is this?" I ask, afraid he may be right.

"Very far away. Across the great lands that stretch to the south and east, beyond rivers and mountains. But soon they'll come here."

"Further than the Voyagers?"

"That's why the Voyagers are here, they want help," Brodi responds. "They travel all over in a big boat, they want to gather people to go back with them and protect their people and land."

"Six are coming here," Croom asserts, looking around.

He is right, we heard from the Bards that six are here – but one of them is Áine. But still, they wore dark cloaks, they may be hiding why they are here. My stomach starts to churn. It seems that Croom and Brodi know a lot about the Voyagers, and Brodi is sure that people are coming to attack us. I press my hands together and sweat rises.

This is a bigger picture than Mona or the Bards have painted. At the Imbolc celebration, Mona talked of big changes, but she did not tell us more. The Bards told a beautiful story of their journey and Áine said they were here for the energy of the Grand Cross. Maybe Brodi is just telling a big story.

"Where do they live?" someone asks again.

"Melita, it's far away, on the other side of the Middle Sea," Brodi replies.

He is right about that. But if Melita is so far away why are these big changes coming here? I sit quietly as cups of mead are passed around and after a while, I breathe more easily. Croom and Brodi talk about getting men together to prepare. Women can help too, we are all strong, we all use knives and axes, and work together. More mead goes around.

I drink many cups of mead at the fire, more than ever before. Tension leaves my body, and a lovely heat fills my belly. I blend into the group, joining in laughter and singing. It is different from the fires at Carraig or Cill Dara. People come and go, move around groups, start songs and then move on to other songs that I don't know. Silence falls then voices rise again with more stories and laughter. The drums start and stop, sometimes drums on one side of the fire have a different beat from the drums on the other side. One side starts a song; the other side starts a different song. People kiss by the side of the fire, pressing into each other. Some people dance, others sit and watch. More people come along, more mead is passed around. Everything goes out of my head. The fire feels scattered; everyone does what they like. I drink more mead, my head starts to spin, and I flop back on the ground.

The ground feels hard when I wake up the next morning. My body is heavy, my head throbs, my mouth is dry, and light hurts my eyes - no Glan. I push that away; I don't want the Grove, Brú, the Voyagers, or anything in my head. Still, my body wants to do the daily movements. I stand up, unsteady, and look for someone, but see no familiar faces. People are scattered on the ground, and bits of food and empty cups lie by the fire. Even clothes are left on the ground.

How can I do my daily movements here in chaos beside the fire? I don't even know where to get water or food.

"Briona." Croom calls me to join a small group of men, who look older.

They are wearing shirts of brown and green, and some have animal fur around their necks. I stop for a moment. Croom was warm in the forest, but not last night. He waves a plate with food, and I go over and sit down.

"What can you give us for food?" Croom asks with a laugh, but he does not offer to share anything. "Tell us what happens in the Grove. Reveal their secrets and we will share our food."

Croom looks at the others and laughs. I want to get up and go, but Croom's gaze draws me in.

"We do our daily movements," I begin.

"We know that. We broke free to live out here now, there's no need for that."

"What about Brú?" I ask.

"Some of us go, some of us don't go. Why does it matter?" he asks.

Nods and murmurs arise from the group.

"For joy, for our connection to the stars," I say, the words stumble out.

"Ah, there are other ways to get joy," Croom affirms. A current runs through the group. Some look uneasy, but nobody speaks. They all watch me now. "Have you taken mushrooms?"

"No," I reply.

I sometimes hear of people who take mushrooms and get joy, but Mona says this is a Geis for me. I wonder if she is wrong about this too.

"That's why we're here with our own fire and supplies. Mushrooms are special, we get a rush, see stars and spirals, we get to feel part of the web," Croom tells me.

That is what I hear happens at Brú. I'm unsure if he is teasing me with a story. But maybe mushrooms can do that. Mead is lovely to drink; it makes us warm and joyful.

"Nothing is better than Brú," I say.

There are so many stories about joy and ecstasy at Brú.

"Some of us think it's as good," Croom claims and looks around.

I sit in silence - Croom has a hold on me. He puts an arm around me again, and tingles rise in my body.

"Stay here and join the party," he invites me. "We don't go to An Uaimh for Lúnasa or help with the harvest. We just stay here until it is over."

I press my lips together. Back home, people always go to help with the harvest. It is hard work, but they come back glowing, with stories about dancing and feasting. They bring boats of food to last us through the winter. Pictures of the Seekers flash into my head - Gormley, Neasa, Ollie, Felim. Soon they will all go to help with the harvest. I stir with an urge to get up and leave.

Croom jumps up and holds out a hand.

"Stay for longer. Come and help with the food and get the fire ready."

I look at my blue gown and see green and brown stains all over it.

"What do I wear?" I ask, aware that my Seeker's gown doesn't fit.

"Erris can give you clothes," he replies with a smile.

We walk over to the fire just as a group comes down from the forest with a big load of wood. Some wood goes to the fire; some is used to build a small shed to store food and build shelters near the fire. More people arrive carrying bags of food. The air is full of excitement.

"We're preparing for our Lúnasa celebration. We need plenty of food, it's still more than a moon away," Croom explains.

"Where's the food from?" I ask.

"All places - the forest, the Cistin, the river."

"We need water."

"The river is over there," Croom tells me, pointing to the north.

The camp takes shape. It is a strange landscape, a little hollow between two ridges, with a good stretch of grass going towards the river and trees behind. It seems far from the Grove, far from Mona. It is fun to work, to carry pouches of water from the river and leave them in the shed.

"Erris!" Croom calls over to the woman from last evening.

She comes over and they embrace. She is small and slight with a strong face and sharp blue eyes. He asks her to lend me some clothes.

She looks me up and down, then beckons me over. I feel unsure but I follow her.

"Croom and I are together", she says, her voice cold and sharp. *"Keep away from him."*

My belly lurches at the words. No one speaks to me like that. Shula, Dori and Gormley can get angry, but I know they love me. Erris is tense, she walks quickly. We arrive at a shelter, and she hands me a tunic in brown colours.

"Put this on now, you look out of place in that gown," she tells me, and tears sting my eyes. She shakes her head. "You're too soft."

She strides away. I stand there and look at the robe of dull brown colours. What do I do with my Seeker's gown? A longing for a familiar face fills me. Shula always knows what to do. I pull the robe over my Seeker gown.

I go back to the fire. Croom is there with a group, and he waves me over. He puts an arm around me and holds me close against his body. Heat from his body sends tingles through me, and I lean into him. I don't care if Erris sees, I want the touch of his body. He slides a hand down my back and caresses my waist. My eyes close as pleasure rises through my body.

He raises my face to his and kisses me, his warm, strong lips hungry for mine. His fingers trace slowly down my neck to my chest. Even as pleasure courses through my body, I begin to feel tense and uncomfortable. Who touches like this in front of other people? A picture of Erris comes into my head, the sound of her angry words. I wriggle as Croom's fingers caress my nipple and his other hand slides between my legs.

"Come on," Croom snaps, a frown on his face.

My face flushes, I am caught between pleasure and fear. No words come to my lips, and my body goes still.

He tightens an arm around my shoulders and pushes my legs apart. I put a hand down to stop him; he flicks it away and moves in closer to the heat between my legs. I grip his arm, but he shrugs my hand away again.

He grasps the back of my neck and pulls my head to him and grinds his lips against mine. I try to elbow him away. Panic rises. Why does nobody notice? Why does no one help me?

"Easy there," Brodi says as he stands with Erris beside him. Croom shifts away.

"*This* again," Erris says, and she shoves against his shoulder. She stands with both fists clenched by her side. Croom jumps up.

"We *just* kissed," Croom protests.

"It was *more* than just a kiss," Erris declares.

"It was just a kiss, *leave us*," Croom insists.

"You like her."

"She wants it."

"That's *not* what her face says," Erris snaps back.

"Look at her!" Croom exclaims and points at me, his face dark and angry.

People watch; they seem to enjoy his anger. Their gazes shift from Croom to Erris to me. I lower my eyes, my face still red, the heat of pleasure long gone. I just want to disappear. His eyes sweep over me, looking me up and down. I want the ground to open up and swallow me. There is no warmth from Croom, just the dark tension of anger.

"She's young, you like that," Erris continues.

"She's the one who *wants* me."

"*You went after her*," Erris presses.

"*No*, she came to *me*."

"You *love* young ones. *Look at her!* She's still wearing her Seeker gown."

"You're wrong," Croom denies.

"You know she's a Seeker, you know she doesn't do mating."

"*She can*, she's old enough," Croom answers back, his voice rising.

He and Erris stand face to face. Erris is full of anger, her eyes flash with her hands on her hips.

"You want to mate her. Use her and leave her, just like Ellie," she says in a loud voice.

Silence falls. The group gasps. I put my hands to my head, I want to get out of here, but for now I am unable to move.

"*Erris,* you promised not to say her name."

"You're doing it *again*," Erris says bitterly.

"*No, you are wrong,* she..."

At that, Erris stamps her foot and turns to the group.

"Now you all know. Croom mated Ellie before she was ready, then turned his back. She stopped eating and she lost the baby."

More gasps from the group. Croom still stands facing her.

"It's not like that," he tries to protest.

"You mated her when she was just a child," Erris states flatly.

People move away. Tears come to my eyes, my body goes hot, I want to run off. But where do I go? I look around. No hut, no shelter, no place to go. All around us there is just grass and mud.

Erris walks away, and Croom follows. I gasp for breath, then jump up and turn the other way. It is hard to see with tears in my eyes. I stumble into a shed where tables with food are scattered about - barley, piles of hazelnuts from the forest, some greens and roots. Tears sting my eyes and roll down my cheeks. I wipe them away with a quick sweep of my hand and lean against the table, trying to slow my breath.

"Are you new here?" a young woman asks me as she comes over, curly black hair tumbles down her face, and she wears a lovely bright tunic.

"Croom brought me."

"Oh. That was you at the fire?" she asks, her voice softening.

"Yes, why does he?"

"Croom is like that," she interrupts, her tone flat.

"Like what?"

"I don't like him," she says bluntly. "Keep away."

"Why don't you like him?"

"He plays with people. Croom and Erris are often angry. They like to fight. He likes to poke at her."

"But why do they act this way," I ask, confused.

"Some people have that energy,' she asserts, and then asks "Are you hungry? We can get food." She hands me a bunch of hazelnuts and berries and sits on the ground. She tells me her name, Dervla. "Forget them. We can go to the fire and have some fun."

But I don't want to go back to the fire, I don't want people to stare. I keep my head down and munch on the food. Tension slowly eases out of my body as I listen to her bright talk. I can be safe if I stay with her.

She jumps up and holds out a hand.

"Croom and Ellis are gone," she tells me.

At the fire people from earlier nod to me but I'm unsure if they are friendly. They look away and talk to each other. We settle by the fire and Dervla tells me she is from An Uaimh, where everyone goes for the Lúnasa festival. It is a big farm like Cill Dara, where two rivers meet, but Brú is close by so there is no temple. I ask Dervla about Brú, but she has no interest in temples or energy. She does not do her daily movements or know her birthstone. She just laughs when I ask. She didn't want to help with the harvest, so she left An Uaimh. She wants to be at the Hollow and have fun.

"When you go back to An Uaimh, what happens then?" I ask.

"They like me this way. They like me wild."

She laughs.

"What do you do at an Uaimh?" I press further.

"Make people laugh."

"*Just laugh?* You don't help with the land and the animals?" I ask, a little surprised.

"No, I make people happy and bring laughter."

"And they give you food and shelter?"

"Yes, like here. Look. I just arrived and there is food and mead and mushrooms."

"I like mead," I say with a smile.

"Yes, it's fun."

"I'm not too sure about mushrooms," I continue.

"It's a different kind of fun. But not if there is tension with Croom and Erris."

"Why?"

"If there is tension, mushrooms are bad."

"My Geis says I must not take mushrooms," I add.

"Mushrooms are great fun. Here we take mushrooms any time we like if we have someone to look after us."

This doesn't sound simple.

"What do mushrooms feel like?" I ask, interested now.

"They make you joyful, and you see wonderful visions, Erris says it's better than Brú!"

I'm excited now. Could mushrooms be like Brú? Maybe I can take mushrooms here. A rush runs through me, but I hesitate. I know it's not good for me to take mushrooms, but Dervla lifts my heart - this may be a way to have fun and put Croom out of my head.

"This is a chance for you," Dervla points out. "We're taking mushrooms this evening. No mead, we do a ceremony and then take mushrooms."

"You do a ceremony here in the Hollow?"

I laugh and Dervla laughs too.

"We sit in a circle, Erris - or someone - takes charge and chants with us. We take mushrooms. It feels good. We stare at the sky and see shapes in the stars. We talk and tell stories about what we see. We lie on the ground together and see what sparks happen!" Her eyes widen and she gives me a big smile. "Later, there is music and dancing."

People stir around the fire - Erris and Croom arrive, arm in arm. They look past me and sit down across from us. My body stiffens.

"Briona, let's have *fun!*" Dervla says and squeezes my arm.

"*Not* with mushrooms, I said it's my Geis."

"No mushrooms now, we can wait until tomorrow," Dervla affirms and smiles at me.

I can just breathe easy and stay beside Dervla, she can look after me. Dervla is fun, lively and friendly with everyone. People come and go, sometimes in pairs, sometimes in groups. Dervla whispers in my ear, tells me who goes for pleasure, who is coming back from pleasure, who does not like who and who does not talk.

"Come with me, they're going to do mushrooms!" Dervla exclaims as she grabs my arm and brings me over to a group of people who sit in a circle.

Some people call out to Dervla and want her to sit beside them. I follow Dervla and sit down.

"I don't want mushrooms," I say to Dervla.

"You can pass them on to the next person, don't take any," she whispers in my ear.

Just then Erris arrives. Like a Keeper, she holds out her arms to the group. She starts a low hum, and everyone joins in. She passes a basket around and each person takes some mushrooms. My mouth goes dry as it comes close, and my head spins. When it comes to me handfuls of small juicy mushrooms with long thin stems stare up, like breasts, each with a nipple. My mouth waters and my hand reaches out, takes some and pops them in my mouth. Dervla gasps. I laugh. It feels good to break rules.

But now Dervla takes a mouthful as well. Tension fills my body. I look at her, but her eyes are closed, then I look at Erris, she stares right through me. People flop on the ground. I don't want to lie down. Unease sweeps over me. This is wrong, this is wrong. Who can help? Just then, Dervla flops back.

I lie down beside her and try to get her to talk. My head starts to spin. I close my eyes, but it spins faster. Stars and dots dance. Strange sounds come from around me. My mouth goes dry, my belly heaves. Everyone closes in, the circle whirls, shapes and shifts. Some people lie on the ground; others get up and start to dance. Shapes loom; my head spins more. I roll over and try to stand. A rush of drool fills my mouth and waves of sickness come from my belly. I pull up onto my hands and knees and let my head hang between my shoulders. My breath is heavy; drool drops from my mouth and nostrils. I shiver, unable to move.

Someone puts a hand on my back. What is this - someone to take me away? Is it Erris, is it Croom, are they playing with me? Where is Dervla? What can I do?

"Briona! Briona, I can help you." Croom says and kneels beside me as he speaks in a low soothing voice. "You must do one thing." He strokes my hair. What, more caresses, does he want to mate with me? "One thing, you hear?"

I nod. I want to get out of this, please get me out.

"Stick your fingers down your throat," Croom tells me. I shake my head. How can that help? "You must get it out of your belly, now." I shake my head again. "Now, Briona, or it'll be too late."

His low voice catches me, his strong words ring in my ear. He presses a hand on my back. I stick my fingers down my throat; it catches and my belly heaves. Sick rushes up and spurts out of my mouth. I collapse on the ground. Croom hands me water. I sit up, gulp, and lie down again.

"*You again,*" Erris says, her voice sharp as she stands there.

"She needs *help,*" he tries to explain.

"Not from *you.*"

"Erris, *stop it.*"

Croom stands up.

"You better leave," Erris warns me.

She turns to me. She stands with her hands on her hips, her eyes sharp. I close my eyes, she is right, I need to get out of here, but I can't stand up.

There is pain everywhere when I wake up the next morning. A dark cloud fills my head, and my belly hurts. I get water. There is no sign of Croom or Erris or Dervla. I look to the forest. Where do I go?

I don't want to go to the fire or look for food. I don't like anyone here and I don't want to hear their stories about the Voyagers. I want to be back with my group, with Gormley and Felim.

-12-

Away to Follow Dreams

"Briona! Briona!"
Is this a dream? Shula and Dori walk towards me with smiles on their faces. They are here! I jump up and run over. Their warm hugs wrap around me like fur. I close my eyes and drink in the touch of their heads against mine, their arms around my back, their bellies pressed against me. My breath eases as I look at their familiar faces. Shula and I are always good even after sharp words, and Dori and I healed the hurt between us.

"How did you find me?" I ask.
"We looked all over, the market, the tents, the Cistin. No-one saw you," Shula answers.

She glows, not like my body, it is full of tension with clouds in my head.

"Then someone said there was a Seeker at the Hollow," Dori adds.

They both look over to the group that sits by the fire, where they see empty plates spread on the ground and cups of mead already in their hands.

"I met someone in the forest, and we had a party," I say, and my face darkens.

"Oh?" Dori asks.

They gaze at me for a moment and then hold me close. Tears well up.

"It looks like a mess and dirt," Shula says as she pats my back.

The urge to leave fills me. I glance around, Croom is talking to his friends and people are scattered around the fire. Croom looks over and waves. It is still hard to walk away from Croom. After the mushrooms I feel like a snail that wants its shell. This is not my group, this is not what I want.

Croom gets up and comes over.
"Who is this?" Croom asks.
"Shula," I answer.
"Another Seeker?"

He takes Shula's hand, and she stiffens.

"And Dori," I gesture.

Croom keeps his eyes on Shula.

"Join us for a while," he says as he looks at me. Shula does not move. Dori touches my arm. "Come to the fire." Croom gestures to the group. "We can have a party."

"I want to leave," I murmur and look away.

"There is plenty of food, mead, and mushrooms!" Croom exclaims as his eyes travel over my face, and my cheeks flush.

"It's time to go," I say firmly.

I want to move away now; I don't want to talk about mead or mushrooms.

Croom turns to Shula. I look at Shula and Croom side by side - she is bright and light, while Croom is heavy. I can see the cruelty in his eyes and the curl of his mouth. How can there be sparks between us? Anger flares in me at Croom, he lives here and takes food, he plays with people, and he laughs at our ways, he uses stories about the Voyagers to bring fear. Shula shakes her head, and Dori tilts their head towards the forest. Croom looks me up and down, holds up the palms of his hands, turns and walks back to the fire.

"Is that who you met?" Dori asks.

"There were strange sparks between us."

"He's not for you."

"And Dervla, she's from An Uaimh, she doesn't care about birthstones and Glan. They don't care about Brú here," I say.

I want to tell them everything, about Croom and Dervla, the talk of the Voyagers, what they say about the big changes, the mushrooms.

"Let's go to the forest," Shula states, then looks to Dori and me. "Leave that brown tunic here." I flush as I take it off and look at the stains on my Seeker gown. "We can wash your Seeker gown later."

We walk arm in arm to the forest. They squeeze me close as we walk. My chest opens to their familiar touch and the tension eases out of my body. The beautiful light of the sun shines through the leaves, and shadows dance on the ground as the trees gently sway. The strange draw of the Hollow fades as we go deeper into the forest. We pass clearings with shelters and small fire pits where people meet and sleep. Like magic, we stumble on an empty clearing - a small patch surrounded by trees where the grass glows and invites us in. We sit between two trees, their leaves caress our hair, and they hold us in a warm embrace.

"Tell us about the Hollow," Shula says and touches my arm.

"You tell me first. Why did you come to Tara?" I ask.

"Shula wasn't able to stay away," Dori says and tosses Shula's hair. We laugh.

"Bres and I went to the Summer Festival, Bres wanted to trade." Shula explains. "We joined in the big dance at the Sun Standstill. I saw you all in blue gowns between the wooden posts, I wanted that, so I went to the Grove and talked to Mona. She said she knew that I would come back." Shula smiles. "Mona was right again!"

Shula's eyes sparkle, she is happy with Mona now, she does not care about the questions and the push from Mona or why Mona was wrong about the Voyagers. But it is different for me; Mona is like a mother to me, and it hurts to have doubts and questions about her.

"I can go back to the Grove, and talk to Mona," I say

"Everyone has gone to An Uaimh for the Lúnasa festival," Shula points out.

"My pack is still there!" I exclaim, my voice rising.

"Did you leave your birthstone?" Dori asks.

"In my pack," I answer.

"Gormley is taking your pack to An Uaimh," Shula informs me.

She and Dori look at me, I know what is in their heads - how could I leave my pack with my birthstone there? How could I walk off into the night and leave it behind?

"I can still go to Brú?" I cry out in a burst.

"You know they want us all at Brú," Shula reminds me.

"But the Hollow took Glan away..."

"Briona, Glan comes and goes. We still have time to be ready for the chamber by the time we get to Brú," Shula says and links my arm. "Tell us the story of the Grove."

"It was fun for a while," I begin in a low voice. I try to describe Croom and Erris. "I like mead, it's warm, and it makes us all laugh. There were no daily movements and no work."

But I do not tell them about Croom's rough touches or the mushrooms. I don't know how to talk about that strange feeling.

"Where do they get their food?" Dori asks.

"People bring it from supplies at the river."

"They just *take it?*" Shula exclaims.

"They don't think of where their food comes from. There was no talk of sowing and planting or helping with the harvest," I continue. Dori purses their lips. "They said the Grand Cross will bring tensions and big changes."

"No. The Keepers said that Summer Standstill is the best ever and now we're ready for the Lúnasa Festival!" Shula declares, full of excitement.

"We watched the Fast Star shine in the evening - did you see it? The stars are moving close to the Grand Cross and bringing strong energy," Dori says and points to the sky.

"But the Keepers told us so little about the changes," I say. "They didn't tell us *everything.*"

"Briona, they don't need to. We can trust them," Dori responds.

They lean into Shula; they both want me to stop asking questions. The heavy tension from the Hollow stirs in my body. I still feel unsure and confused.

"Croom said something about mushrooms?" Shula asks, a serious look on her face. She knows that it is my Geis, she was there when Mona said it. "Did you take mushrooms?" I nod. "Briona, that means Glan is gone, you can't come to Brú."

Shula has tears in her eyes. I close my eyes; I hope Shula is wrong.

"I got them out of my body."

"*How?*" she asks.

"I stuck my fingers down my throat."

Shula shudders.

"But it's your *Geis*, Briona."

"They didn't go through her if she spat them out," Dori says and touches my shoulder.

"Still, you took them. You broke your Geis, that means the end of Glan for you," Shula cries, tears streaming down her face.

"My body said no to them. I wasn't able to sit or lie down. I had to get on my hands and knees," I explain. I am glad I can finally tell them. "I threw them up, out of my belly. I hope that means I didn't break my Geis."

The mushrooms brought me to my knees, I know I will never take them again.

"Only Keepers can tell," Shula says and shakes her head.

She purses her lips, then closes her eyes. Questions about Keepers come into my head, and then I hear Coll's words - that Keepers do not know it all.

"Who knows? Who can say?" I question.

Shula's eyes widen.

"We need food if we want to sleep in the forest tonight," Dori says and jumps up.

We soon find berries and nuts and branches to make a shelter. It is so lovely to be in the forest together again. We take strips of bark off a tree, tie them together with ivy, and lean them against a tree to make a small shelter. We gather twigs to make a fire that Dori lights with a firestone from their pack.

As the light fades, we sit in the forest with a small fire. Low murmurs drift around us; the forest is safe and peaceful. We lie back and talk about the Voyagers, about Áine, about the Bards, about Lia Fáil. At last, I tell them about Croom and how he touched me at the fire and did not stop when I said no. Shula holds me close and lets my tears flow. She says there is no way to know how sparks can go with someone like him. Dori hits the ground with their hand; they want to go and stop him. Dori and Shula know that Croom is wrong, that he hurt me. My heart feels lighter.

I tell them what they said in the Hollow, that the Voyagers want people to go with them to their land. Dori is surprised to hear this, but it is not new to Shula.

"Áine asked for help at Cill Dara," she points out.

"Some people may travel with the Voyagers," I say.

"Leave here and go with them?" Shula asks.

"You don't want to travel across the sea?" I ask as I make a swishing noise like wind over the ocean, and we laugh.

"Sail across the sea? It's very hot, where they live!" Shula says and looks at me with eyes wide.

"Do *you* want to go?" I ask her.

"I'm not sure..." Shula hesitates and brings her lips together.

"I want to know how they do incubation," I explain as I stumble on the word.

I tell Dori how Áine described the long sleep in a temple. I want to do that, go into a deep sleep for a moon cycle and have special dreams. The draw to the Voyagers pulls me.

"My visions are enough for me!" Shula exclaims and laughs.

"We can learn from them, and they can learn from us," Dori suggests.

They may be right, the Voyagers are just here for our temples and cairns, to charge their crystals with Beo from our land. But the talk at the Hollow plays in my head - the Keepers did not tell us everything.

We lie down and cover our bodies with bark, grateful for the heat of the fire. Questions go around in my head and Shula and Dori half listen as I fire them out at the stars in the sky. They twinkle back, they promise answers, and they seem to say - be patient. I sigh. Mona tells me that too. Gentle white moonlight glimmers through the trees. My hands touch the grass and leaves on the forest floor. A warm stone draws me. I grasp it in my hand, hold it to my belly, and let out a big breath - it is so good to be away from the Hollow. It is time to focus on the next step - meeting the Voyagers. The dream of the Voyagers in a circle with a beam of white light from their cauldron comes into my head as I drift off.

A bird chirping loudly on a nearby branch wakes me. The stone throbs on my belly and a vivid dream fills my head.

A cave on top of a mountain. Early morning. The sun lights up the valley below where a group of people walk in a line by a winding river. Most of them wear dark cloaks but in the middle, some people wear colourful cloaks. One has their hood down; their hair is curly black. They are carrying banners on poles.

The Voyagers! I'm sure of it. I leap up, ready to run to meet them. Shula wakes up and looks at me.

"Briona?"

"I *need* to leave. I *need* to find the Voyagers," I say, my voice shaking with the wish to leave now.

"But..."

Shula's face goes dark.

"My dream says that they're travelling to Sliabh na Caillí."

"Not now," Shula responds firmly, standing up to block my path.

"I need to go find them!" I insist.

"Briona, *stop!*" Shula says loudly. "You need to come to the Lúnasa festival and get your pack. You need to go to the Labyrinth. You need to get clear."

She has her hands on her hips and her eyes hold mine. I look away, I want to move now, to meet the Voyagers where they travel, before they get to Sliabh na Caillí. Shula shakes Dori's shoulder; she wants them to stand with her.

"You must come to Lúnasa," she repeats.

"*I want to follow my dream!*"

"They need our help at the harvest," Dori murmurs as they get on their feet and rub their eyes.

Shula places a hand on my arm, her eyes pleading me to stay.

"*Everyone*, the Keepers and the Seekers are going to An Uaimh for the Lúnasa festival," she says.

I know - it is a big feast, where the energies are let loose, and after that, everyone helps with the harvest. I pause for a moment. What if I don't get Glan back? But the dream calls to me. The Voyagers are close by, it is time to meet them, to hear their story of why they are here.

"My dream tells me to go," I repeat softly.

"*You already left* the Grove. Now you don't go to Lúnasa!"

"You stopped at Troim and didn't come with us. *Then you came back*," I point out.

"But I *came* to Tara!" Shula says.

"I need to go to Sliabh na Caillí. *Now*, to meet the Voyagers."

"Your dream - did it come from the mushrooms?" she questions, and her words stop me. But the rush of energy in my body tells me the dream is right.

"This dream is like the other dreams of the Voyagers; it has the same feel."

"Maybe you're too late, they're already at Sliabh na Caillí," Dori says.

Dori and Shula stand side by side, look at each other, and then look at me. For a moment I wonder if they will walk off and leave me. Dori reaches out and we take hands. My heart settles - we have known each other for so long now, and we each have our own path to follow.

Shula turns to me.

"Let's do our movements. Then see if you still want to go," she suggests.

She is right to tell me to slow down. I can only find the Voyagers if I am clear enough to follow the signs. I put the dreamstone in a bag that Shula made for me. We scatter ashes from the fire and leave the little shelter for someone else to use. We stand in the clearing, side by side and slowly do our attunements. Tension and confusion seep out of my feet and into the ground. A flutter sweeps through me, like a wind from the stars. It tells me to go on a journey to find the Voyagers. When we finish, Shula turns to me and looks into my eyes.

"We need you at Brú with your birthstone. You're part of the great web of life," she repeats and takes one of my hands.

"You're born to be there this year," Dori adds and takes the other hand.

I look from Shula to Dori.

"I'll go to Brú no matter what," I promise them.

"And Lúnasa energy?" Shula asks.

I know what she means, at Lúnasa we forget about Glan and let out our doubt and confusion. We drink mead, we dance as fast as we can under the full moon, we swirl and twirl, we shake bodies and heads, we roll down hills and have fun in the forest.

"The Hollow is my Lúnasa!" I exclaim.

Shula and Dori laugh as if they agree a little bit. The mead and mushrooms and chaos at the Hollow teach me - the Keepers' way is not the only way to learn the lessons of Turas, it takes us on our own path.

We leave the clearing. Leaves waft us gently out of the forest on a path that leads to the river. A hive of activity fills the riverbank, there are many more people than when we first arrived. People crowd around the fire at the big Cistin, stand or sit to eat and drink. Groups wander through stalls at the market in summer clothes. I see groups from different lands with bands around their hair. Boats come and go, full of food, jewellery, flints and stones, plants, skins, furs, cloth, woodcuts. One big table is full of crystals that gleam in the sunlight. People crowd around and talk about how to use them. Tables stretch up the river full of colours from rugs and tapestries and tunics. Skins stretch out over poles with different colours of fox and deer and even bear. Shula points to a table full of plants, another with flowers of Summer. There is so much I want to stop and see. But my legs itch to set off.

We go to the Cistin, it is full of food for people to take - bread, nuts, seeds, eggs, berries, dried fruit, dried meat. A boat comes in from the river with baskets of fish. We fill our bags with food. I take some bread but mostly nuts and seeds, I don't want a heavy load and there is plenty of food in the forest. We sit side by side, our bodies touching, eating slices of bread piled with dried meat and plants.

"I want to go with you," Dori says.

I hesitate.

"I love you Dori, but this is *my* dream."

They hand me their light summer wrap.

"This will keep you warm," they say lovingly.

"See you at An Uaimh," Shula and Dori say together.

We warmly embrace before they set off downriver in a boat going to An Uaimh for the Lúnasa festival. We wave goodbye.

A boat takes me across the river, and I jump off onto the bank on the other side and walk fast into the forest. I want to move away from here, away from Tara, from the Grove, from the Hollow, and find the Voyagers. A trackway snakes through the trees and stretches far ahead.

My arms pump as my legs spring from the solid earth and air sweeps my face. Pictures of the Grove fill my head - Mona arriving in bright Keeper's clothes and how I longed to run to her, but my questions stopped me. Mona saw me but she didn't care how I felt. Then Neasa walked away, and Coll did not help. Anger rises in my chest. Why did they not see? Why did they not help?

I run and run until my breath is ragged and at last, I slow down. I lean my forehead on a tree and watch sweat drip from my nose. A breeze ripples through the trees and sends shivers down my back. The breeze is moist - I follow it and it brings me to a small stream. I sit and drink and try to calm my body.

After a short rest, I run again, my feet pounding on the forest floor, and more pictures from Tara flood my head. I left the Grove to find some fun and met Croom. Why did I have sparks with Croom? Tears prick at a picture of his touch by the fire, at his refusing to stop. Anger explodes in my head. Blood boils as my feet pound, my body shakes, and red sparks fill my head. But he helped me with the mushrooms. The conversations and questions from the Hollow go around in my head- Can stones be enough? Why are the Voyagers here? Do we know what big changes are to come?

The sound of water fills my ears, and I pause. I put my hands to my head. I want stones, I want to see and smell, I want to bring stones to my face, run stones and water over my body. I find the stream and crunch my bare feet on the pebbles as the breeze cools my face. I go to my knees by the stream and sink my hands in the wet pebbles and stones that I rub over my arms and the back of my neck and head to wash away the sick and sweat of the Hollow, the touch of Croom, the mushrooms, the stains on my Seeker gown. I sit by the stream as my body eases and my head calms.

The light changes as the sun goes down and I look for a place to sleep for the night. A twig on the ground points to a big oak tree with a hollow in the base. I gather branches and fit them in the hollow to make a fence, then gather more twigs and strips of bark for a little nest. The bark on top keeps me warm enough to sleep. My ears strain for the sound of big animals but I only hear rustles of small ones - they are all around. My body and head are quick to rest after a long day - at last, the questions, tears and surges of anger fade away.

The forest full of birdsong wakes me. I jump up, eat some nuts and berries and find eggs in a nest nearby. A path opens in front of me in the direction of where the sun goes down. My body still wants to move fast but my heart is more at rest as I follow the path through the forest. Branches reach down and caress my head - it is like the forest at Carraig, which seems so far away. I always felt safe in Carraig, surrounded by people who love me. Murta was always by my side and Mona was full of love. Shula is right. Why does it matter if she is wrong? What if she was so busy at Tara that she did not see my confusion or hurt?

I sit on a branch by an oak tree. Pictures of Shula come to my head - of us walking arm in arm, and then her strong words at Troim when she told us she didn't want to go to Brú. Then doubt rises - Mona pushed her, did she care how Shula felt? She wants us all at Brú, she just says words to get us there. But why is this so important? People at the Hollow said there was no need to go to Brú. Shula did not want to go, Bres said it was not good for him, Dervla did not care. Maybe there is no need for us all to go to Brú. My head spins.

The sudden noise of a big animal crashes through the forest. Quickly, I look for a tree to climb. The animal is close, it smells me. I press my back to the oak tree beside me, no time to climb, and freeze. The animal stops and sniffs. I stay still as my heart pounds, my mouth goes dry, my hands sweat and my eyes dart around searching for a way to run. Then I see it - it is a boar, a male boar, alone, or a mother boar. A picture flashes of Dori and Teelin back from the forest, so long ago, Dori limping, their leg bleeding. A boar charged at them and gashed their leg.

I ask the tree to keep me safe. It opens and closes around me. But the boar sees me, walks up, pushes her snout between my legs, and sniffs. I stand still, silent, my eyes closed. I try to breathe with the tree, breathe with the tree. The boar slowly walks away.

I take quiet breaths into the tree and thank it for its protection. The boar brings a warning - we need to be ready for the changes ahead. It is time to settle all these questions, keep my feet on the ground, and sense the strength of Beo that runs through this land. The boar tells me no more questions, don't look to anyone else for answers. It is my path to be a Keeper of Stones, to be a healer for my people, as Lia

Fáil showed me. I need to go to Brú and lay my birthstone on the mound of Newgrange.

I walk on slowly and quietly, my eyes alert, and my ears attuned to the sounds of the forest. Birds dart from tree to tree, animals move through the growth on the ground, but there is no sight or sound of the boar. I pick off berries, they are delicious, fresh in my mouth. I find holly trees that make a circle that can keep me safe for the night. I weave more holly for a fence and make a nest inside and lie there.

My eyes open to sunlight. The dream of the Voyagers is vivid in my head; I can see them travelling in a line. Surely, we will meet very soon. Energy courses through my body and I jump up. But there is no sign of the path - the boar got me off track. A branch hits me on the head. Stop, it says, it is time for daily movements. My feet sink into the earth, my arms rise and float, my feet shift, and my body turns. A soft mist drifts through the trees, and the forms of trees around me shift and shape.

Then I hear the gentle plod of hoofs on the forest floor, the snap of twigs and branches. I stand still, hold my breath, my eyes and ears stretch, and my nostrils flare. It is a big animal with a soft smell. Deer. Here to take me to the Voyagers. Many deer appear through the trees, their heads move up and down as they eat food from the forest floor, and I follow them. I want to meet the Voyagers today. But the deer are slow, they take a few steps then stop for food. I gather nuts and berries, plenty of food to last, and stay close to the deer.

The slow walk through the forest keeps me calm until my breath deepens and my feet sense the soft spring of the ground. Step by step, the deer brings me to two big Wishing Trees that reach above my head. Their branches make an archway and on the ground between them is a small circle of stones.

I step into the circle and root myself to the spot. Energy surges from the ground up my legs, along my back to the top of my body. This is like the energy of the stones at Carraig, of my birthstone. After all this time away from the Grove, at the Hollow, in the forest, Glan comes back to my body. I stand unable to move as glimmers of light dance through the leaves and fill my eyes. The light grows dimmer as the sun slips low. I reach out with my hands and ask for guidance to find the path. My ears fill with the sound of wings flapping and I turn to see ravens flying up from nearby trees. They fly towards the sun and beneath them, I see a path that climbs gently up the hill. I follow the path until the trees thin, and I climb out of the forest to arrive at a hilltop that is flat and clear of trees.

I gasp in awe at the beautiful sight. The golden ball of the sun sits on the horizon in front of me, and light shimmers all around it. Behind me, the full white moon hovers. I stretch out my hands, one to the sun, one to the moon. I bathe in the pink and red light that holds me in a field between the two globes. The dark blue canopy of the sky sweeps above the valley below. I glance down at the valley as it catches the last dim light - it is the valley of my dream! It stretches out below with trees growing along the low-rising hills beside the curve of the river. The Voyagers are there somewhere. Great Spirit guides me to the right place and shows me the path to meet them.

Darkness hovers - I have no food or water; I need shelter for the night. A pile of rocks on the ground draws me to a cave nestled in the hillside with a big, wide entrance. The cave is very dark. I stand, watch, listen, smell, sense. No sign of animals inside. I pick up a stone and throw it in, clap my hands and shout into the cave. There is no response. I slowly walk in. The cave is perfect, not too deep, with a little hollow in the ground to sleep in and a pile of twigs for a fire. This is a special place, somewhere that other people, maybe Seekers, come to clear their bodies and heads and get Glan.

My head is light, but it is too late for food or drink, so I settle in the cave and watch the moon climb high in the sky. I drift to sleep with moonlight on my face. My eyes open now and then to see the stars get brighter and brighter. The stars glisten and the moon glows as my eyes close again. When the light changes on my face, my eyes open. The full moon hangs so close I can almost reach out and touch it. I watch the clouds play with light and dark on the surface of the moon. My hand reaches into my pack and takes out the stone from the dream at Tara, it throbs strongly on my palm.

The clouds shift in front of my eyes, shimmer, and shift again, teasing my eyes with shapes of animals and humans, trees and lakes, hills and mountains. They form into the familiar shape of an island, our beautiful, shimmering island with its jagged coastline of beaches and cliffs, inlets and headlands. Shadows of mountains rise from its surface and silver ribbons of rivers crisscross, meander from mountain to coast, stream in and out of dark pools.

It is a strange sight, but I know that shape - it is Éire, the island where we live, bathed by moonlight, our island, where the earth feeds us and stones heal us and fertile land teems with life, the island that we love. Light and dark give way to colours.

Green splashes across the island, lighter greens in the valleys by rivers and lakes, darker greens on hills and mountaintops, and pale green along the coast. The colours brighten, blades of grass shine, and trees glisten. Rocks throb in greys, black and white. All the seasons come to life all at once. Flowers blossom in reds, yellows, and blues. Trees and shrubs are filled with colourful berries of black and red. Leaves change to all shades of red and orange.

This island is so beautiful, rich with water, plants, animals, a land of green trees and rolling hills, swept by wind and rain, warmed by the sun. Like the tapestries at Cill Dara, the seasons unfold, the wheel of the year, the cycle of life, turns over.

The bright lights fade to green again, and the contours of hills and valleys shape into a familiar form - the body of Spirit, Great Spirit. Rolling hills show the contours of her thighs, hips, belly, and breasts. White light shimmers from head to toe. She ripples and moves closer.

Light fills my body, the hairs on my neck stand on end, and my body tingles from head to toe. She shows herself to me, Buí, the great Source of life, who grows and gives birth, who breathes earth to body, water to blood, air to breath, fire to spirit. We are all one with earth and sky. We dance and hum, our bodies open, and she pours love through us.

Her body shifts back to the shape of the island. Silver light-beams pulse from earth to sky across the island. Tara throbs brightly, and just beside it Brú on the bend of the river. Sliabh na Caillí rises above the forest, there is Cill Dara, Uisneach, many places. The web of light connects them all. Little spots of dancing lights appear and weave around in circles and spirals - people dancing.

We follow our ancestors who walked the earth to find places on hilltops, by rivers and lakes, where earth energies throb. They built cairns and dolmens, carved stones, and gathered crystals. We follow them through the seasons, we gather for the joy that pours from

Great Spirit, we store it in the stones and our bodies, hold it for healing, and look for signs of what is to come. Love for my people throbs through my chest, I want to embrace us all - a people who live for love, who live for harmony with earth and sky.

That night, eyes, head, body and heart are on fire for a long time, until the moon shifts close to earth. I stay awake as the first colours of sunrise appear on the horizon and my eyes close to sleep.

It is clear and bright when I wake and sit with the stone in my hand. All doubts are gone. We are all part of the web of life. A picture of Mona at the Imbolc festival as she says these words flashes into my head. My anger is gone; she is wise and kind. The stone throbs in my hand and tells me this is my path. Then the wind stirs and clouds hover on the horizon. I need to get food and water quickly. I gather berries and further into the forest find nuts and eggs. A small spring gives me water.

I hurry back to the cave before the clouds come, and the rain falls. Many days pass. I watch over the valley, collect food and drink water, find a stream to bathe in, do daily movements, and sit with the dreamstone. I don't want to move until I see the Voyagers in the valley below. The moon gets smaller each night. My vision seems like it is from long ago, but waves of love for the land and my people still course through my body. I have a smile on my face for the gift of days of calm and quiet. Brú is still many moon cycles away, but the year is turning and bringing us closer.

-13-

Meeting the Voyagers at Lúnasa

Morning wind gathers, trees sway, clouds grow big and dark. I give thanks for the cave and the shelter in the rocks, go and collect more food for the storm and return to the cave. I stand and scan the valley below. Where are the Voyagers? They must be there. I gaze through tree-tops to the forest floor and along the bank of the river, looking for signs. I want to find them before the big storm.

My eyes catch movement - a group of people walk in line with banners, but more than in the dream at Tara. Surely, they are the Voyagers. They move steady, focused, the wind at their back, the river running beside them. Most are dressed in the greens and browns that we wear. Some wear bright cloaks, reds and yellows, just like in my dream.

I stand for a moment and watch them snake along. They are too far away to see their faces. They slow down, turn, veer into the forest and go out of sight. Quick, I need to move, I need to find them. I turn to get my pack, clean up, set off downhill, and then pause to feel my feet on the ground for daily movements. I ask the earth for guidance.

The wind changes direction and blows hard, pushing me down the hill. It fades when I arrive on the forest floor. The damp smell of the river drifts from the left and I walk that way, my ears and eyes open. A gust of wind brings voices across the forest. They are close now. The voices fade, drift closer, and then fade again. I pause, listen, and follow. The glitter of the sun through the trees beckons me and I quicken my pace as I hear voices again.

Flashes of colour and movement tell me that people are nearby. A gap opens in the trees to a beautiful sight. A woman stands right in front of me. She is wearing a long cape of dyed wool in many colours over a purple gown. Her legs are planted firmly on the ground, her arms outstretched, the curve of her breasts and belly and hips visible through her gown. She is about my height, with curly black hair, skin the colour of dark oak, and beautiful full lips. Around her head is a purple headband with small, coloured beads. One hand holds a wand, a long thin stick with crystals on top.

I stop. Our eyes meet. A jolt runs through my body. I stand there, rooted to the spot. She stares right at me with a gleam in her eyes. My head tingles, my forehead pulses, my mouth waters, and my face stretches into a big smile. I am not able to move. Fire rises through my body. I want to take her into my arms, gaze into her eyes, and beam at her.

I take a step towards her. Light beams surround her, reds, oranges and yellows glow. Before I get close, other hands take mine, one on each side, and draw me into a circle of wonderful energy that flows out and through me. I keep my gaze fixed on her. From the corners of my eyes, I see the people around us in colourful clothing. A ribbon of white light whirls around us then slows down and forms a spiral between me and her.

Words ring out, sounds I've never heard before, strange strong words spoken clearly one at a time - oma, gaba, kali, punda, sula. As the voices chant, each word sends jolts through my body. It is not like the hum in the forest or the Labyrinth, not like the sound of drums or pipes, not like the roar of Summer Standstill. Big breaths, short words, lips smack, tongues click. Then the clap, clap of hands cracks through the forest. Energy jerks from my body and the light disappears. She stands there, looks up at the sky and raises her wand. Feet shuffle on the forest floor. The hands that hold me let go and I stumble back and fall to the ground, barely sensing the crackling and movement around, the swish of clothes, the low murmurs, the rustle of leaves and the smell of earth beneath me. My eyes flicker to see the canopy of leaves sway above me. The sound of ravens fills my ears as a flock takes flight. Then all is dark.

I wake up in a daze on the forest floor with a picture in my head of the beautiful face, bright eyes, and full lips. The charge between us still fills my body with fire. My chest stretches, I long to see her and hold her in my arms. My eyes open but there is no sign of her, and I stand up. The sun is now high in the sky, and a group of four people stand nearby. They wear brown and green travel cloaks.

Someone smiles at me.

"She touches you with magic," a voice says. It is Conor, from Tara. "Are you ready? We want to get to Sliabh na Caillí today."

We hug.

"Who is she?" I ask, wanting to hear more.

"We can talk later," he replies, eager to get going.

The other three people are a little older than me. They form a circle, and I join as they greet me, tell me their names and say they are from Sligeach. We face the four directions and do the familiar movements.

We set out through the forest in a single file at a steady pace. I am in a daze, glad to be in motion in the line of walkers with no conversation. I move with the group, step by step, one foot after the other, head down as I shut out the forest sounds. Pictures flash through my head of the strange, beautiful woman with the spiral of light. Around and around in my head, the pictures shift and change, fleeting, powerful, moving. The vision on the mountain tells me that I live for the love of my people and the land we live on. I want that love to survive and thrive. Then the picture of the woman in the forest fills my head, so sudden, so charged, that a fire lights in my body. I want to run and find her. I long to meet her again.

Clouds close in, the light turns grey, and a sudden chill surrounds us. The rain starts, but we keep walking. It gets heavier, darker, and as we struggle through the forest, the cold drops sting my face. Then a huge tree appears with thick, wide branches dense with leaves that can give us shelter.

"Let's stop here!" Conor exclaims.

Without words, two of them go to gather branches to make a shelter and someone digs a small fire pit. I can hardly see their faces through the rain that pours down.

I help one of them to collect firewood. Sheelin is her name, she is not much older than me, tall and strong with black hair. She picks up twigs and branches, and I carry them. We make a good team and soon we have enough wood for a fire. The rain is heavy, but someone with a fire stick is able to get a spark, and the fire catches and flames build up even as rain hisses on top. We build a shelter against the tree, big enough for all of us to huddle in a circle and share food - hazelnuts, eggs, and dried meat. Conor sits quietly, his wish to get to Sliabh na

Caillí shows as he taps his foot on the ground. Sheelin talks about Sligeach - that is where the Voyagers came to land from their boats. She tosses her hair back, eager to tell me about the Voyagers. Words pour from her mouth.

"Mara and Finn went out to sea in a boat. We waited on the shore until they arrived back with the Voyagers. We could not hide our surprise at how they looked. They wore big, heavy cloaks and walked to the shore in a tight group. They had bundles and a cauldron with precious crystals. When they saw the great Cairn on top of Sliabh Mór they came to a sudden stop and talked to each other in a different language. They stared at the Cairn and then looked around at the ring of mountains with cairns on top." Sheelin pauses and turns to me. "You know Sligeach?"

"No, I come from the south, near Cill Dara," I reply.

"Cill Dara! *I want to go there!*" she exclaims. "I hear there is a wonderful temple with beautiful tapestries. Did you visit the temple?"

"Yes, at Imbolc," I answer, but I want to bring the conversation back to the Voyagers. "Have you met all the Voyagers?"

"Yes, they stayed at Sligeach, and now we're showing them the way to Sliabh na Caillí," Sheelin replies.

I want to know more about the woman in the forest.

"Do you know their names?"

"Two of them, Arzu and Mata, they're like our Keepers."

"Who's the woman with the wand?" I ask as my face flushes, but I need to know.

"That's Arzu."

I turn the name over slowly and feel it in my mouth. I keep my eyes down and hope she tells me more.

"Arzu has magic, she touches *everyone*," Sheelin says as she leans into me.

"Not everyone," Conor points out.

"Soon after they arrived," Sheelin continues the story, "we went in procession to the Cairn of Great Spirit on top of Sliabh Mór. When we got there Arzu and Mata climbed on top of the Cairn. Arzu held up a cauldron to the sky. Her hair was floating as she said special words that Mata repeated after her. The sun rose above and filled her hair with light. A glow spread through us."

"What words did they speak?" I ask.

I only want to talk about Arzu.

"I'm not sure. Áine said the words out loud to us, she knows their language."

"She called the Spirit of her island, the fire Spirit of Melita," Conor explains.

"The Voyagers stay together; they don't talk much to us. Áine stays with them. Arzu and Áine are very close," Sheelin continues.

"Are they together?" I ask, my heart beating.

"Yes, they go to the forest together."

My lips tremble when I hear this.

"But they didn't stay together for long. Áine went with Mara and Finn to Cill Dara. Arzu and Mata stayed at Sligeach. Do you know Áine?" she asks.

"She came to Cill Dara with Mara and Finn, they told us about the Voyagers and their land," I answer.

"They had to leave their land," Conor speaks in a sharp voice.

We go quiet. The fire glows in front of us as rain falls steadily on the leaves above us, and raindrops break through.

"I heard that too," I say. "That there are too many people on their land."

"They don't have enough food," Conor adds.

"How do you know this?" I ask in a sharp tone as my unease rises.

"Sheelin heard them talking, she learnt their language," Conor explains.

I turn to Sheelin.

"I know some words," she says, and pauses. "Enough to understand that they may have to leave their land."

"Why are they here?" I ask.

"To bring special crystals to Brú," Sheelin replies. I take a breath; this is what the Bards told us at Cill Dara. "They went to Cruachan to dream for many moon cycles."

A sudden gust of wind catches the fire and raises sparks into the wet night. I've heard stories of Cruachan; it is a deep passageway into the belly of the earth. People say it is hard to get into and harder to get out of, that only people with special magic can go there, and it is a passageway for the ancestors to go to the Otherworld. Why did the Voyagers go there? That is not a place for their ancestors.

The wind gets stronger, the flames surge, the rain hisses on the fire and droplets hit our faces. We huddle back further into the tree as the wind rises and swirls around us, and the trees and branches sway. The shift in energy puts my hair on end. It seems to tell us that the Voyagers can bring big changes ahead that we don't know of.

"May Spirit protect us," says Sheelin.

"From their magic," Conor adds.

"No!" Sheelin exclaims, looking at him. "They're here for Beo at Winter Sun Standstill."

"They want to take our Beo and our people," Conor answers back.

"Conor, no one can take our Beo, it belongs to the land and the stones," Sheelin states and looks away. "Dreams help prepare the Voyagers for Brú; they want our Beo in their crystals at Winter Sun Standstill."

The wind fades as she speaks, the whispers in the trees seem to say she is right. A picture of Arzu comes into my head - she has a special magic, and I want to see her again.

"Where are they now?" I ask.

"They are hurrying to Sliabh na Caillí before the storm," Sheelin replies.

I want to get up and run to find Arzu, follow her to Sliabh na Caillí, but the steady rain and the dark forest keep us under the tree.

A song starts. The conversation ends for now. We sing more songs, lie back on the ground, and drift to sleep. As soon as my eyes close, a vivid picture of Arzu with her smiling face and beautiful curves comes into my head and sleep falls quickly after the long day.

I wake up from a dream, it has the same energy as the vision on the hilltop before I met Arzu.

Clouds form and undulate in front of me and become a small island. But there is no sign of lakes or rivers, no trees, just bare earth. The island shifts shape into the body of a woman with big breasts and buttocks. She sits on her haunches. Red light fills her body. She glows.

This is like the statue of the big woman that the Bards showed us at Cill Dara. This is the island that Arzu comes from. Is this the Spirit of her island, why is she calling to me? Heat rises in my body. I lie there in the darkness, the vivid picture of the hot island in my head. How can I be a healer for my people when I dream about another land? I wonder if our energies can come together, if they have a Spirit of their land like us. Maybe Spirit brings me to Arzu. But I don"t know when I can see her again or how she feels. I hope that Spirit will bring us together for the Grand Cross at Brú.

The glimmer of sunlight and the sound of birdsong wake everyone. It is easy to find nuts and eggs in the forest. Conor still has some dried meat and bread. We eat quickly, we are excited, we hope to get to Sliabh na Caillí today. We set out again. Visions and feelings swirl in my head, but I focus on the forest floor and the trees drifting by. I want to meet Arzu and the other Voyagers again soon. All I know about them is what I've heard and from my dreams and visions. I know their names, what they look like, how they dress, and where they come from. But still, they are mysterious and different. Unease rises in my belly as stories from the Hollow come into my head. Do the Voyagers bring an energy that is different from ours? Can they block us? Are they looking for more? I keep my head down - I want to see Arzu again and have that spark between us.

"There it is - Sliabh na Caillí!"

Everyone stops. In front of us, two big round hills rise above the tops of trees, each with a cairn on top like familiar breasts beckoning us.

"Like Sligeach," Sheelin says. "Like the Cairn of Great Spirit."

"Where our ancestors live," Conor adds.

They hug each other. The sweep of hills and cairns draws us on and soon we hear the sound of a river. A low, cool breeze wafts around us. We move to the riverbank with a landing bay where boats are tied up. A pathway follows a row of fencing away from the bank and we walk a long time through the forest until we come to a big gateway. Just as Sheelin lifts her hand to knock the gates open, someone beckons us to come through.

"Welcome. My name is Dectin. This is the gateway to Sliabh na Caillí," a man says. He is wearing a Keeper's robe over his long, thin body and has a big smile on his face. "Join us by the fire."

We step into a small clearing. Branches of trees lean over two longhouses set behind a fire where people sit with cloaks of browns and greens, their hoods thrown back. They look like the group that travels with the Voyagers. I hurry over, but there is no sign of the colourful clothes or dark faces. This group has travelled for days, just like us, to get here for the Lúnasa celebration.

I sink onto a bench beside Sheelin and Conor. Someone hands us bowls of thick hot soup and slabs of bread. No one talks as we eat. I sit in a white cloud, I can barely see out, or sense energies around me, as if I am going to take off and hover above our island, ready to fly, but I don't know where. All I can see is the vision, all I can feel is a longing to meet Arzu again.

Dectin comes to sit beside us.

"Are you going to An Uaimh for the Lúnasa festival?" he asks us.

"No. We travelled from Sligeach with the Voyagers," Sheelin responds.

"Oh, they aren't long here," Dectin says. People lean in, they want to hear more about the Voyagers. "They're in the Sanctuary, our temple area, with their special crystals."

"Can we meet them?" I ask.

"Soon, when they come to the Lúnasa fire. We have a small ceremony here at full moon, most people are away at An Uaimh for the big festival," Dectin explains and stands up. "You have been travelling for a long time, here you can wash and rest."

He points to a longhouse and a large washhouse in the corner, with a big barrel of water and a small fire in front.

We jump up and take turns at the washhouse. In the longhouse, there are piles of furs and wraps. I take a deer fur for a bed and lie under it. Everyone from Carraig - Mona, Murta, Shula, Dori - and Seekers from Cill Dara are so far away. I am here, alone for the moment, but I know I am in the right place. The dream at Tara pushed me to leave and find the Voyagers, boar and deer guided me, the wind took me to Arzu. The stars are pushing me to follow my own path. I lie there with a picture of Arzu in my head. I know she is close, and I ache to see her again.

I step out of the longhouse the next morning. Many pathways lead out of the clearing. How do I find the one that will bring me to Arzu? Dectin sits by the fire and waves me over.

"Where do the pathways go?" I ask.

"One leads to the gardens, where we go later. Some to the Sanctuary, where we watch over ancestors, others to cairns on top of the mountains, one to the Labyrinth. These paths are not for all," Dectin replies.

My eyes widen and the hair stands on my neck. I have the sudden sense that Sliabh na Caillí is different from Cill Dara or Tara. It is a place where the Keepers look after our ancestors, it is strange and mysterious, not a place where we wander in the forest.

"Can we go to the Sanctuary?" I question.

"Only when the Keepers take you there," Dectin affirms, his eyes narrowing. "We will go later, at Sun Balance, when the other Seekers arrive after the harvest."

That is a long wait to see Shula and the other Seekers - Sun Balance is more than a moon cycle after Lúnasa. Dectin stands up as Sheelin, Conor and the others from the longhouse join us.

"Are all of you here for Lúnasa?" he asks, and everyone nods. "Follow me. We have bigger longhouses and a Cistin for people who come to stay."

We follow Dectin along a pathway and arrive at another clearing with the familiar Cistin, fire in the centre, stores for food, longhouses, and a big shelter for firewood.

We take food from the Cistin and sit by the fire. Dectin points to the longhouse where visitors sleep.

"We have gardens here, but we get most of our food from An Uaimh. You can help us gather the barley that we grow here. After the harvest Sliabh na Caillí gets very busy, as many people arrive for Sun Balance and stay for Samhain."

"We can stay here after Lúnasa?" Conor asks.

"Yes, if you want, you can help at the Cistin, in the gardens, with the buildings. We have many longhouses and buildings. There are cairns and pathways. There is much work to do."

Murmurs rise in the group. There are many stories of Sliabh na Caillí, where Keepers look after the ancestors. Already it seems bigger than that, there are more people, more buildings hidden in the forest, and many cairns on the tops of mountains. Dectin holds up a hand.

"Sliabh na Caillí holds the spirits of ancestors," Dectin continues. "We need to stay calm and keep Glan."

I catch Conor's eye. He pulls down the corners of his lips to make a funny face. I smile back.

"Surely we can have fun at the Lúnasa celebration!" Conor calls out.

People laugh and Dectin smiles and claps his hands. He gives us tasks for the day - to go help at the fields, work on buildings and fences, and gather firewood. After work in the morning, some people go to the Sanctuary or up to the cairns on the mountains. I'm not sure if they are all Keepers, they are friendly, but they are very focused on work. After dark, I sit by the fire with Conor and Sheelin and we watch for the full moon, but only patches of white peep through the clouds. After a few days, the sky clears, and we see the moon getting bigger in the sky - we are close to Lúnasa. My breath stops as I gaze at the moon and the urge to see Arzu fills my chest.

It is quiet before Lúnasa, not like the celebrations at Carraig, where we have mead, music and dancing on the day before the ceremony. At Cill Dara we heard so often of the big festival before the harvest that brings many people together for days of fun and games. Surely it is the same at An Uaimh. An ache to see Shula, Gormley, Neasa, Felim and Ollie fills me - they are there now, maybe leaping over fires as we sit here.

On the night of the full moon, we meet for the ceremony. A tall pile of wood, higher than a person, rises in front of us. Logs are cut down the middle with space between, and many small twigs are piled at the base to make the fire burn quickly. Conor jokes that this may be a fiery festival after all. My body thrums, my eyes are bright as I scan the pathways for the Voyagers. I watch for the dark faces and curly hair, for bright cloaks or headbands. Beside us, a big table is cleared, ready for new food from the fields and gardens. Heat rises from the oven where bread bakes.

Horns ring out. A procession approaches. At the front Dectin carries a torch with a burning flame, followed by a Keeper who holds up a long, thick staff with a sharp stone blade. The familiar carvings of spirals and wavy lines dance in the light of flames. More Keepers follow with baskets of food fresh from the forest and the fields.

Behind them are the Voyagers. I am sure of it, even though I can't see the colours of their clothes. They are smaller, they move in rhythm, and as they get closer, they raise their hands to us. It is them; they are here in front of us. One of them carries a drum, not like ours, it has a long body with a small skin on top. Beside her, a big smile beams out from Arzu as her eyes sweep over the group. My face lights up. She is here beside me, by the fire.

A Keeper steps forward.

"We welcome the Voyagers who come from across the Middle Sea. They are here to learn our ways, especially how we place stones on places where the earth's energy is strong." As the Keeper speaks, two Voyagers step forward. "Mata and Arzu. They bring crystals for the Grand Cross at Winter Sun Standstill."

Mata steps forward and raises her arms. She speaks different words that we don't understand.

"Hendri, Gora and Saleem guide their way across the seas," the Keeper continues.

Smiles on their faces tell us they are glad to be here.

The Keeper raises the staff with the blade on top.

"At Bealtaine we lay seeds in the ground
We ask Great Spirit for bounty.
Now we see that seeds grow into plants,
Wheat and barley wait in our fields.
Fruits and nuts sprout in the forest.
We ask Great Spirit to smile on us,
Allow us to gather these riches."

Two Keepers move to set flames to the base of the wood. Fire flares up, burns into the twigs at the base and licks up the sides of the wood. My eyes widen to see it burn so fast. I gaze through the flames at

Arzu's face as the light of the flames dances on her skin. People cluster around and I stand on the tips of my feet to keep my eyes on her. Too soon she blends into a group of people moving around.

The Keeper raises and lowers the staff so that the stone blade dances in the firelight. Cheers ring out as people raise baskets of food in the air and others join in with platters of bread still hot from the oven. The rich foods from the harvest come alive in the glow.

Gongs sound.

"This is a good year - wheat and barley grow well, the fields are full of plants, and the animals are strong and healthy. The forest is filling with ripe berries, apples and acorns. We thank Great Spirit for these gifts of food."

Our words of thanks to Spirit and the earth ring out to the sky and draw us together. Even though we are a small group, we can still sense the energy of Lúnasa rising between us, moving us through the next turn in the wheel of the year towards Samhain, when the light starts to fade, and our ancestors call us.

The Keeper turns to the Voyagers.

"The Voyagers wish to show us how they dance with fire."

Saleem beats her drum with the palm of her hand, a loud, rich beat, then pauses.

Mata speaks in her language. Sheelin translates what they are saying.
"Fire burns, embers hot."

Saleem plays a slow, soft beat. All eyes are now on the fire as the tall beams of wood burn through and collapse onto the wood near the base. The flames reach through small pieces of wood and eat through the piles of burning twigs. Soon all we see are red-hot embers on the ground.

Two Voyagers step forward. They use long sticks to spread the burning pile into a long strip, the length of three people. The Voyagers stand in a line at one end of the strip. All along the strip twigs and wood glow as flames snake through. It looks like a ribbon alive with fire. They take off their boots and show us the bare skin of their feet. Saleem plays out a loud, deep beat and Mata moves forward. People gasp as she steps onto the strip and dances across to the grass on the other side. She turns and raises her arms to the group. The smile on her face shows she is pleased to be there. We cheer.

Flames still flicker and burn in the embers as Arzu steps forward. The drum rolls. She dances across the red-hot embers to join Mata. We cheer again. How can they do this? We take a breath as we watch Hendri dance across. Then Gora and Saleem follow, and they all stand together on the other side. They put their arms around each other and with a big shout, step forward and dance back across the embers to the other side. They bow to the group. We all burst out into cheering and clapping. We move forward to touch them and tell them how brave they are. Is this fun, is this magic, is this dangerous?

People surge towards the Voyagers, but gongs ring out just as I push forward. Dectin gestures to the Voyagers to join them at the big table, where baskets glisten with fruits, nuts, plants and flowers beside warm loaves of bread. Arzu's curly black hair gleams through the group of Keepers surrounding them.

"Seed and earth come together to bring this great bounty. We thank Spirit for this bread, the first from our harvest this year."

A Keeper steps forward, holds a knife up, and cuts the bread into pieces that she hands to each of us. We thank Spirit, take handfuls of food from the baskets and go back to the fire where new wood picks up the lingering flames. The Voyagers are so close, I can hardly eat. They sit together with bright faces and smiles, with the Keepers beside them. All around us is talk of the Voyagers and the fire dance.

"How can I meet them?" I whisper as I turn towards Conor.

"We can go to talk to them now," Conor answers and jumps up as I try to hide the beam on my face.

The Voyagers are surrounded by people, but when Mata and Arzu see Conor and Sheelin they call them in, and I follow. They kiss Conor and Sheelin on both cheeks.

Arzu turns to me. Her beautiful brown eyes gaze into mine. She places a hand on my cheek, glances at Mata, and speaks some words.

"She knows you from the forest," Sheelin says.

Arzu drops her hands and kisses me on both cheeks. Our cheeks brush. A charge from her smooth, soft skin surges through my body. I take her hand as I lean forward and kiss her on each cheek. I want to close my eyes, have her arms around me, nestle into the warm, lush skin above her breasts, and press my body against hers.

More people step up to greet her and soon there are many people between her and me. Everyone wants to greet the Voyagers. Then the Keepers start to move away, and the Voyagers follow. I watch as they walk down a path into the forest, my heart thudding in my chest. My dream tells me that fire shines through the Spirit of their land. It flares between me and Arzu. But she is a leader of her group, she may be with Áine, she might have many sparks. Who knows what is next?

"There is her magic again," Conor says. He stands beside me, and I look down. Can Conor sense how fast my heart is beating? "Time for fun. Come with me."

We go over to the longhouse with Sheelin, where she picks up a bag and pulls out a pouch.

"I heard they don't have mead at Sliabh na Caillí!" She exclaims, and she and Conor laugh. We sit on the floor of the longhouse and share the mead, spluttering as we drink too fast, and talk about the Voyagers. They listen to me as I tell them about the Bards, about Áine and the huge clay figure. Conor wants to know more about why they are here; he thinks we have not heard it all. Sheelin laughs and tells us they have come from the land of fire, maybe we need more fire. She smiles at me, and they touch my shoulder and tell me I am not the first to be touched by the fire of Arzu. I am unsure what to say, for now I am happy to be in the little group with my big feelings in my body. Eyes gleam and faces beam as we talk faster and laugh together. Outside the sound of drums grows louder. We jump up. A few people are still there, enough for fun and dancing. I throw my body into the dance, weave and twirl until sweat breaks. My body and face glow as energy flows.

-14-

Building Cairns

A strange quiet falls on Sliabh na Caillí as Lúnasa ebbs away. The Voyagers are away in the forest at the Sanctuary. The Keepers and others who live at Sliabh na Caillí come to the Cistin for food and then leave to go down one of the paths that lead to different areas. Dectin has many tasks that keep us busy. I go with a group to bring barley from the fields and store it in the Cistin. As we walk back and forth, my body feels heavy. It is a long, long time until Sun Balance, when the Voyagers may join us again, when Shula will come here with Gormley and Neasa and Ollie and Felim. I want to see Mona before then even if it is different between us. I walk back and forth with heavy feet, even Conor and Sheelin are not able to make me laugh. I sit at the fire in the evening with my head down, unsure if I can wait until Sun Balance. The moon seems to crawl across the sky.

One morning Dectin comes to sit beside us.

"You and Conor are Seekers. We might have a special task for you," says Dectin. My head lifts, and my eyes shine. Conor leans in. "You can take food to the hill nearby where they are building a cairn, maybe they can let you help there."

We jump up, beam at each other, and run to the Cistin to find baskets and fill them with food. Dectin points to a path and tells us to stay on it, and we will soon see a hilltop. A short walk through the forest brings us to the bottom of a hill, smaller than the two big ones that rise above the forest, and we climb quickly. At the top of the hill, two small cairns sit with entrances facing different directions, like the cairns for stargazing at Cill Dara. Summer huts sit in a cluster around a small fire pit where a group of people sit. The hilltop is light and open to the sky.

"Welcome to Sliabh Rua. My name is Cael." Cael is tall, with a deep blue band around their grey hair that tells us they are a Keeper and a weave of hazel around their neck that shows they are Flowing Spirit. "Let us take your gifts and present them to the ancestors." They rattle us in the four directions as other people join in. We hand Cael a loaf of bread from the basket, and they raise it to the sky. "We thank those who go before us for this gift of life."

We weave slowly around the cairns as they break off small bits of bread and place them inside the passageways.

Cael pauses in front of the huge stones that stand beside piles of earth and stone.

"Here we're building a new cairn for the Grand Cross," Cael explains.

My eyes widen.

This is my first time seeing a cairn before it is covered in earth and stones. Three huge stones as tall as my shoulder are placed side by side in a row opposite another row of three to make a short passageway. At the end of the passageway, the stones are placed side by side in a circle big enough for three or four people to sit inside, with flat stones layered on top to make a roof for the chamber. Cael scatters crumbs of bread as they take slow steps down the passageway. They bend their head to go into the chamber and then return to the group.

"Do you work with stone?" Cael asks me.

"I am practising to become a Keeper of Stones," I answer.

"Where are you from?"

"Carraig, up the mountain, near where the river, An Life, springs from the ground."

"Ah, that is where the white stones at Brú come from!" says Cael, excited, and I smile. "And what did Lia Fáil show you at Tara?"

"A Keeper in front of a big cairn."

"You can help us carve stones."

My breath catches as I hear the words.

"*Now?*" I ask, hesitating.

"Yes, until Sun Balance," Cael affirms and smiles.

"*Me too?*" asks Conor as he leans forward.

"Do you work with stones?"

"Yes!" Conor replies quickly.

"Where are you from?"

Conor pauses for a moment and looks at me.

"Ard Mhacha."

He told me one night of the big wooden temple at Ard Mhacha, but he didn't say if there were carved stones there.

"And what did you see at Tara?"

"I'm in a cairn gazing at stars," answers Conor.

"You can help us with the stars," asserts Cael.

Cael turns to the stone passageway. We sit in front of a big stone, and they show us how to place our hands and feel across the stone. Slowly, the palm of my hand senses the shape of ridges and rises on its surface, and fingers touch notches and edges and bumps. Cael tells us we must know a stone like our own body before we can start to carve. We spend the whole day touching the stones. Cael points to places on the stone where we might carve a spiral or a circle or a diamond, how we might fit it around the curves and bumps on the stone. As the day goes by the tingle in my hands grows hotter and spreads up my arms through my body. My belly reaches for the stone, I want to embrace it, hold my body to it, and press my cheek to the cool surface.

"You have the gift of stone," Cael states and smiles at me. "Tomorrow, you can start to make carvings on the stone." They turn to Conor, who faces them with a concerned look on his face. "We are building this cairn so that the Bright Star shines in at the Grand Cross. You can help us draw a chart of the stars."

We walk back downhill with light steps and smiles on our faces. At the Cistin we say to Dectin that Cael wants us to help. We hear that they want Sheelin at the Sanctuary to help the Voyagers and Keepers prepare for Sun Balance, since she knows some of the language of the Voyagers. I want to go with her, but the tingle of stones in my body tells me to stay here and keep calm until Sun Balance.

Day after day we walk up the hill with baskets of food and pouches of water and work with the stones. Cael shows us how to carve using small, sharp flints, bigger hand-sized stones with sharp edges, and stone hammers. I find a place on the stone where a lozenge can fit, and Cael agrees. I trace the shape with a sharp flint. Slowly, carefully I pick away to make a deeper groove, only stopping when sweat drips on my nose, or my hand gets scraped.

The hilltop is like the Haven at Cill Dara with a lovely, calm focus, hands on tools, and my eyes fixed on stone. Sometimes it feels the same as the time alone on top of the mountain after Tara, with sun and moon and the beautiful vision and white light in my body. I grow to love the pulses of stones that connect us with earth and sky.

Slowly I see carvings take shape on the stone. My hands and eyes learn to attune to the big stones. I'm pleased now for all that time at Cill Dara, for how Sorcha taught me to sense stones. I find a place for a beautiful spiral. I take a long time to pick and polish the circular grooves and then carve out little dots nearby. Conor carves the shape of stars with dots. Cael makes a circle inside a circle and a dot with eight lines out for the wheel of the year. Others make rows of diamonds and columns of half diamonds.

As the days get shorter, Dectin says we can stay on the hill and Cael gives us a summer hut to share. I like Conor. He is excited to work with stone; he knows about stars and the patterns that they make. Each day after we carve, we help to haul big stones with ropes to place on the ground in a circle around the passage and chamber. Then we cover the passage and chamber with earth and stone - it takes a long time to make enough layers so that the mound rises to a soft curve.

At nighttime, we sit by the fire and hold different stones in our hands, gaze at stars, watch the moon grow small and then big again. Cael points to the White Band and the Swan Star that shine over Brú. They tell us our ancestors took a long time to bring special stones along the sea and up An Bhóinn to build the three huge cairns at Brú, bigger than any at Sliabh na Caillí. When I describe the tapestry at Cill Dara Cael beams and tells us that is what Newgrange looks like.

"You two are strong on your path," Cael says, their voice warm and encouraging. "It's good that you're going to Brú this year. You'll see how our great culture grows and grows. More people come to live here, to learn our ways."

Their eyes shine with joy.

"Are the Voyagers here to stay?" I ask.

My longing for Arzu stirs. What if she has come here to stay?

"The strong energy of the Grand Cross moves many people," Cael says.

"And after the Grand Cross?" Conor asks with curiosity.

"The Augury at Sun Balance may tell us what's next."

"What's an Augury?" Conor asks.

"A message from stones," replies Cael.

"How do we get the message?" Conor questions.

Cael's voice goes deep and steady as they speak.

"At sunrise on the day of Sun Balance, the sun shines on the carvings on stones in a pattern that gives us signs of what is to come. This year is special; we are all coming here to prepare for the Grand Cross at Brú."

I catch Conor's eye and a current of excitement runs between us. Cael turns to others at the fire. I push my feet into the ground; I want peace and calm for now.

The steady rhythm of the days brings us closer to Sun Balance. The Sun is not so strong, the light does not last as long, the evenings grow colder, and we are glad for the warmth of the fire. We work at a steady pace back and forth as the days get shorter, even sometimes after the sun has gone down, to make the mound over the passageway and chamber. At the end of the day, our bodies are so tired we barely see the night sky. Other people come and go with food, water and wood for the fire to help us finish.

The shadow of the sun tells us that Sun Balance is close. Cael gathers us at the entrance to the cairn.

"We worked long and hard to build this cairn for the special time of the Grand Cross. We know the Grand Cross will bring changes to our culture. Whatever comes, this cairn holds our strength. It sits here with the other cairns, large and small, at Sliabh na Caillí."

The hair on the back of my neck prickles as I listen to Cael. The words of Mona at Carraig come into my head - they speak the same way. Many prophecies and dreams for this year foretell that the Grand Cross brings strong energy. Others predict that the changes are not all good. My time on the hill with stones put all this out of my head.

Cael steps forward with a basket of stones and hands each of us one to take with us. A small round stone sits in my palm, it says we are ready for the changes to come. I turn to Conor; he has a smile on his face.

"I've good Glan after the time on the hill," Conor says, beaming with joy.

"So do I," I say, and we laugh as we leave.

Even on the way down, I am filled with hope to see Arzu soon. I am excited that Mona, Shula and the other Seekers will be here soon, and we can all come together again.

As I lie in the longhouse that night, a picture of Arzu dancing across the fire brings the sense of her touch to my cheek. I pick up the stone that Cael gave me and hold it against my belly. Cael said I have the gift of stone. I loved building the cairn and carving the stones as much as I love healing with stones. I wonder if that is why the spark with Arzu is so strong, maybe she has the gift of stone as well.

The next morning a familiar figure appears at the Cistin - Mona.

I jump up and we embrace. She is staying at the Sanctuary and is here to see me before Sun Balance. She strokes my hair, pats my face, touches the marks of stones on my hands, smiles and laughs. My arms open to her; it has been too long since I saw her at Tara. Joy fills me as love flows between us. She tilts my chin and holds my eyes.

"You left Tara very suddenly," she says, and I lower my eyes.

"I left for the night, not to stay away," I reply quickly. "I had so many questions after Sun Standstill."

"Why didn't you talk to me?"

"We heard at Troim that the Voyagers were not at Tara. Then Shula said she didn't want to go to Tara or Brú. I felt unsure of what to do." Mona waits. She knows I can tell her more. "I was confused that you said that the Voyagers would be at Tara," I say in a low voice.

"That's why you stayed away from me?"

"And Shula says you pushed her," I add.

"I want to see you and Shula at Brú," she explains.

"But maybe that's not what Shula wants."

"You're young, you need to listen to the Keepers."

"But you don't always know, you may not always be right," I blurt out.

My face flushes at the words, and I hold my breath, afraid she may pull away. But she takes my hand.

"I may not always be right, but I always look for the best for you. Briona, you're like a daughter to me. I'll always love you," Mona says and places her hands on my shoulders and looks into my eyes. "Now tell me about after Tara."

Tears well as the feelings of the Hollow and the night on the ground after mushrooms rise in my body.

"I took mushrooms..." I say, the words bursting out.

Mona drops her hands, her eyes narrow and a frown shows on her face.

"Briona, you know if you break your Geis, that means that Glan is gone. You may not go to Brú."

My stomach sinks.

"After I took them, my body said no, so I threw them up," I speak in a rush. Mona closes her eyes and sits in silence. "Later I had a vision on the mountain. Our people, this island, my path. It's all clear before me."

I want to show Mona that I still have Glan.

"What's clear?" Mona still has a frown on her face as she opens her eyes.

"My path is to be a Keeper of Stones, a healer for our people."

"You saw this in a vision?" Mona raises her eyebrows.

"Yes, Great Spirit came to me." My head fills with the vision on the mountain-top, the clouds shifting, the moon shining. "Would she show herself if I broke my Geis?"

Mona raises two hands above my head and slowly brings them down along my body, past my hips, down my legs to my feet. She sits with her body still and her eyes closed. I hold my breath.

"I don't sense mushrooms in your body," she confirms and puts her arms around me and holds me close. "Great Spirit has a different path for you, testing you with mushrooms." I sense questions in her body, she seems unsure. "We'll wait and see how things unfold, how well you keep Glan."

"I saw the Voyagers in a dream and then met them in the forest. They're here now."

"Yes, they're in the Sanctuary, we're preparing for the Augury."
"They danced on fire at Lúnasa," I continue.
"They bring fire energy."
"I have a strong connection with one of them," I say, my voice shaking. "Arzu. She touches my heart."
"There is so much energy from the stars as the Grand Cross grows stronger. That's what brings your vision and your spark with Arzu. You don't know yet what the Voyagers want, or where your connection comes from," Mona says. She is right, so much can come from the stars, who knows what comes next. "You're close to being an adult now, Briona. You must stay strong if you want to follow your destiny."

A small tremble rises in my belly, and I press my lips together - I need to keep my focus, practice Glan, stay on the path with the other Seekers if I want to get to Brú.

Mona stays at the fire until the sun is high in the sky. Love runs tender between us as we sit together, eat some fresh food from the harvest and enjoy the quiet of the day. Her warmth and love embrace me; she is strong and wise. She knows me even though I do not show her all that is in my heart. As people come to the fire at the end of the day she stands and says she needs to go to the Sanctuary, we will meet again at the Sun Balance ceremony. I smile softly as I watch her walk down the path. I feel strong now.

The next day, Dectin shows Conor and me how to get to the Seekers' Lodge, and we hurry along the path that snakes through the forest and brings us to a huge clearing with many buildings. There is Shula! We run to embrace and hold each other tight. Body to body, her warmth fills me, familiar, steady, our bellies, chests, arms tight together.

"It's so long since Tara, did you meet the Voyagers?" she asks. There is so much I want to tell her - of the vision and the encounter with the Voyagers, of building a cairn on the hilltop. I want to hear about the Lúnasa festival at An Uaimh. I gaze at her, words swirling through my head. "We came from An Uaimh, we're staying in the Seekers' Lodge."

The words suddenly flood out.

"I stayed on top of a mountain and had a beautiful vision, Shula, it was *wonderful!* Then I saw a group travelling across the land and went to find them, they're the Voyagers, like the dream at Tara. They drew me into a circle with one named Arzu. I have a strong connection with her."

My face flushes as I speak. I just want to talk about Arzu. I long to see her again. I shift from foot to foot.

"Another spark?"

"More than that."

"A strong connection?" Shula asks, her eyes wide. I nod. My eyes glisten, and my cheeks are hot. She catches my arm. "Briona, this is the first time I see you like this. There is a huge spark in you, bigger than anyone before, it's like a fire."

I press my palms to my eyes. Shula knows me. I look at her in wonder.

"So sudden, can it happen like that?" I ask.

"Look at the stories, they tell how it's like lightning or a waterfall or a ray of sun or..." Shula speaks fast. I don't know if she is laughing or if she shares my excitement. Her eyes shine, and she beams at me. "Like me and Bres, our heart bond grows stronger."

"This is different from what happened with Dori or Gormley…" I say.

"Maybe she's the special one that Mona saw in your stars?" Shula asks questions I don't think of.

"*Oh*, maybe she is."

This is too much for now.

"Tell me about Lúnasa," I urge her.

"After you left, we went downriver to An Uaimh. Oh Briona, it's a huge farmland, bigger than Cill Dara."

Shula describes the harvest festival and laughs with joy as she speaks. She talks of connection to the land, with people at the harvest, and the fun of the festival. She is light and clear.

"Where are the others?"

"They're here, at the Seekers' Lodge in the temple area, they call it the Sanctuary, I can take you there."

She links my arm and soon I see Gormley, Neasa, Ollie and Felim in front of a longhouse. My body lights up to see them and I run over. Gormley wears the familiar red headband. Felim has a huge smile, and Neasa's eyes shine. Ollie looks brighter than ever before. Their strong arms embrace me, tunics and cloaks blending as we stand close, arms about shoulders, heads bent towards each other, kisses to cheeks and foreheads. We go to the fire and sit with Conor and the other Seekers to prepare for Sun Balance the next day.

-15-

Augury at Sun Balance on Sliabh na Caillí

"*Hurry hurry*, sunrise is soon," a voice calls.

Outside the early morning fire welcomes the light of the day. We are ready for this special day of Sun Balance and the Augury on the hill. There is an ease in my body as I melt into the attunements with the group of Seekers I have known for so long now. I hope that the Voyagers are on the hill and that I will see Arzu again. Cael raises a torch, and we silently follow them onto a path through the forest in the dim dawn light. Shula is beside me, and the other Seekers follow.

We arrive at a clearing with an archway of carved wood that opens to the foot of a tall hill rising in front of us and blends with others that come from different pathways. Silence falls as we circle the foot of the hill and begin a slow spiral that streams around and upwards. Shula tugs my arm and points to a large cairn covered in stones that sits on top of the hill with smaller cairns scattered around. They seem asleep, waiting for dawn, or maybe for us to visit.

Excitement fills my body as we reach the top of the hill. The big mound of the Cairn of Augury looms over us, covered in white stones that look grey in the dawn light. We follow Cael to gather in front of a huge stone chair that is the size of two people. On top is a colourful rug with beautiful spirals. The stone chair sits in a circle of big, wide stones that stretch around the base of the mound.

"Keepers wait for rays of the rising sun to fall on the carved stones and give us a message," Cael says and gestures for us to face east.

The sky lights up gently as the sun peeps and then rises above the horizon, sending long shafts of golden light shining onto our faces. The stones on the mound come to life in the soft glow.

The sound of drums and pipes draws our eyes to a procession. It comes out of the cairn and streams around the side of the mound. Drummers and pipers play a low lyrical beat. Keepers wear colourful gowns with indigo bands around their heads. Mona is in the middle, one of the elders; she looks splendid and wise.

My body trembles - there are Arzu and Mata. The group stirs with gasps and intakes of breath. They are stunning in their bright robes, their hair plaited and woven with ornaments. They carry big drums, unlike ours - a carved hollow log that is wide at one end and covered in skin, and narrow at the other end with an opening. The drums make a deep boom boom as they come around the mound. Arzu looks wonderful. I stand transfixed, my eyes wide. She moves with her head high and her face beaming. The golden light of the sun bathes her and sparkles off the crystal stones in her hair. I follow her with my eyes as she walks slowly with the other Keepers to form a crescent around the big stone chair.

A Keeper steps forward in a yellow robe, and two others lift her onto the chair. My gaze is fixed on Arzu, but I see from the corner of my eye that it is Áine. Áine raises two arms, ready to speak. The drums and pipes stop. There is silence.

"Sun lights up stones
Stars speak
Love pours from the sky.
This is a time of turning.
Dark clouds cover the sun for many moons.
Rain pours from the sky and washes the earth away.
Trees and plants cannot grow strong.
Our special ones, our Shining Ones,
Keep us strong.
We will hear more at Samhain."

Ripples run through the crowd, sounds of "no" and "when" and "how". A whoosh surges through my ears, wave upon wave. Words echo in my head - "time of turning", "dark clouds", "Shining Ones". Around me, people turn to talk and gather in groups. Shula, Gormley, Neasa, Ollie and Felim move together. Shula tugs my arm. We huddle and catch each other's eyes, surprise and fear on our faces.

"Dark clouds wash the earth away," Ollie sobs, tears flowing from her eyes as Felim wipes them off her face.

"We must stay strong," Neasa murmurs.

Gormley nods his head.

"We have so much cloud and rain, which help us grow food. How can the earth wash away?" Ollie asks us all.

"Our Shining Ones keep us strong," Gormley repeats the words.

The line of Keepers steps forward and begins a chant.

"Love pours from the sky. Love pours from the sky."

Everyone links arms and holds tight. We stand intertwined and chant the words back to the Keepers. We sway together, our gaze on the Keepers. The strength of love can help us through hard times. But some people look around with frightened faces, others stare at the ground. I block out the words of dark clouds and trees that cannot grow as I say the chant over and over. Voices ring out the chant to the Keepers, and they call the words out again, back and forth, louder and louder.

Suddenly my eyes meet Arzu's. A jolt jerks through my body as lightning flashes between us. My body is back in the forest where we first met. My mouth still moves to the words of the chant, but the sound of the group fades away as Arzu holds my gaze. Energy spirals between us, from me to her and her to me, growing ever stronger until there is just her and me in a band of white light that pulses between us. Then someone touches her shoulder, and she looks away. The energy fades from my body. I shiver.

The Keepers raise their arms and the chant dims, its echoes fading out across the hilltop. I turn back to the Seekers, we share embraces, but our bodies are still tense. Ollie stands with her lips in a straight line as Gormley and Neasa continue to repeat the words, and Felim and Shula are silent. People begin to quietly move downhill. Just before we leave, I look back at Arzu. The Keepers are moving away from the big chair. Áine stands beside it and Arzu steps forward and embraces her. They hold each other's eyes and bodies like no one else is around. My breath leaves my body, my mouth goes dry, and my feet come to a stop.

"Briona..." Shula calls and catches my arm as the others move away down the hill. "What?"

She follows my gaze. But Arzu and Áine have moved apart to hug other Keepers. I look at Shula, I have no words, as tears fill my eyes.

"Let's go to the Seekers' Lodge," Shula suggests.

She holds my arm and brings me over to the other Seekers. They are calmer now as we spiral downhill together. They talk about the time of turning and the Shining Ones and keeping strong. I hear it all as if from far away. Shula talks about the changes to come, and others talk about the Grand Cross. Someone reminds us that Áine is a Shining One who can keep us strong.

At the bottom of the hill, I stop. The forest opens in front of me, away from the path that leads to the Sanctuary and the Seekers' Lodge. How can I go with the group when Arzu is somewhere nearby? I turn to walk back up the hill, but people are still streaming down. I want to look for her.

"Briona, stay with us," Shula says, tugging my arm.

I shake my head and walk away to the forest. She doesn't come after me.

In the forest I don't know which direction to go in. It is so different from that time in the forest when I first met Arzu. Already the leaves show yellows and oranges, and blackberries grow on brambles. I wonder - is Arzu the one for me? Then a picture of her hugging Áine fills my head. They lived together on her island, they travelled across the ocean together, Sheelin said they were very close.

I stumble through the forest, unsure of where to go, who to talk to. My feet trip and I reach out for a branch to steady me, but it breaks off and I fall on the ground at the base of a huge oak tree. I nestle into the trunk. Swirling energies in my body settle and flow from my back into the tree and seep down into the ground. I rest my head on the trunk. I am sure of one thing - I want to see Arzu.

A flock of swallows startles me as they rise from the trees, hover above me and then fly off. I stand up and follow their path. It leads me to the edge of the forest. Through thinning trees, I see a small winter lodge where a group of people sit around the fire outside. I recognise Arzu instantly. It takes me a moment to see that her eyes are closed. I gaze at Arzu, at her shining black hair, peaceful face, and strong hands. She opens her eyes, sees me, and waves me over, her finger on her lips. She pats the bench beside her, and I sit down. My body trembles to be so close to her.

She points to the other Voyagers and makes a gesture of sleep. A laugh bubbles in me, joy floods my body, and I want to dance. I gesture to my chest and draw a spiral slowly in the air. She raises her eyebrows, then points at the sun and fans her face. I walk my fingers in the direction of the sun. Now we are lightheaded and light-hearted as we laugh and gesture more. We stop and sit quietly, almost touching. I long to take her hands, put an arm around her. I catch her eye and gesture to the forest. She stands up. As we walk, she puts an arm around my shoulder. Heat surges through my body. I turn and smile at her.

"Arzu," she says as she points to her chest and speaks strange words.

"Briona," I respond, and speak some of our words.

They are so different! We talk back and forth. Her words are strange; I only hear her rich and melodic voice. She stops at each tree, touches the leaves, nods at me, presses leaves to her face, and smells and tastes them. We gather berries and nuts until our hands are full, then stop at a tree. I place a berry in her mouth, catch her eye, watch her lips close over it, and see the juice seep through. We wander on, bodies bumping together as fire rises and spreads through my body.

We enter a small grove of trees. Arzu turns and pulls me into her arms. The heat of her body radiating through her clothes matches mine. She runs her hands up and down my back and presses me close. Our cheeks touch before she takes my face in her hands and presses her soft lips to mine. She slowly widens her mouth, and our tongues meet in a long kiss. Our arms tighten. We pause, gasp for air, and laugh, looking into each other's sparkling eyes. She trails her lips down my neck, pulls back, takes my hands and kisses my fingers, then leans against a tree, her eyes still on me. I step forward to melt into her and she takes me in her arms again, her mouth on mine. We kiss and kiss, letting the world around us melt away.

The air shifts around us as birds begin their evening songs. Arzu places her hands on my shoulders, lowers her eyes and sighs. My body still tingles but my face falls. She places the palms of her hands together and puts them to the side of her face with her eyes closed, the gesture of sleep. Maybe she means we can be together. She flashes her fingers at me several times, then does the sleep gesture again. I bite my lip, unsure what she means.

She stands for a moment and looks at the sky. Then she bends to the ground, picks up a stick and draws a small round cairn on the ground. Beside that, she draws a circle that she divides into eight for the wheel of the year. She draws the sun at the top for Summer Sun Standstill, and one at the bottom, that is Winter Sun Standstill, then a dot at where we are now, at Sun Balance, and fills in the space to Samhain. She makes the sleeping gesture again and points at the cairn. I laugh and repeat her gestures, still unsure of their meaning. She laughs back and takes me in her arms again and strokes my hair and face. We hug, pleasure still in our bodies, then pull apart and walk back through the forest, arms around each other. Maybe she is going to the cairn to sleep - or we are both going to sleep.

We linger in the forest until the light fades. Back at the winter lodge, she gives me a long kiss on the lips and turns away. I watch her walk over to the lodge. I want to sink to the ground and hold onto her. My skin feels bare, missing the touch of her body. Arzu turns around, waves, and points to a group of longhouses with a fire in front. I watch as she disappears into her lodge with a last wave to me. An ache to see her again rises in my body. I stand until I can barely see, then hasten over to one of the longhouses and go inside. It is dark but I find a place near the wall where I lie for a long time, my body trembling, Arzu's face in front of me.

The next morning someone shakes my shoulder. My eyes open, and Shula is standing in front of me. I get up and follow her outside, blinking at the light of day. She smooths my hair and brushes me down. I look around for Arzu's lodge, but I'm not sure which one it is. The forest sweeps around the huge clearing with buildings everywhere - longhouses and many huts in circles with layers of wattle and thick thatched roofs. Shula takes me to a fire where Gormley, Neasa and the other Seekers sit. I want to nestle in beside smiling faces, talk and laugh like at Cill Dara, but they have serious looks on their faces.

"Good, you're back!" Felim exclaims as they touch my arm and smile.

"You left us at Tara and again yesterday," Shula speaks in a firm voice.

"We didn't see you for three moons. You left your birthstone all that time," Gormley adds.

"We want to hear all about your adventures," Felim says in a gentle voice.

"So much has happened…" I start.

My legs itch to jump up and find Arzu. Why are they talking to me like this?

"Is Glan good?" Neasa asks.

"Yes," I answer, with pictures of Arzu still in my head.

"How can you be sure?" Neasa's eyes are sharp.

"I got the vision at Lia Fáil," I mumble and look away.

"You need to go to the labyrinth with your birthstone," Neasa states.

My body stiffens at her words.

"Go, Briona," Gormley adds as he takes my hand and I snatch it away.

"You aren't my Keeper," I snap.

Silence falls in the group, all eyes are on me. A picture of Arzu flashes through my head, I feel our kisses on my lips and heat fills my body.

"Just leave me."

"We want you at Brú; you know you must work on blocks and clear your energy," Ollie speaks, in a voice that is so much stronger than at Cill Dara.

"Briona, you heard the Augury. Our people need us to be strong," Gormley says.

I don't want to hear about the Augury; it seems like a dream.

"Who knows what we may hear at Samhain? Briona, we need you!" Ollie exclaims and leans into me with a look almost like Sorcha's.

Now they all crowd around me with a mix of smiles and cross faces.

"Come with me," Shula says as she jumps up and holds out her hand. Our eyes meet; she looks at me with a steady gaze and firm mouth. "Let's get your birthstone." I stand up and Shula links my arm and pulls me close. "Then we can go to the washhouse to clean up."

We go to the longhouse, and I take the box with my birthstone out of my pack. We walk through the forest. Buildings peek from all around, I still don't know what some of them are for, or where Arzu's lodge is.

"Briona, this is a special place, where we meet our ancestors," Shula affirms and sweeps her arm around the clearing.

The two hills of Cailleach, the Wise One, rise above the trees in steep slopes, one to the left, one to the right. The Cairn of Augury gleams in the sunlight and on the second hilltop, another big cairn reaches to the sky. I scan for the small hill where I helped to build the cairn, but the trees stand too tall around me.

Shula holds me tight on the path to the washhouse. She keeps talking about how the Seekers missed me, how we need good Glan for Brú, and how we are all part of the web of life. Her words echo in my head; we hear them so often.

"Briona, we all need to help our people. That vision I had at Cill Dara showed me what the augury says – that dark clouds are coming. Sorcha shut me off, but now I know it was right," she says.

I shrug, I barely know what the Augury said. I just want to talk about Arzu. I say her name and talk to Shula about her and the wonderful time in the forest. The pictures in my head and my feelings for Arzu are stronger than any before. Shula does not question if this is yet another spark- she just listens until my words slow down, then brings the talk back to Mona.

"Mona helped me with my visions. She sees it all. The Voyagers, the Grand Cross at Winter Sun Standstill, the changes to come, and even that we find love," she continues.

A picture of Mona showing us our birth charts comes into my head. She said a special one will come to me before Samhain. Maybe that is what flares between Arzu and me. I want to go and find Arzu now. I pull away from Shula.

"No, Briona. The Seekers need you to be clear," she exclaims and takes my arm.

"But I have such a strong pull to find Arzu."

"You can find Arzu later," Shula insists, squeezing my arm. "We all need Glan for Brú, for the clouds and big changes that are to come.

Briona, we must stay focused." She speaks so clearly, her doubts seem to be over. She believes in her visions again. "We both need a wash!"

Shula touches my hair, and we laugh together. She loves me, she draws me back to my body, she helps me sense the earth beneath my feet.

We walk through the forest to the area where I first arrived. A barrel of water sits at the washhouse with a small fire beside it. We heat the water in the pan over the fire and go into the hut together. We pour water over our bodies and wash ourselves with some soap we find on the shelf. Shula rubs soap over my back, and I do it for her. A rough towel hangs on the door, and we dry our bodies. Afterwards, my body is lighter, and my breath comes easier.

"Now let's go to the Labyrinth," Shula suggests.

We stand together and do daily movements, facing east, then south, west and north. Tensions sink from my head to my body and into the earth. I turn my head to the sound of chirping and see a path in front of me. Shula waves me off, and soon I come to the Labyrinth, it is easy to find, close to the Landing, not deep in the forest. It has three domes that connect in a spiral, like at Carraig and Cill Dara. Mona stands there in her fullness, warm, strong and wise. She holds her arms open, her face beaming. I hurry over, hold her tight and breathe in her smell as her robes touch my skin. She takes my face in her hands and looks into my eyes.

"I met Arzu again, there are huge sparks between us," I speak quickly.

"Strong energies flowed at the Augury, I saw you both."

"We had a wonderful time in the forest…"

She smiles.

"Arzu has fiery energy," she states.

"Surely she's the special one that the stars see for me," I affirm and stand firm with my feet on the ground.

"She's going to the Cairn of Dreaming until Samhain," Mona informs me. My heart sinks to my belly and my legs shake. That is what Arzu was showing me with her drawing, it means she is gone for more than a moon cycle. I can't wait that long to see her again. Why take her away just after we had a beautiful time in the forest?

Mona touches my hair as my head drops. "And then she's focusing on Glan for Winter Sun Standstill at Brú."

I press my lips together, unsure why Mona is saying this. Does she want to quell the fire between us?

"I can wait for her, she's part of my destiny," I declare, raising my head and looking into Mona's eyes.

"Wait and see how it unfolds," Mona says.

"Is she with Áine?"

"She and Áine are alike, they draw people to them. Áine is a Shining One, and Arzu protects her people. They must follow their path," explains Mona. Why does Mona not answer my question about Áine and Arzu? Maybe she wants to keep us apart. Anger flashes in my body. Then, to my surprise, tears spring to Mona's eyes. She grasps my shoulders. "Briona, you have a starburst in your chart, you have many different energies. You must bring these energies together to help your people."

"I can do that and be with Arzu. The stars show a special one for me to love. Arzu is special."

Mona's tears touch me, but now I want to stand on my path and follow what my heart is saying.

"We only know some of what the stars tell us," she continues. "We know you are born with a starburst. You may be one of the Shining Ones that they saw in the Augury."

My body goes quiet as I hear Mona's words. She says I may be a Shining One, with that strong, beautiful white light flowing through me. I take deep breaths as tremors run up and down my body. Turas brings us on our own paths to become adults. How can it offer two different pathways?

"Like Áine?" I can barely speak. "How can I be a Shining One?"

"The Shining Ones have Glan as well as strength, they follow the stars and the stones. This is why you must focus on Glan, go to Brú."

"I can go to Brú with Arzu!" I exclaim.

"Who knows for how long she'll be here or where she may go after Brú? The Grand Cross brings strong energy. If the stars say you are a Shining One, you may get a sign when you lay your birthstone on the mound."

My head spins, there is so much in Mona's words. She says I can be a Shining One, but she seems to say that my spark with Arzu comes from the Grand Cross. I want to be with Arzu, and I want to bring my birthstone to Brú and be a healer for my people. Mona is right about conflicting energies.

"Let's do Sos, that will balance your energies, so we can be sure your birthstone is clear," Mona states as she takes the box with my birthstone and brings me inside the Labyrinth.

We arrive in a small room with a robe laid out. Candles light the walls painted with spirals and wavy lines, just like at Carraig. Mona shakes her rattle up and down my body and we move through the four directions. She pauses and repeats the movements. She stands still for a moment, senses my body, and repeats the movement through the four directions.

We enter a large circular room with a rug on the floor and candles all around. My eyes widen to see Coll, Sorcha and Cael standing there in their Keeper robes. Coll places his hands on my shoulders and smiles; his warm touch calms me. Then Sorcha places her hands on my shoulders and gazes out over my head. It seems so long ago that I shook and flushed under her gaze. Her strict way of teaching taught me to listen to my body, and now I stand firm as her deep, dark eyes look into mine. Strength flows through my body from Cael's hands on my shoulders. Mona shakes her rattle around us all and gestures for me to lie on the rug.

I lie down and close my eyes. A low, steady drumbeat begins. Cool stones with a strong pulse touch my feet and hands. The stones draw energy from my body in different directions, pulling at my arms and feet and stretching my chest. Pain fills my chest, it seems like it is being torn apart. My head swirls with pictures of Carraig, the Imbolc gathering, the Temple at Cill Dara, and the wonderful dance on the Hill of Tara. My love for Mona, Shula, Dori, Murta, Gormley, Felim fills me. They are my tribe, my people. The vision on the mountain bursts into my head - of this beautiful island, of Great Spirit. The vision shifts and shapes into the smiling face of a Shining One. She looks like Áine, but she is not Áine. A bright white light flows from her to me. The pain fades, now love and joy fill my body. Glan! I am overjoyed as the familiar feeling of a clear body opens me up to the flow of Beo.

Mona takes my hand and places my birthstone on my palm. The white stone pulses as I hold it against my body and lie in the warm glow. Drums stop. I want this, I want the energy of a Shining One. Mona, Coll, Sorcha and Cael surround me as I stand up.

"Did you meet Great Spirit?" Mona asks.

"She looks like Áine, but she's not Áine."

"That shows you may be on the path to becoming a Shining One," Mona declares.

"If you have Glan," Sorcha adds.

"And the stars come together," Coll says.

"It may be a long journey," Cael affirms.

My face falls. They all seem to say that nothing is sure.

"Briona, you must keep Glan," Mona asserts. Tears well in my eyes as she takes my hand. "Keep your birthstone with you, it can help with the balancing of energies." She takes the birthstone and places it back in the box. "You're special to me, daughter of my daughter."

They turn to leave the chamber. Prickles rise on the back of my neck as their robes swish. Mona puts her arms around me and hugs me tightly.

We step outside, and there is Shula, waiting for me.

"Briona, you look," she pauses, searching for words. "Light? bright?"

She laughs and hugs me.

"The energy of the Shining Ones flows to Briona," Mona says.

Shula looks from me to Mona. I gaze back at her; I have no words.

"Briona can be a Shining One?" Shula asks, surprise in her voice.

"Briona's too young to know for sure, we can only know after Turas if that is her path. We must wait for this to unfold. We keep Glan, and we will learn more at Samhain," Mona replies. She places her hands on my shoulders and looks into my eyes. "Arzu has a strong pull on you. Try to stay balanced." She touches Shula's cheek. "Stay by her side."

They both smile. Shula links my arm, and we walk down the path away from the Labyrinth. She stops to stand and face me.

"You *can't* let Arzu take you away from the path to a Shining One," she says

"I follow *my* path, maybe with Arzu, maybe to being a Shining One".

"Briona, *how* can you say *that*? A Shining One is your path!" Shula exclaims as her eyes flash. "You have a starburst, dreams come to you."

"The Keepers say it will unfold on Turas, that we can't be sure."

"But it can help us understand how your path is different if you tell us all about it."

"It's too soon to say this to the other Seekers, let's wait and see what happens at Samhain." I end the discussion.

I don't want anyone to tell me to choose between Arzu and my people. I know that I will meet Arzu again at Samhain. We can find a way to be together.

At the big fire that evening, people talk in low murmurs and hunch in small groups to talk about the Augury, the Voyagers, and what is to come at Samhain. I huddle in with Shula, Gormley, Felim and the other Seekers.

I know now that Mona moves energy, that she is part of the shift in the Labyrinth, she knows the big picture of the stars and the changes to come. Her words about the Shining One echo in my head. She has questions about Arzu. I slip my hand into my pouch and touch the box with my birthstone. Mona is right about one thing: now is not the time for Arzu, it is time for focus, for Glan.

- 16 -

Ancestors Speak at Samhain

On the night of the full moon, Cael calls us to go to the Lodge and bring our warm furs. They rattle in the four directions, strong and loud.

"Tonight, we go to the Cairn of Augury to visit our ancestors," they say.

We stir and stretch and glance at each other - maybe this can help to settle us. Since Sun Balance unease rumbles through Sliabh na Caillí as we wait for Samhain. We hardly see the Keepers. Mona and some of the others have gone to the Cairn of Dreaming to stay with the Voyagers; maybe they are learning about incubation. Some Keepers come and go from the fire. Sometimes they seem calm, other times they move around and talk in excited voices, then they disappear into the forest to their lodges.

Pictures of Arzu and the Shining One flash through my head every day. I hold the box with my birthstone in my hand to calm the tremors that rise in my body. On clear nights, I look up to the hilltop where a small bright fire burns in front of the cairn where the Voyagers incubate. Often wind and rain keep us in our longhouses.

Tonight, it is clear and the full moon shines on us as we follow Cael and spiral uphill under the sharp night sky. At the top of the hill, the big Cairn of Augury looks so different. The bright moon brings a gleam to the white stones that cover it, and small fires flicker in the dark around it. Beside it, many small cairns stand alone with a small fire in front and a solitary figure covered by a cloak sits in silence beside each fire. Shivers run down my back. We circle the big cairn three times and gather in front of the entrance. Cael lights a torch.

"Let us enter the passage. May our ancestors welcome us," Cael says, then divides us into two groups that can each fit into the cairn.

We climb over the big stone lying in front of the entrance and enter the short passageway lined with standing stones that are almost the same height as me. Inside the chamber, we can see the circles, wavy lines, and wheels of the year that are carved into the stones. Cael shines their beacon into three small alcoves with beautiful carvings that dance in the flickering light. Then they whistle through their teeth and rattle around us. The quiet presence of stones surrounds us as a cool breeze wafts through the chamber. We all stand in silence with our eyes closed.

Suddenly a young woman stands in front of me. She has a bright face and laughing eyes, she looks familiar, but she is not anyone I know. I hear the words - "I am the mother of your people. I bring you strength." She holds her arms out, and the white light of a Shining One flows into my body. My chest fills with love that courses through my entire body and into my bones.

She fades away. My eyes open to the dim light of the moon in the chamber. For a moment I wonder if she brings a warning - we hear so often that we need strength for the changes ahead. But a vivid picture of her face and the feel of the white light in my body sweeps my doubts away. My ancestor speaks directly to me. She tells me to be sure - I can be a Keeper of Stones, a Shining One.

Beside me, Shula's eyes gleam. Slowly everyone opens their eyes. Cael opens their arms for us to form a circle. Warmth fills the chamber.

Outside the cairn glows in the light of the full moon. We wait for the next group to leave the chamber.

"I saw the mother of our people," I say to Shula.

"I saw her too," Shula replies. "She gave me strength."

"To all of us," Felim adds.

"She gave me the light of a Shining One," I say, her energy still glowing in my body.

"*How can you tell?* You needed to go to the Labyrinth; you don't follow the path!" Neasa questions me.

"Briona, *only special people get that.* Why did you get it? You left Tara, you didn't come to the Lúnasa festival, you wandered off after the Augury." Ollie agrees with Neasa.

I feel surprised to hear her speak like this. Maybe she sees blocks that I don't see.

"Briona was born with a starburst." Shula supports me and moves to stand beside me.

"*Only* Turas shows us if we can be a Shining One," Neasa affirms. She is so against what I say, maybe she wants to be like Áine too.

I place my two feet apart and face Neasa.

"It's *my* path," I say.

"Only if you follow Glan, *and you don't do that yet!*" Neasa snaps at me.

"There are different ways to Glan, ...," I begin.

"You must clear your energy all the time, *you know that,*" Ollie interjects.

"Surely we all got a vision," Gormley says just as Cael comes out of the cairn with the other group and gathers us together.

I feel the strength of the ancestors around us in the dark, but the words of Neasa and Ollie make me uneasy - even Mona cannot be sure if my path is to be a Shining One.

Cael gestures to the small cairns where figures sit in stillness.

"The Keepers sit with our ancestors," they say.

There is Coll and Teelin. Teelin takes Shula and me close to his chest, arms around us, and holds us tight. He places a finger on his lips and gestures for us to follow him to one of the small cairns. We circle it three times and sit by the fire at the entrance. Teelin picks up a small rattle. As he shakes the rattle, he lists names of people from Carraig who left for the Otherworld. Tears flow down my cheeks when he speaks the name of Bríd, my mother and Shula squeezes my hand. People go to the Otherworld, but we still hold them in our hearts. We drop our heads as the names change to people we don't know, people we hear stories about. The hair stands on my neck as the long line of ancestors goes on and on, back to the first people who came to the island. Around us, we hear soft rattles at other cairns. We are all connected to mothers, to fathers, to those who lived here before us, to earth and sky.

Teelin stands and goes into the passageway of the cairn. He brings out two small pots with lids.

"These are the ashes of our ancestors from Carraig," Teelin explains. "They're a special part of you. You'll bring these to Newgrange so they may lie in the chamber at Winter Sun Standstill." Shula and I stand face to face, our hands trembling as we take the pots. Teelin embraces us. "We'll meet again at Samhain." He gestures to return to Cael at the big cairn.

We walk downhill with the precious pots and gather around the fire at the longhouse. Deep conversation about our ancestors keeps us entranced. Cael tells us we are all related, that we share ancestors, that they are part of the web of life, and that they can help us to stay balanced. They inspire us and bring us gifts and challenges. Cael says their energy is strong at the Cairn of the Augury, that they are there to guide us. They speak in a low, strong voice, and we lean in to hear every word as a deep connection settles between us.

The moon grows smaller as the days get shorter. We count the days until the moon goes out of sight. Then we will have our dark moon Samhain ceremony. When wind and rain keep away, we gather outside by the fire. High above us small fires burn through the dark on the two hills where the big Cairns sit. Someone says they are for our ancestors, to ask them to come and help us. My neck tingles at these words. I gaze up at the firelight flickering in the dark high above us. A strange cold wafts around my body - the feel of our ancestors. My heart reaches out to Arzu, up there in the darkness. I ache to see her, to hold her, to go to the forest with her.

On the day of the dark moon, we gather before sunset to help with preparations for the ceremony. We carry firewood for the fire and help lay food out for the ancestors- the harvest of wheat, apples, nuts, berries, plants. On a wooden platform beside the fire, drums and pipes are laid out. In the middle I see the special drums that the Voyagers brought. Tremors run through my body as I picture Arzu in the forest, her body against a tree, pulling me towards her.

The evening is dark and crisp. Burning torches cast light on the beautiful clothes and jewellery, colourful headbands and painted faces. Quickly we gather in a half circle around the fire pit and face the direction of the setting sun. The fire on the hilltop in front of us suddenly grows bigger and blazes up in the dim light. My body lights up - the Voyagers are emerging from the Cairn of Dreaming along with Mona and other Keepers. A ribbon of torchlight flows from the top of the hill and slowly winds down. It comes closer and closer and then goes out of sight. I can hardly breathe. In a moment I will see Arzu.

Pipes ring out. A gate opens in front of us and the Keepers enter. What a sight! They all look alike - they wear black robes, and each Keeper has a white mask on their face. They walk forward to the stage. My eyes widen and my mouth goes dry at the sight of Arzu. No robe or mask can hide the beautiful black hair and graceful body.

The Keepers stand in a row on the stage facing us. Rattles sound a long, slow rhythm that makes the hairs stand on the back of my neck. Shula takes my hand. Around us, trees loom. Above, only one or two stars gleam as a cover of cloud moves in. A Keeper steps forward and speaks in a strong voice that rings out in the night air. It is Teelin.

We are the face of our ancestors.
They ask us for help.
In the darkest dreams they show us
That blood spills on many lands.
People come from the east
Knives and shields in hand.
Times are turning.

Tension rises and gasps and murmurs ripple through the group. "No", "It can't be", "What does this mean?" "What can we do?" I tighten my grip on Shula's hand. Gormley is beside her, Neasa, Ollie, Felim and Conor just behind us. All around us people shuffle, turn to each other, move into small huddles and pairs. Teelin continues.

We must strengthen the Beo in our stones,
For our stones can protect us.
We draw on the bounty of our land.
We know the power of our ancestors.
Our cairns hold the force of Beo.
One day we may cover them all.
We must be strong.

The group stands in silence, facing Teelin. We are not sure why we would cover our cairns. How can that help the power of stones? Our ancestors speak through stones; we need Beo from the stones. We know how to use this energy for healing, but how do we use it to protect us?

The Keepers take their masks off just as murmurs rise in the group. The familiar faces touch us - Mona, Teelin, Coll, Sorcha, Áine, Gráinne, Cael, and others. They stand shoulder to shoulder in front of us, their faces calm. Beside them, Arzu and Mata remove their masks. I beam at the sight of Arzu's beautiful face.

"*We must be strong; we must be strong.*"

They start a steady chant. Their eyes catch ours, one by one. Slowly people join in, repeating the words. It calms us.

"*We must be strong; we must be strong.*"

Our ears fill with the words calling out to the night sky.

Suddenly Arzu and Mata move to the front. The chant fades. Arzu pulls a knife from the band at her waist and holds it up to show how the light glistens on its surface. She steps behind Mata, throws one arm in front of Mata and puts the knife to Mata's throat. Gasps and shouts fade as Arzu releases Mata, steps forward and speaks very slowly in a deep voice in her words. What is she saying? She pauses and speaks again slowly in words we know.

Raiders kill our people.
They take our land.
They want our temples.
Help us!
Come with us.
Save Great Spirit.

Arzu steps back as voices rise in alarm. Arzu wants us all to go with her to their land - to leave here. This is the land where our power lies. Our ancestors are here. People cluster together as fear rises in the group. My face burns to hear the voices around me. How can Arzu ask this of us? How can the Keepers let this happen? My heart thumps at the strong words. Arzu's people are in danger, she is in danger.

Voices pause as Áine steps forward, flanked by Keepers who carry burning torches. She glows in her yellow gown and purple headband. Her face is lit up by the torches, her hair shines, and her gown sparkles. Surely, she is the Shining One who can save us. Áine speaks.

They may not come here in our lifetime,
But we must be prepared.

We must join together, all our lands.
We have our stones, our temples
Our stone-readers and stargazers
Our healers, our seers,
Our farmers, our fishers.
We can move mountains
Raise boulders, carve stone.
We love earth, sea and sky.
Let us light our fire
Let us call for strength from our ancestors.

Her words ring out into the night air and bring us together. Mona, Teelin, Coll and Sorcha step down from the stage and walk through the group. Their steady movement calms us. All eyes are fixed on the burning torches as they move forward. They surround the firewood and set it alight from all directions. The fire surges, flames rise, heat and light fill us. Áine is right. We are strong. We all link arms.

A huge burst of drumming brings our eyes back to the stage. The Keepers and Voyagers beat drums together in a loud rhythm. Arzu and Mata hold their big drums between their legs and slap and pound with their hands. The deep beat adds to the familiar sounds of our drums. Arzu and Mata beat out a strong, deep burst, then pause. The drummers beat in return. They go back and forth, back and forth and lull us with the steady rhythms that tell us we can work together. Then they merge into one again. A loud, long beat breaks over the crowd, and we cheer.

Fiery energy sweeps through the group. We let go, stamp our feet, and become one with the rhythm of the drums. No one can take our land away. With one last long, loud beat the drumming stops. The echo rings out in the night air as we stand by the fire, our faces red and shining. I look at the faces around me and feel the fierce strength of Áine's words.

Gongs sound. Coll and Teelin step forward carrying a black cauldron painted with white wavy lines and spirals. They place it in front of the fire and Áine casts a handful of wheat into the cauldron. Gongs sound again - time to share food.

We go to the long table where the food is laid out. Everyone - the Keepers, Áine, Arzu, Mata - mills around. I take a few steps towards Arzu. She sees me and we move towards each other, our hands reaching out. But Mata links her arms with Arzu's as some people turn towards them with angry looks. The Keepers move to surround them. This is not the time for us.

The Keepers bring Arzu and Mata to a group beside Áine. Arzu beams at Áine, they stand close, their shoulders touching as Áine murmurs in Arzu's ear. I look away and take a plate over to the fire to sit with the Seekers. I can barely taste the food as I try to calm my fears. Surely Arzu does not have the same fiery sparks with Áine. Around me the Seekers talk about the words of Arzu and Áine.

"More energy, more clarity, more strength. Our tribe needs us," Gormley speaks in a low, strong voice. Fierce focus unites us as we sit in a group and eat. There is so much talk, we sound like a swarm of bees! Unease, hope, strength, and fear ripple through us.

We finish our food and gather around the fire. Teelin comes and sits with me and Shula, his strong presence keeps us calm. I watch Arzu and Mata leave, surrounded by Keepers while others lull us with songs of our ancestors. A Bard stands up and recites the familiar poem – the voice of our ancestors telling us about walking the land to find special places.

> *We walk this land of plenty*
> *And follow the lines of land and water*
> *To rivers and hilltops where Beo throbs.*
> *We mark the movements of stars on stone and bone*
> *And find times when the sun, moon and stars are strong*
> *Times when joy pours from Great Spirit.*
>
> *We gather huge stones and build our cairns*
> *Where we can read the stories of stars and stones*
> *As the year turns from winter to spring, and summer to autumn.*
> *We store energy in the stones for healing and prophecy.*
>
> *At last, we find a perfect spot at the bend of a great river*

*The place to build our finest cairns for the energy of Beo
When the sun stands still, and earth is in balance.
We clear trees and gather huge boulders from nearby hills
and send out boats to gather more.
For many years, we build our cairns
And carve them with patterns of the earth and sky.*

*Year after year people journey to Newgrange,
The great mound that faces the rising sun.
They carry their birthstones and lay them on the mound
They cover it with beautiful white stones
Until it gleams in the morning light.
They bring the ashes of their dead
and lay them in carved basins inside the cairn
Ready for their journey to the sky
When the golden beams of the Winter sun shine in.*

*Ah what times, what times, these are
When the great temple pulses between the earth and sun
When we gather to feel the joy of Great Spirit
As the dead depart and new light enters her womb.*

We return to the longhouse, but that night no one sleeps. We gather in the longhouse after the songs and poems.

"More energy, more strength," Gormley starts.

"We must ask Spirit for help," Neasa says and tilts her head.

"What if Spirit can't help?" Ollie counters.

Silence. How can she ask that? Spirit is always there, always ready to help.

"Spirit gives us strength," Neasa replies.

"But they asked us to protect Great Spirit. How can men with knives attack Great Spirit? If we lose our Keepers and our temples, if they attack our stones and learn our ways…" Ollie says as her voice trails away at the bleak picture. Maybe the Raiders can take the strength from our stones. "We could lose everything."

"We have our stones, our cairns, and our ancestors," Gormley responds.

"Gormley, that *isn't* enough. We *can't* just wait," Ollie asserts and leans forward.

"Our Tribe needs us," Felim affirms and leans forward beside her. They take Ollie's hand, the spark between them still strong.

"We have to help the Voyagers and their people," Shula declares and looks around the group.

"Shula, do you want to go with them?" I ask.

"No, I want to stay here," she replies. "And you?"

"If we can help the Voyagers stop the Raiders, that's one way to keep us safe," I respond.

"But why us?" Felim questions and looks at me with a frown. "We're so far away. We need to stay here and keep our strength for our tribe."

I am surprised to hear Felim speak against me, they are always gentle with me.

"You can't go, you have the gift of stone, we need that," Shula remarks as she touches my arm.

"That can help the Voyagers," I respond.

"Why *them* and not *us*?" Shula asks. "Why do you want to leave your people? The land you love?"

"They need our help. We need to stop the Raiders on the Voyagers' land. We can get a big group to come together and send the Raiders back to their land." I explain, the words tumbling out of my mouth. "We have the power and strength of stones."

"Let's wait and see what the Keepers say," Gormley interrupts as he holds out his hands to the group.

"*We can't just wait!*" Ollie speaks again.

"The Keepers know best," Neasa tries to calm us.

"Maybe the stars will decide for us," Shula says.

In my head, I wonder why the stars brought Arzu and me together.

"Shula, the Raiders are a big danger," Conor snaps.

Who knows what is next? Keepers may decide who can go with the Voyagers or the stars will decide. Maybe our hearts will guide us. I close my eyes and see a picture of Arzu on the stage with her arms out to the group. Does she want us to go with her, to travel to her land and stop these Raiders? Is that why the Voyagers are here?

Round and round we go that long night until our heads hurt and our bellies ache. I put my head to the ground and let my eyelids droop. A picture from Cill Dara of the beautiful big statue comes into my head and Áine's words about a sun-baked land ring in my ears. Is this the way to be with Arzu? But the vision on the mountain says to love my people. Our ancestors are here; they give us strength.

Voices murmur overhead, back and forth, about how to decide, and who decides. As the light of dawn seeps into the longhouse, Gormley stands up.

"We must be strong. Our tribe needs us," he repeats.

"Great Spirit give us strength," Neasa adds as she stands beside him.

"We must be strong," Ollie and Shula say and stand together.

They look at Felim, Conor and me. I join in with Felim. The familiar chant soothes us. Conor sits in silence, his head down.

"We must have Glan, and go to Brú, to be there for the Grand Cross," Neasa states and reaches out to take our hands. "The Grand Cross at Brú will bring us strength."

We take hands, and even Conor joins in.

Coll enters the longhouse, and we crowd around him, speak together and ask questions. He holds up a hand.

"Listen now. Where does our strength come from?" he asks, looking to each of us.

We give different answers.

"From the land."

"Stones and cairns."

"Our ancestors."

"Where do they get their strength from?" Coll questions.

"From Buí, Great Spirit, Mother of us all."

"What does she give us?" Coll asks.

"Beo,"

"Strength."

"Love."

"How do we get the strength of Beo?" Coll enquiries.

"In our bodies."

"In stones."

"Glan."

"How do we see what is next?" Coll asks.

"The stars tell us."

"Through dreams and visions."

"Who knows most about stars and stones?" Coll has a big smile on his face.

"The Keepers," all our voices ring out and we laugh.

Coll raises his arms.

"We know there are questions, fears, and many changes to come," Coll adds. "That is why we must focus on Glan, and store Beo in our stones. If the Raiders get here, we must have the strength to stop them, they don't know the power of our cairns and stones."

"The Voyagers want us to go with them," Conor speaks up.

"How can we wait?" Ollie asks.

Coll raises his two hands to the group.

"Soon we go to Brú na Bóinne for Winter Sun Standstill where the Sun lights up the chamber of Newgrange and fills us with Beo," Coll announces. "And at the next Summer Sun Standstill, when Beo is strongest, when our stargazers follow the skies, when we hear more from other people from across seas and other lands, we will meet at Tara. There we'll decide how to help the Voyagers. We must channel the energy of the Grand Cross into our stones and into the special crystals that the Voyagers bring here. For now, that's how we help ourselves and the Voyagers."

Coll begins our daily attunements. We move together, facing the direction of the rising sun, full sun, low sunset and dark. He takes us around and around. At each turn our feet sink into the ground, our breaths settle in our bellies, and we connect to the earth beneath us and the stars above us.

"Keep your body calm," Coll says. "Go to the Cistin, eat, go to the forest and help gather wood for the fire."

We walk slowly out of the longhouse and go to the Cistin. It is still early, the Cistin is quiet. We eat with Coll and then follow him to the big wood store. I take an axe to help with chopping wood, and we all spread out in the forest. As the steady movements clear the questions in my head, fire stirs in my body. I want to find Arzu.

I put the axe down and look around. The glint of fire catches my eye, and there I see the Voyager's lodge at the edge of the forest. I quickly walk over. A group of people, some Voyagers, eat by the fire. Arzu sees me, she jumps up and hurries over, our bodies press together and our cheeks brush as we beam at each other.

She takes me to the fire to sit beside her. Sheelin is there, and we smile at each other. Arzu presses her hand to my back, then turns to the other Voyagers. They are excited as they talk. They include me in their looks and gestures, but it is strange, I don't know what they are saying. They look away as Mata touches Arzu's chest and they talk back and forth. I sit close to Arzu and wait.

Arzu turns to me, takes my hand and brings me into the lodge. She lights a small candle, takes me in her arms and kisses my cheeks and forehead. I nuzzle into her, my body already on fire, as my skin tingles with longing for her skin against mine. She gestures to a pile of furs on the ground, and we lie down. Her arms encircle me, our legs entwine, and our bodies press together. Fire blazes through our kisses, our lips are hot and wet. I slip a hand through a gap in her robe. Her warm, soft skin sends more pleasure through my body.

She takes my hand away and draws back. She turns on her side, props her head on her hand and with the other hand she strokes my hair and trails down my neck. She holds my gaze and touches my lips, then drops her head and kisses me again, strong and slow. Her hand brings my mouth to hers, then she pushes my mouth away, gazes into my eyes and rolls me onto my back. Slowly she moves her fingers down the centre of my chest as pulses of pleasure surge through my body. Then she traces her fingers on my body, lower and lower. Pleasure rises with her kisses and slow strokes.

We toss and turn, stroking, teasing, caressing, tasting, energy rising, and bringing us to bliss. She holds me in her arms, her head buried in my neck, her strong hands pressed against my back. We drift until Mata calls out and Arzu turns her head. She touches my hair, draws me up and brings me outside.

Sheelin and Mata are still at the fire. Arzu speaks to Sheelin and Sheelin turns to me.

"Arzu wants you to come to Melita," Sheelin says.

My body trembles and my head fills with a picture of me in Arzu's arms, on a big boat, travelling over the sea and landing on a sunbaked island.

"To be with *you?*" I ask and look directly at Arzu.

Sheelin speaks some words to Arzu. She nods, smiles at me and speaks again.

"And to learn our ways, to help us," Sheelin says to me.

There is a silence. Mata says something to Arzu and Arzu speaks back to her, then turns to me and puts her hand on her chest. Mata and Arzu speak again in sharp voices.

Sheelin looks back and forth at them.

"They speak too fast," she whispers.

Mata and Arzu stand face to face, their voices rise. Mata is angry. Arzu shakes her head.

"I think - Mata asks about someone in Melita, Arzu says she wants you," Sheelin explains and raises her eyebrows. I hope she is right.

Arzu suddenly turns from Mata and places one hand on my face and the other hand over her heart. She says something, but all I hear is "Melita." She moves her hand from her chest to mine, then she clasps my hand and pulls it to her chest. She gestures for me to come with her. I nod, touch her face, sway and make the whooshing sound of wind on the sea. Her face brightens with a big smile. Mata steps forward and speaks to Arzu in a calmer voice.

"It's time for the Voyagers to leave for Brú," Sheelin tells me.

Mata places a hand on Arzu's shoulder as they talk in low voices. Arzu turns to me and presses the palms of her hands together in front of her heart, then opens her palms toward me. We turn to the fire and stand together as the flames flicker and flare. We hold each other tight, then step back, our hands brushing each other.

"Melita," she says and turns to go with Mata.

I stand and watch. Just as they go into the lodge, Arzu turns back to me again and a beam of light joins us and sends shivers through my body. She waves and goes inside. Tears sting my eyes.

"There is a big spark between you," Sheelin observes, then laughs. I nod and walk away. There is more than a spark, this is a huge heart bond. I go back to the longhouse, lie on the bed and gaze into the dark. Pictures of her fill me with longing and my body throbs. I want to go with her to Melita, but how can I travel when my people need me here? Tears fill my eyes.

"Briona…"

Shula's voice lifts me as she enters the longhouse. I tell her about my time with Arzu, and of the wonderful, strong feelings I have for her, that she wants me to go with her. I say that I want to be with Arzu and that we have a bond even stronger than hers and Bres's.

"Are you going to go with her?" Shula questions.

"*I want to.* I want to be with her."

"Leave your people? Leave this island?"

"Shula, listen to me. These are *deep* feelings. It's more than I have ever felt for anyone. She *wants* me to go with her," I answer back.

"You're going to *leave us* to go with her?" she asks as her voice rises.

"Maybe. Or to help the Voyagers."

"Briona, you don't *know* Arzu," she says. "What if you go for her and she meets someone else? Or your spark may go. There is so much you don't know." Shula gets a sheen in her eyes. "There are dark clouds ahead."

"With Arzu?"

"For all of us…" she whispers and places her hand on my arm. "Do you *really* want to leave your people for someone you don't know?"

"I want to follow her, and I want to stay here," I respond.

"Do you want to help us, or go with them?"

"Both?"

"How do you decide? What do the Keepers say?"

"They want me to stay. Mona tells me it's my destiny, that my people need me," I answer.

Shula touches my arm. She does not want me to go with Arzu, she wants me to stay here.

"Briona, you have a starburst, you had a vision on the mountain, Great Mother gives you the energy of a Shining One. *We need you here!*"

But in my head, I ask - why then do I have such a big spark with Arzu and why do I burst with love for her?

"You would follow if Bres travelled," I say.

"No."

"*How* are you *so sure?*"

"This is *my home*," she affirms. "Gara, Teelin, and Dori are my kin. This is my tribe, my people. I want to live here; I want to be with Bres here. I don't want to leave."

Shula's strong words remind me of my love for my people and my love for this land. How can I leave that?

"I want to go with Arzu, but it's hard to leave here…"

"Coll says wait until the Summer Sun Standstill. *Wait*, Briona. See what Turas shows, see what happens at Summer Sun Standstill. You want to help your people and be a Shining One."

Shula puts her arms around me and holds me close.

- 17 -
Journey to Brú

We gather around the blazing fire in our winter furs and boots. At last, it is time to travel to Brú. Even in the cold of winter, heat surges through our bodies and our faces glow in the orange-yellow light. We step from one foot to the other, turn our backs to the fire and twirl around again to face it. We laugh and smile at each other, fix each other's hoods, and check that our packs are firmly on our backs. Hair prickles on my body at the sound of horns, and a thrill courses through me as joy surges through the group. The Keepers step forward in their colourful robes and light torches that flare and fill the air with fire as they weave circles and spirals that dance off our furs and faces. Horns ring out again and the Keepers form a passageway of fire with their torches. Coll beckons us through one by one. With whoops and hugs, we set off down the pathway out of Sliabh na Caillí.

We walk with steady strides to get to the river before darkness falls. Rain stays away but drops drip off the trees and glisten on the fern and moss. The forest floor is damp, and the leaves slip under our feet. We keep our heads down, and as we walk deeper into the grey forest, a cold chill seeps through the group. The light grows dim, and suddenly the loud Caw Caw of ravens fills our ears. Their scattered sound stirs unease.

Since Samhain, the Keepers have tried to keep us steady. They sent us out all over Sliabh na Caillí to repair walls, thatches and fences. Cael asked us to cover the wall of the Lodge with spirals, diamonds, half diamonds, wavy lines, arcs and circles to make colourful art and drawings of stars. But the evenings grew long and dark, cold and wet, and we spent much time huddled in the longhouse. We talked back and forth about Samhain until our heads grew weary. Who knows when the Raiders may come to our shore? And how can anyone take our Beo? Some said it was wrong for Arzu to hold the knife to Mata's throat, others said she did it to show us the danger ahead. Talk of

Arzu unsettled me and Shula's questions ran through my head - do I know her; how can I be sure of what is next between us?

The ravens fly up out of the forest just as we arrive at a small stream. Coll gathers us and tells us that the stream will bring us to An Bhóinn. We smile at each other - that is the river that brings us to Brú! The sky clears above us as we follow the gurgling stream that widens into a small river and soon, we come to a wooden platform on the riverbank where two boats lie upside down.

"This is a stopping place, we sleep here tonight," Coll says.

The shed looks old, its thatched reeds sprout, and ivy grows through the walls. Inside are thick animal skins on the floor and baskets of wood. We quickly light the fire and gather around to eat the food that Coll hands out. I glance at our faces lit by the light of the fire. Shula smiles at me with gleaming eyes, Felim sits straight and steady, Ollie sits beside them with her shoulders hunched, Neasa and Gormley stare at the fire, and Conor looks at the floor. How can we bring the joy of the journey back to the group?

Coll jumps up and claps his hands. He speaks words that bring us back to the farewell ceremony at Sliabh na Caillí when the Keepers urged us to be strong. He tells us we are ready for Brú, to enter the chamber of Newgrange for sunbeams, to lay our birthstones on the mound. After Brú we will meet at Tara, where we will hear more and prepare for the changes that are to come. He ends with familiar words - that the web of life needs our birthstones for the Grand Cross and the Bright Star. The warmth of the fire and his firm words help us to focus, but we are still restless.

Coll opens the door of the shed, and I blink at the cold, sharp air that quickly clears my head. Outside a beautiful sky full of stars curves above the river. All around us, stars gleam and twinkle against the deep, dark blue of the night sky. The Three Stars hover in front of us. The Red Star and the Fast Star are high above us. The Swan Star shines brightly and the White Band of stars the colour of milk, streaks across the sky.

"See, the Grand Cross rises in the sky, it is now above Brú," Gormley points up.

We stand and gaze at the vast sweep of stars. My breath catches as white light flows into me from the stars above.

I turn to Shula and Gormley and the other Seekers and all of us come together in a huddle with arms around each other. The light of the White Band reaches down and pours through our heads into our bodies, out our feet and into the earth. A wave of joy suspends us between earth and sky. We are full of fierce focus from Samhain and many moons of practice.

I wake up to the light from the open door filtering through the smoke from the fire.

Coll stands at the door.

"We need to travel fast to get to An Bhóinn before dark," he says.

When we form a circle for our attunements, we move together as one, like a flock of birds. Our bodies move in rhythm as we push boats along through the shallow waters until the river deepens into a steady flow. The currents gather pace, and we paddle as fast as we can. The light of the White Band fills my head as the river flashes by. A picture of the green mound of Newgrange with its shining white wall above the river comes into my head.

The water gets choppy, the boat ahead pulls over to the bank and we follow.

"We'll walk across the forest from here," Coll explains. "It's hard to row through the rushing water and swirling currents where this river meets An Bhóinn. Leave the boats tied up on the riverbank."

The huts in the forest tell us we are close to An Uaimh, where the two rivers meet. We take our packs and set out on the path.

Just as the sun goes low in the sky, Coll stops us in front of two tall standing stones with a big flat stone across the top. A circle of clear brown earth surrounded by small stones sits between them. Beyond, two people sit by a small dome building with a fire in front. Just past the dome is a familiar sight - a small settlement. In the fading light, it looks just like Carraig, with a big central fire, a Cistin and piles of wood nearby. Longhouses and other buildings loom close to the forest.

Coll hands a leather pouch to each of us.

"Here we step into the land of Brú na Bóinne," he announces. "Take out your birthstone and place it on the ground between these stones. Step through then put the birthstone in this pouch."

My hand trembles as I open my box. My birthstone connects me to the Source of life; it brings my energy to the mound at Brú. A charge pulses through my fingers as soon as I touch it. It burns into the palm of my hand, and I quickly bend to place it in the circle of earth and then step into the circle.

As soon as my bare feet touch the bare earth, energy surges through my legs, up my back, into my head and down the front of my body. When I pick up my birthstone, it sends hot throbs to my belly, so much stronger than the time with Mona in the Labyrinth at Carraig long ago. It tells me I am clear, that I am close to being an adult, that I am ready to follow my path. I step out and place the birthstone in the pouch around my neck. Shula is next, she comes to hug me, her warm glow matches mine. We stand together and watch the beam on the Seekers' faces as they each step between the standing stones.

We follow Coll to the low dome building. Stones glow red in the heat of the fire, and just past them in a gap in the trees, we see the twinkle of light on water. We are at An Bhóinn, the river that gives Brú its name. We run to the river and stand in amazement at the calm flow of the water. I want to dive into the river and follow the currents to Brú. Felim and Ollie laugh and start to take their fur off. We laugh as Conor shouts that we can all jump in. Coll holds up a hand and points to the small dome building.

"*Wait!*" He exclaims. "First, go and sit with the cleansing heat that brings out your sweat and then you can plunge into the river. After, you can wear these fresh woollen tunics."

Coll points to tunics that hang from a wooden frame. We strip off our furs and tunics, lay them on the ground with our pouches and packs and hurry to the fire. Our bare skin glimmers as we stand in a circle around the fire. The heat of the fire on my skin brings a sudden flash of Arzu that licks through my body and stops my breath. I close my eyes for a moment. A picture of her that last time in the Lodge fills my head, her smile, her gesture to come with her.

Our breaths catch from the cold night air as we turn from the fire to enter the dome. The dome is low and spacious inside with rushes on the floor, and a round pit is dug into the ground in the middle. We shuffle around in the darkness and find places to sit. A gong sounds and someone outside lifts a flat shovel with a red-hot stone through the door and places the stone in the pit. More stones come through and then the door closes. The gentle sound of bones clicking outside sets a rhythm and soon we breathe as one, sweat trickling down our bodies.

The intense heat empties my head. I flop onto the ground and suddenly find myself back on the mountain with the full moon and clouds shapeshifting into the beautiful body of Great Spirit. She floats in front of me; she beams white light that fills me with joy. Then the red heat of Arzu rises from bush to breast. A picture of her in the forest brings a glow of pleasure and love. My body opens to the beautiful energy that swirls through me. Surely, I can find a path that brings these energies together.

The sound of scraping startles me. The door opens and we stagger out and run down to the river to plunge into the cold water. Wide awake and full of joy, we splash in the river beneath the night sky, the stars twinkling above us. We have good Glan, maybe the best. We jump up and down and whoop with glee. The White Band seems to sweep us towards Brú. We hurry to dry ourselves at the fire, slip on the new tunic and place the pouches with our birthstones around our necks. A familiar figure moves forward - Mona is here. A smile fills my face as I embrace her and feel her love.

"I'll travel with you to Brú," she says and ushers us to a fire in the centre of the settlement.

A tall man in furs with a white beard and long hair welcomes us over to the Cistin where food is laid out - bread, honey, hazelnuts, apples, and a huge salmon.

"I'm Nectin, welcome to Ros, the gateway to Brú na Bóinne."

My mouth waters - this is the finest food I've seen for a long time. We pile food on our plates and take cups of juice over to the fire, still tingling from the cold of the river. We huddle together, full of excitement to be so close to Brú.

Nectin stands and hits the ground three times with the staff of the Bard. Silence falls.

"In days past, we had special visitors," he starts, "the Voyagers, who travelled here from their island far away to the South. They told us stories of their island, and we told them the legends of our land."

A sudden wish sweeps through me to be on a boat heading away with Arzu to her island. I glance over to Mona, and she holds my gaze. Have good Glan, her eyes say.

"What stories?" someone asks.

"And we have the same legend!" Nectin exclaims, his voice ringing out.

"What legend is this?"

"Long ago, snow covered the ground from north to south, from east to west. Giant deer, huge bears and fierce wolves lived in caves. Powerful winds roared across the land. Every day, rain fell like spears, and every living creature had to find a cave or dig a hole in the ground. All this changed overnight when a powerful, giant, wise woman, Cailleach, made her way across the pillars of the ocean, her apron filled with huge boulders. As she travelled across the land, she dropped the boulders from her apron onto hilltops and mountains. As soon as the boulders landed on the ground, the ice melted, the rivers flowed and sprouting trees appeared." Nectin pauses and looks around the group.

Somebody else takes up the story.

"When we told them of the giant Cailleach, the Voyagers started to laugh. They told us that they also have huge temples with spirals and diamonds and wavy lines and that their legends claim that a giant woman dropped huge boulders from her apron as she crossed their island."

Silence falls around the fire. We all lean in, eager to hear more. My breath catches at these words. What if snow and rain like spears come back? Prophecies speak of dark clouds that stop food from growing and men with knives who may take our land away. But the story of Cailleach soothes us, she has the power of the land, she can help us.

"We wondered why we have the same story," Nectin speaks again. "We said we were the first, and that the giant travelled from here to their island. But they said the opposite. Then we told them that we believe the first people came to this island from the north, a long time ago. They believe that the first people came to their island from the south." Nectin beats his staff on the ground and continues. "Many tales from lands far and wide tell of cairns and standing stones with carvings like ours. We are all connected with the sun, moon and stars."

He drops his head and stares into the fire. His words go around in my head.

We are all connected. We are all one. Help the Voyagers, help my people. Go with Arzu to stop the Raiders in her land and that can stop them from coming here and taking our land. That is the way to help my people. Maybe that is my destiny, that is why I met Arzu in the forest so soon after my vision. Mona says my feelings for Arzu may not be real, that they come from the Grand Cross. But what if the stars sent sparks between me and Arzu so that I would go with her and the Voyagers? Blood pulses in my body and head. I want to stand up and run to find Arzu, but my ears prick as the conversation turns to the carvings on stones - the Voyagers have the same carvings.

"What do the spiral carvings mean?" Someone asks.

"As the sun comes and goes, we die, and we are born again," Nectin replies.

Different voices speak.

"The circles are for the Sun."

"Wavy lines are the waters of life and milk flowing from breasts."

"And the dots are the stars in the sky."

My eyes widen as I listen to the conversation. The Voyagers are not so different, they are like us. I look up at the sky above - they see the same stars, they love their land, and they have Great Spirit. The White Band glows back, it seems to tell me to follow the path to Arzu.

Songs start at the fire and Shula nudges my arm as Mona gestures to follow her to the longhouse. Shula is excited as we walk.

"Islands and lands with cairns and dolmens! Carvings like *ours!*" Shula exclaims.

"*We're the same people!*" I call, wanting to dance along.

"The web of life connects us all," Mona says. When we arrive at the longhouse, Mona turns and looks deep into my eyes. "Remember, you have special energy for the Grand Cross. Focus on your birthstone and good Glan until you get to Brú."

"After Brú maybe I'll go with the Voyagers," I assert, the words spilling from my mouth.

"Why do you say this now?" Mona asks. "We wait until the Summer Sun Standstill at Tara and then see."

"Arzu wants me to travel with her."

"To be with her?" she questions.

"And to help her people."

"*You can't leave us!*" Shula cries. "We all love you!"

They both gaze at me.

"Briona, your stars say you're here to help your people," Mona reminds me as she touches my cheek.

"But there are many ways to help," I respond.

"Your vision at Tara said your destiny is to stay here, to become a Keeper of Stones."

"I can do that and still go with Arzu," I say in a firm voice.

"This is your time to be named a Shining One, one who will save our people," Mona declares.

But how can Mona know this? The stars choose Shining Ones.

"But… How can we be *sure* of that?" I question.

Mona is silent.

"Arzu just wants you to help them," Shula says. "She doesn't love you like we do."

"Briona, you love your people, you love this land. Your kin are here - Murta, Dori, Shula. You're the daughter of my daughter who was taken from me. Stay here," Mona pleads as she takes my hands.

"*We love you! How* can you go to a land where no one knows you?" Shula asks.

"For now, I'll go to Brú for Sun Standstill, keep good Glan, and ask Great Spirit to guide me," I declare and blink back tears from my eyes at their words of love.

Tears well in Mona's eyes. She and Shula pull me into an embrace, and we all press together. It is so long since we sat in the Labyrinth at Carraig and talked of Turas. Then we did not know of the many changes to come with this special year.

- 18 -

Winter Sun Standstill at Brú

Mist lies low on the ground, shifting and moving in wisps across the clearing and swirling around us as we gather at the water's edge. My body thrums as I step onto the small flat boat with Mona and Shula. Mona sits calm and steady in the front of the boat and Shula stands behind with a pole in her hand. I grip my birthstone as the strong flow of the river pulls us deeper into the mist. We float through a canopy of leaves and branches, shrouded and hazy with the shadows of boats around us. The damp air cleanses our breath, and the gurgling of water clears our heads. My body attunes to the rich, deep currents beneath and the stillness of the air around us.

Glimmers of light break through as the river curves around a bend. The mist fades into the forest and daylight brightens around us. Rippling water whispers, leaves and branches reach out and birdsong fills the air. Then the gushing of the river grows louder. A cool breeze rises and reeds and water plants sway. Suddenly the boat rocks on strong currents that swirl in every direction, shifting us from side to side. Shula kneels to keep her balance as we all grasp the side of the boat. The beating of heavy wings fills our ears. A flock of swans rises in the air and soars up as one, their long necks reaching forward. The strong beat of their wings stirs the air around our heads and ruffles our hair. We turn to follow their flight. An enormous mound covered in gleaming white stones rises in front of us. It is Newgrange. The magnificent mound radiates energy that calls us and embraces us. The curve of white stones arcs out from the glowing orange-red centre. We step onto the platform built out onto the river and gaze, full of awe.

I place my hand on my birthstone, which pulses to the beat of my heart. Shula holds her pouch as she gazes straight ahead with glazed eyes. We have had so many dreams of this moment. We grew up with a special connection to Brú, and now we are here to enter the chamber of Newgrange for Winter Sun Standstill. Felim, Gormley, Neasa, Ollie, Conor and others arrive. We all stand filled with wonder and awe in our winter furs and blue Seeker gowns, with our birthstone pouches around our necks and the precious pots with the ashes of ancestors in our packs.

Mona and Coll lead us to the mound along a path up beside the meadow that stretches all around us, filled with huts and shelters as far as we can see. Fires burn and groups of people sit in circles. The sounds of talking, laughter, singing and low drumming drift by. The people wear warm winter furs, and some wear clothes, hats and scarves that show they come from across the seas. People near us wave and cheer, and we beam - this is our special place, people come from many lands to be here for Winter Sun Standstill.

We stop by the line of standing stones that separates the front of the mound from the meadow below. The mound is vast; its white stones soar above our heads. Keepers in colourful robes stand with torches in front of the doorway which is covered with a beautiful tapestry of reds and yellows. In front, a huge stone that is as high as my chest and three paces wide, glimmers and draws us over. It is alive, it seems to dance in the sunlight. Carvings of swirling spirals leap out at us, undulating in every direction, wrapping over the top and bottom and weaving around the sides of the stone. A thrill courses through my chest as my birthstone throbs and waves of white light surge through my body. My hands and feet tingle and crackle, my face stretches into a beaming smile, and my eyes widen and sparkle.

Two Keepers move forward to stand in front of the dancing stone. Mona tells us their names - Daire and Boann.

"Welcome to Brú na Bóinne," one of them says. "You're here at a very special time. In two days, we will enter Newgrange for Winter Sun Standstill. First, we will go to Knowth, the mound that holds the stillness of Sun Balance and helps us prepare for Newgrange."

They lift their rattles and shake up and down and around our bodies. A field of white light shimmers around us, as if Newgrange is leaning out and embracing us. They bend to place rattles on the earth and the energy recedes into the spirals on the front stone.

We follow Daire and Boan on a wide path that leads past Newgrange and through clusters of trees. We arrive at a big clearing where another huge mound, the size of Newgrange, sits solidly in front of us, with small cairns scattered around. Huge stones carved with beautiful spirals, circles, curves, and wavy lines form a circle around the base of the mound. Knowth is still and quiet as if it is asleep. To the side, there are longhouses and a Cistin. The Keepers wave to seats around the fire and hand us plates of food - bread, honey, nuts, fresh salmon. We sit to eat and I hear some of the talk about Brú. They speak of the wonder of Newgrange and how it dazzles with light.

The talk pauses as a group of Keepers come to the fire - Arzu and Mata are with them. Sparks flare in my body. Arzu looks splendid, strong and focused in a colourful cloak that matches the band around her dark hair. Shula places a hand on my arm.

"Glan..." she murmurs.

She smiles at me. I want to throw down the food and run to Arzu. She turns and our eyes meet. A beam of light joins us, like the first time in the forest. She comes over and touches my cheek.

"*Melita...*" Arzu whispers.

She beams and my face lights up. She turns to sit with the Keepers.

I stay beside Shula and try to stay focused. Arzu looks over and back as she talks with Mata. My gaze moves to Mona. She reaches out to me with her eyes full of love. Maybe Mona is right, this island is the best place for me. I look back at Arzu. She is different from anyone here, yet we are so connected. A sudden sigh rises in my body. I want to settle, to focus on Sun Standstill. No one knows what is best for me - only the stars and Glan.

"What if the stars say that you'll travel, like Áine," Shula whispers.

She nudges me. My eyes move to Áine. She glows in her yellow robe, her face calm with a big smile. What if my destiny is the same as Áine's? To travel away with the Voyagers, like her, and then return to my people. Maybe my path is like Áine's path to a Shining One.

My eyes widen as my body trembles, my feet tingle, and white light fills my body. This is the answer. My body tells me this is my answer. I put a hand to the birthstone in the pouch and sense its warm glow. I can travel with the Voyagers and come back to this land and the people I love. That is my destiny - to help stop those who take land and food from the Voyagers, so they can't come here and take our land. I breathe in and out to calm my body. This is right. This brings me Glan. This is what the cleansing heat at Ros told me - that the fire of Arzu and the white light of Spirit can come together.

"*I know for sure*," I say as I turn to Shula. "Like Áine, I'll go with Arzu, with the Voyagers, learn their ways, help them, and then come back here."

We startle as a big drum beats out three loud beats. Boan and Daire stand and go to the entrance of a round building that looks like a Dreamhouse.

"This is the ceremony for Glan," Shula says.

Unease rises in my belly - what if Glan isn't good? I catch Shula's arm.

"Ceremony for Glan?"

"Yes," she says.

"How do you know?"

"They told us."

"When?" I ask, surprised.

"At the Grove, at Samhain. This is the ceremony that decides whether we can enter the chamber of Newgrange," she says.

I missed so much at Sliabh na Caillí, lost in my feelings for Arzu.

"I'm not sure I'm ready," I say in a low voice full of concern.

Shula rests a hand on my arm.

"Briona, you're here now." Her eyes meet mine and hold them, they say - be strong. I know that I want to travel with Arzu. Now this ceremony will tell me if this is my destiny. I smile at Shula, she helped me to get clear, just in time!

Boan and Daire step forward.

"Bring your birthstones and the pot with the ashes of your ancestors," Boan says.

Silently we take the pots with ashes from our packs. They move us through our attunements. We step forward one by one and stand at the entrance. The Keepers shake rattles up and down our bodies and we hand the ancestral pots into their care. I clutch my birthstone; its steady pulse tells me to stay calm.

Inside the chamber, tapestries are covered in spirals that flicker to life in candlelight. They are like whirlpools, moving and undulating.

In the middle of the room a big beacon stands on a table surrounded by a circle of bowls painted in beautiful red sun signs. The Keepers close the door.

"Place your birthstones in a bowl," Daire instructs. He steps forward and lights the beacon.

We move forward one by one. My body feels bare without my birthstone and sudden fear rises - what if I am not able to find my birthstone? What if I am wrong about travelling with Arzu?

"Now we perform a circle dance for the wheel of the year," Daire says.

The beat of drums brings us back to Imbolc, the start of Turas. We take slow steps around and around in a circle. Drums beat out the wheel of the year. As we weave around the room, the drums speed up and our steps get faster and faster. My head whirls with visions and familiar faces. Round and round we go. Pictures flash in my head of the dream of the Voyagers, the Temple at Cill Dara, the Bards, Bealtaine fires, Lia Fáil at Tara, Lúnasa, Arzu, the Augury, and Samhain.

The drums settle to the rhythm of Winter Sun Standstill. Daire quenches the beacon and leaves us in total darkness. We slow our steps and focus on the ground as the drums stop. A spiral of energy roots us to the earth and connects us to the stars.

"Your birthstones hold energy for the first part of your life," Boan explains, her voice ringing out. "Your Turas ends here at Brú. Let the energy guide you to your birthstone."

How do I find my birthstone in the dark? I don't know what direction I face or where my birthstone is. We must find our birthstones by sensing them.

I take a deep breath - I know I can do this. I stand and wait as someone steps slowly forward and then another and another. I step in the direction of the table with my hands out but don't sense my birthstone. My hands brush past empty bowls. Blood rushes to my head. I focus on my feet, on calm breaths, and shuffle slowly around the table. There it is. The familiar throb of my birthstone draws in my hands. As I take it out of the bowl, its energy flows through my body. I stand with my birthstone in my hand until one by one the Seekers find theirs. The candles are relit. We all stand, our faces glowing in the light.

"You're now ready to enter earth's womb, to be reborn for the second part of your life, to fulfil your destiny. Soon you will leave your birthstones at Newgrange, where they become part of the energies of the mound," Boann says.

Boan and Daire lead us out and point to the low cairns scattered about.

"Choose a cairn, you'll stay there through the night until the end of the day tomorrow," Daire tells us.

The other Seekers walk away, but I pause and look around. Arzu is sitting by the fire. My birthstone tells me that I can travel with Arzu, that is my destiny. My body trembles as I walk over to her. Energy crackles as we get close. She makes space on the bench, and I sit beside her. Shoulder to shoulder, hip to hip, we take each other's hands, and our eyes lock. I long to kiss her and go with her to the forest. But not now, as we prepare to enter Newgrange. I touch my heart with my palm and reach to touch her chest. She places her hand on mine. Our hands entwine.

"I will go to Melita," I declare.

Arzu reaches into her clothes and takes out an amulet, a tiny carving of a woman with breasts, belly, hips, and thighs like the huge statue that the Bards brought to Cill Dara.

"Melita..." she says.

All I can do is beam and nod my head. We sit in silence with our hands clasped and let our spark flicker and set our bodies aglow.

"Briona, you must go and choose a cairn," Mona says, leaning over to catch my eye. This is not what she wants, but now I know that this is my path.

Arzu squeezes my hand, and I get up and walk towards the cairns.

My birthstone draws me to one of them and I crawl up the short passage to the chamber at the centre. As my eyes adjust to the pitch dark, I see layers of warm furs lying on the ground in the centre of the cairn. It is very low and very small, with just enough space to stretch out my legs. I lie down with my birthstone and turn to gaze out through the passageway to the horizon, where bright lights of the stars twinkle in the sky. So many clusters and bursts of light dazzle me at first, then I pick out familiar groups and focus from one cluster to the next. I watch as the White Band moves down to the horizon, and I look for the Swan Star. The sky reaches out to touch me and I fall asleep with stars dancing in my eyes.

I wake to the pale light of dawn in the cairn. The Bright Star shines low on the horizon. Glan in my body tells me I am ready for the chamber. I lie in the dim light of the cairn as energies shift through my body and head. I can travel with the Voyagers, help them, then return to my people. I want my spark with Arzu to grow. A flutter runs through my body at a picture of us on a boat with big sails. A vision of this island, of the people who dance, comes to my head. I know this is what I want - to live on this island of love, with people who live for love, maybe be a healer or a Shining One who can help to save our people. This island may not survive if we do not stop the Raiders from taking the land and food from the Voyagers.

I know Mona wants me to stay, and also Shula, my people at Carraig, and the Seekers. I hope the people of Melita celebrate the wheel of the year! They are like us, they have spirals and diamonds, they love the Mother Spirit of their Land, and they have Cailleach. We are not that different. I know now that this is my destiny. I drift until loud drumbeats call us to gather again. It is still daylight when we come out of the cairns, but it seems like many days and nights have passed since we gathered here. We stand together in front of the fire.

Daire steps forward.

"It's the eve of Winter Sun Standstill," he says. "Now we go to Dowth, the mound that faces the setting sun at Winter Sun Standstill. We'll bid farewell to the sun and then prepare for dawn. The Stargazers say we'll have a bright sky in the morning."

Shula, Gormley and Felim draw us into a quick embrace as currents of excitement run through us - we are so close to entering the chamber.

We hurry after the Keepers, the bright colours of Arzu and Mata in their midst. Dowth appears - a big mound, almost the size of Newgrange and Knowth. It rises in front of us, covered in grass, but there are no white stones in sight. Big stones surround its base, but carvings are hard to see in the fading light. Boan and Daire step forward and beckon to Arzu and Mata. They hold up a cauldron between them - the cauldron that holds their special crystals, the one I saw in my dreams. A faint white light seems to reach out through the cover of the cauldron.

"Arzu and Mata will stay in the dark chamber of Dowth tonight," Daire says.

They move into the cairn. Small shuffles among the Seekers quickly quiet as Mona, Coll and Cael stand side by side to face us. The Voyagers are here to bring crystals to Brú, not to bring harm, their steady faces say. We stand and watch as the fading sun gives a glow to the entrance. The low-lying ball of the sun moves towards the horizon, and twilight descends on us. Boan and Daire come out of the cairn and chant the words for the eve of Sun Standstill.

"*Darkness reaches its fullness,*
We enter the longest night of the year.
This time of darkness is the birth of new light.
Every year we gather at this time
To help our ancestors on their journey through the skies
Not just on this island but in further lands.
Let us thank the earth, the sky and our ancestors
For the great gifts they have bestowed upon us.
Tomorrow, we welcome the return of light!"

The ball of the sun slips below the horizon. Boan and Daire turn, and we follow, with just enough light to walk back. Stars sparkle above and only the sounds of birds chirping disturb the stillness of dark closing in.

The Seekers walk along together. Shula links my arm, and we talk in low voices. She knows I want to travel with Arzu, but she thinks I should go later when the days are brighter. Gormley touches my back, he seems to say to follow my path. Felim is unsure, they want me to stay here for the Tribe. Neasa and Ollie put their fingers to their lips; this is not a time to talk of leaving.

Back at Knowth people are already at the Cistin, taking food to eat by the fire. We sit silently in a circle. One more night of sleep and then we can enter Newgrange. We hope for a clear morning so that golden sunbeams may enter the chamber. We eat our food and then crawl into the cairns to sleep with the stars.

My eyes open to the darkness of the small cairn. At last, it is the morning of Winter Sun Standstill. I turn to look out through the short passage - the Bright Star shines low in the sky and its sparkles reach my eyes before it sinks below the horizon. Outside the remains of a fire smoulder and people move around in the darkness in furs and boots. In the longhouse, we change into our blue Seeker robes and touch our pouches with our birthstones. I stand in a circle with Shula, Felim, Conor and the Seekers from Cill Dara - Gormley, Neasa and Ollie - and we hold tight, arms about shoulders with our heads down. We stay silent, fierce focus on every face, ready for the chamber.

A gong sounds and we take our furs and go outside where the Keepers stand ready for our morning attunements. In the grey light I can see that they are wearing flowing robes under their furs, and around their heads are bands with big feathers that reach to the sky. Slowly, step by step we move as one, easy, dreamlike after the long nights in the cairns. We set off on the path through the forest. The bare trees seem to lean into us as we walk, their looming forms taking shape as the darkness eases. Ahead we can just see the torches that Boan and Daire carry. And then the sound of birdsong welcomes the beginning of dawn. Deep calm settles around us as we arrive at the edge of the forest and follow those in front to leave our furs under a shelter.

The big mound of Newgrange sits in stillness in the dim dawn light, waiting for the sun. We gather at the back of the mound, where the light of the fire reveals a beautiful sight. The Keepers stand in ceremonial robes with swan feathers around their heads, each holding the pots with the ashes of our ancestors. Arzu and Mata wear colourful cloaks that flow around their bodies. My face lights up at the sight of Arzu, but I focus on my birthstone and my feet on the ground. Mona is wearing a splendid green robe decorated with golden spirals, Teelin's robe is dark blue with tiny crystals forming the shape of stars. Áine is wearing her bright yellow robe with a purple shawl, and Coll's robe is a deep, dark red. The other Keepers are wearing robes of red and purple, blues and greens, yellow and oranges - their colours dance in the light of the fire. The Keepers draw us into the circle and our light blue robes blend in with theirs.

Daire and Boan step forward and shine their torches on the big stone at the back of the mound. Beautiful carvings of swirling circles and diamonds come to life in the light from the flames. Boan raises her torch:

The Sun comes to a standstill
The Grand Cross is high in the sky
The Bright Star shines strong.
The Voyagers are here with their crystals
And the Seekers carry their birthstones.
Let us give thanks for their long steady journey.

Gentle cheers from the Keepers fill the air. The words fill me with joy and love for the Seekers who stand beside me as we reach the last step on Turas. Boan and Daire turn and sweep their torches across the carved stone. Boan continues.

As the sun grows stronger
And shines through these stones
May its light reach us all.

We chant back, "May its light reach us all".

Soon the brightening daylight tells us that the sun is rising, ready to appear above the hill opposite Newgrange.

Boan and Daire turn, and we follow them towards the big bright lights of burning torches that sit on top of two rows of wooden posts. They make a long passage of flames that curves around the side of the mound. As we walk slowly through, feathers bob and weave, colours shimmer in the heat, bringing a glow to our bodies and lighting up our faces and robes. The gleam of the mound sets my birthstone pulsing. Shula touches my hand, and we glance at each other, our shining eyes reflect our joy and excitement.

The sounds of pipes and drums greet us when we come around to stand in front of the standing stones that stretch around the temple. Crowds of people are gathered with drums and torches. The meadow glows in the dawn light from little fires that are scattered across and down to the river where a steady flow of people arrive in boats. Across the river, trees at the top of the hill seem to wait in line for the sun to rise above them and shine its golden beams into the chamber.

Gongs ring out. The sound of drums and murmurs and songs fades. People step forward with children at their sides and tiny babies wrapped in fur at their chests. The Keepers hold the pots with the ashes of ancestors out to the crowd and then up to the sky to the chant of Winter Sun Standstill.

We gather at this time when the sun stands still
We honour the great spiral of life
We welcome newborns into our world
We carry our ancestors to the Otherworld.
May the sun, moon and stars shine strong
Bring Beo to our cairns, our land and our people.

The people gathered in the meadow chant back.

May the sun, moon and stars shine strong
Bring Beo to our cairns, our land and our people.

The words ring out across the meadow and down to the river. Waves of joy and love for our people ripple through the crowd. Hope fills me - Beo flows strong in this land, in our stones. The Bright Star shines, we have the strength for the changes that the Grand Cross brings. We chant the words over and over until the brightening of the morning light tells us that the sun is about to rise above the hill across the river.

Gongs sound and the chants fade into silence. We turn and step through the gaps in the standing stones into the pulsing energy of the wall of white stones. Spirals dance on the beautiful carved stone in front of the doorway. The door slides open. A deep, dark portal pulls us in and my birthstone throbs in my palm. I take Shula's hand to steady my feet, and she squeezes my hand and leans forward with her eyes fixed on the entrance. The Seekers press together as energy swirls through us.

One by one the Keepers step forward to swing their bodies over the top of the dancing stone at the front. They step down and melt into the passageway. Arzu and Mata lift the cauldron over the stone and follow the Keepers. Then it is the Seekers' turn - Ollie, Gormley and Neasa are in front of me, Shula, Felim, Conor and other Seekers behind.

The huge spirals shimmer and swirl around me as I lift my leg over the dancing stone at the front. Heat sizzles up the front of my body and down my back, around and around until body and stone are one. I can barely sense my feet on the ground as I step forward to enter the passageway. A Keeper holds out a hand and I lower my head and step through the lintel into a long, dark passageway that seems to have no end. My breath quickens at the sudden strong draw of the passageway. I hold out my hands to feel the dark, solid stones that guide me to the end.

I bow my head and enter the chamber. My chest opens to the strong flow of Beo and my hands tingle as Mona guides me to place my birthstone on a basin in the centre of the chamber along with other birthstones and the Voyagers' crystals. Shula and the other Seekers place their birthstones. Finally, the last person enters. We stand to face the passageway as the door at the entrance closes over and we are in total darkness.

Large standing stones surround us with the energy of all those who have come before us. They loom over our shoulders as if they want to join in, waiting with us for the wedge of shimmering light. Suddenly an orange-red beam appears and advances up the passageway. It shines through the stones in the basin and comes to rest at the back of the alcove. The chamber floods with beautiful light. The three-spiral carving at the entrance to the alcove dances and the greens and oranges of stones on the roof come to life and arch above us. Beams of light shine onto the basin of stones and the pots with the ashes of our ancestors. Stones and crystals sparkle in the sunlight, sending light in every direction, dancing off spirals, diamonds and wavy lines carved on stones all around.

My body comes alive - my skin prickles, my hair tingles and heat rises from my feet, filling my hips and chest. My face flushes and tears of joy well in my eyes. We join in a circle around the glistening birthstones and crystals and stretch our hands out over them. Their energy pulses through my hands, up my arms and across the back of my neck. My head fills with bursts of light and my body melts as I whirl on a spindle that rises from the centre of the earth to the great Bright Star in the sky. Waves of energy spread out in circles all around us, connecting us to long lines of ancestors, then spread out to settlements and villages around the island. Waves spread further and further across fields and forests, rivers and lakes out to oceans and beyond, where people in every direction gather at stone circles, in cairns and on hilltops for Winter Sun Standstill.

Hums start - odd low hums here and there that pull energy back into the chamber. My belly thrums as the hum steadies and gathers force. We open our mouths and throats and become one with the vibrations of the earth. My ears fill with the low, steady sound that holds us rooted to the ground until the hum fades and stops. As it echoes around the chamber, a flood of love washes over me. I want to laugh and hug and dance for joy - we are all part of the spiral of life. Faces glow with love in the beautiful light. We hold hands and watch as the golden yellow light pulls back and fades down the passageway.

Dim daylight lingers in the chamber as an answering hum calls us from outside. We form a tight circle with our arms around each other and stand for a moment to steady ourselves for the passage out. Mata and Arzu place the crystals in their cauldron. The Seekers take our birthstone from the basin. My birthstone leaps into my hand, its heat burns my palm and courses through my body. The beautiful energy in the chamber enfolds us as we turn to leave.

My hands brush stones as I follow Shula and walk down the passageway step by step. The sound of drums and pipes grows louder. I step out through the doorway past the spiral stone that pulses to the joy in my body and I go to stand with the other Seekers. Horns sound. Daire and Boan, Mona, Coll and the other Keepers stand in front of us and hold out their arms to the crowd. Áine steps forward and announces in a ringing voice that the rising sun has entered the chamber! Her yellow robe seems to blend with the sun, and beautiful white light glows from her face. Whoops, cheers and drum rolls come from the crowd. The Keepers move to sit with their backs pressed to the mound as people come over and stand in front of them, ready for healing. Others move forward to enter the chamber and bathe in the wonderful energy.

Shula holds out her birthstone and we join Gormley, Ollie, Felim, Neasa, Conor and the other Seekers in a circle with our hands holding our birthstones reaching to the centre. In one move we lean in and press our birthstones into the white stones of the mound. A thrill crackles through my body - this is our last step on Turas, our passage to becoming an adult. We stand in a circle, arms about our shoulders and jump up and down, beaming at each other. We turn to see some of the Keepers smiling at us, ready to embrace us as adults.

My breath stops as Áine steps forward, takes my arm, and brings me over to Arzu. She brings Arzu and me together on each side of her, then draws us all together. Her beautiful energy surrounds us and joy surges through me. She smiles into my eyes and hands me a white stone that throbs in my palm, then she pats my cheek and moves away, leaving Arzu and me in a cocoon of white light.

We turn to dance up and down the meadow, filled with joy. The sun shining into the chamber means that Beo will flow for the year ahead. Áine has shown me that my path forward is with Arzu. Beaming faces meet us at every turn. Swirling and twirling, we dance to the beat of the drums. Mona takes my hands and dances in a circle with me. Coll whirls me around and around. Shula and Gormley catch me, and we shimmy down the meadow. I breathe in the familiar smells of the earth. The waters of the river reflect the cold, crisp sky. The soft green grass caresses my feet. Newgrange holds us in a healing embrace.

Acknowledgements

Writing a novel was a challenging and fascinating experience. Workshops and courses were all immensely helpful. A Master of Fine Arts in Creative Writing in UCD fostered a range of writing skills, and I would like to thank Gavin Corbett, Ian Davidson, Katy Hayes, Frank McGuinness, Eamon Jordan, Éilís Ní Dhuibhne and Paul Perry. I am particularly grateful for the support and advice of Mia Gallagher and fellow students of the Stinging Fly fiction workshop.

The resources and support of the Irish Writers Centre were invaluable. The teaching of Catherine Dunne, Claire Kilroy, Conor Kostick, Lia Mills, Annemarie Ní Churreáin, and Adam Wyeth were wonderful, and Claire Hennessy provided outstanding feedback. A bursary from the Irish Writers Centre/Arts Council came at just the right time, and a stay in the Tyrone Guthrie Centre in Annaghmakerrig enabled me to finalise a complete draft of the novel.

I was fortunate to join the Brooks Writers' Group shortly after leaving University College Dublin (UCD) in 2016. Over the years, several members of the group read and gave invaluable feedback to drafts, namely David Butler, June Caldwell, Julie Cruickshank, Micheline Egan, Aingeala Flannery, Lauren Foley, Kevin Gildea, Lisa Harding, Joanne Hayden, Jennifer Lynn, Oona Marian, Henry McDonald, Elizabeth McSkeane, Aiden O'Reilly, Manus Boyle Tobin, Susan Tomaselli and Stephen Walsh.

I very much appreciate the solidarity, support, ritual and ceremony, site visits, and expertise provided by people I have met or trained with in shamanic and pagan communities. These include Cáit Brannigan, Eimear Burke, John Cantwell, Gabriel Cooney, Martin Duffy, Mary Edwards, Luke Eastwood, Margot Harrison, Sandra Ingerman, Caitlin Matthews, Amantha Murphy, Anthony Murphy, Annette Peard, Lora O'Brien, Frank Prendergast, Manda Scott, Clare Tully, Deirdre Wadding, Karen Ward and Dolores Whelan.

None of this would be possible without the love and support of the wonderful people in my life. Sonya Mulligan, my partner, is the most loving, creative and generous person I know. Over the many years of working on this novel she offered unrelenting love, patience, inspiration, and practical support of every kind. She read and re-read the entire novel and provided line by line commentary.

I grew up in a family of eight children with parents who were dedicated to fairness and equality and who provided a safe and stimulating environment. Both they and the extended family were consistently supportive as they listened, read, shared interests, and attended readings.

Many friends were generous with their time and feedback on the text, especially Gráinne Blair, Mallory Courrell, Eileen Costello, Tricia Daragh, Aileen Donnelly, Mary Egan, Orla Magill, Susan Miner, Irene McIntosh, Siobhan McMahon, Carmel O'Reilly, Ger Ormond, Dee McDonnell, Eilis Stanley, Hilary Tierney and Elaine Wall. Particular thanks go to Vicky Barron, Mari Maxwell, Kate Meleady and Alison Mulligan-Carroll who read the novel in its entirety. And thanks to Ciarna Hackett, also known as Kiki_na_Art, who created a vivid image of Briona.

Finally, I would like to thank Tribes Press, and particularly Marguerite Tonery, for critical feedback, endless encouragement, and practical assistance. The editing and editorial assistance I received from her and her colleagues at Tribes Press were invaluable at every level from plot and character to the novel structure and language. I am also very grateful for the great efficiency and enthusiasm of Marguerite as she brought me through the publication process. I would also like to thank her illustrator Ana Slattery who provided beautiful illustrations of the map of Briona's journey and the wheel of the year along with a wonderful cover.